Sitting in the Memory

MALCOLM BULLER

Also by Malcolm Buller

Parallel Lies – a novel set in 1964 London

What's in the Box? – a poetical miscellany

Leeds Castle – a poetic tour

ISBN: 979-8-7673-1208-5

Many of the locations in this work existed, at least in the author's memory. Some events of his childhood are also reflected here. Descriptions of the medical provision in the era are imagined, as are the characters.

ACKNOWLEDGMENT

Andrew's expertise in this world of publishing has meant that I have been enabled to write freely. He continues to aid others fulfil their dreams of turning ideas into reality. He writes and publishes his own work too and further information can be found at www.andrewbuller.co.uk.

Malcolm Buller
November 2022

1 SIT THERE

"Sit there please Dearie while I talk to Matron." She means well, but hasn't the time to help anyone properly.

This room is a mess with shelves of scattered books. I like to read. I like these machines with their blinking lights in regular rhythms, pulsing to prove they have a heartbeat. At least the closed door gives peace from all but her verbal diarrhea. "No, no name – and no-one's reported her missing." There are cobwebs above the curtains – not much of a view out – no escape route.

They're both staring at me. I'll not see them. I wish these trousers they put me in didn't itch so. My hands look too old. "Just that bag. It's got her clothes in that she was wearing." I wish –

"Come along then. Let's show you your room." The portly Matron puts a firm hand around my arm and squeezes me up. Her face is smiling, but her eyes are elsewhere. I detest that grip with fat fingers and a cheap agate ring. Control is hers. I have no choice. "This way." She pulls and I follow through the door, along the corridor. I keep my gaze on the maroon carpet, dotted with patterns of cream diamonds that stretch ever onwards. Paintwork chips reveal a ghostly green beneath the magnolia skirting boards that give way to brown doors at monotonous intervals. "Here we are. Number ten." Prime Minister at last. Now we'll see who's in charge.

I'm ushered inside. "Sit there please Dearie." There's a small armchair in the corner. I obey. It's what I do.

Matron opens another door and pokes her head in. "This is your bathroom. I'll get some soaps and toothpaste. Out here are some drawers for things. We'll find some more clothes for you soon. Okay Dear? Someone will be along soon. Just sit there." They leave without a backward glance.

I lift my eyes to the bed with its neatly folded corners. I think my Mum would approve. I must have a mother. The walls are the same magnolia colour. No pictures. Huge red roses droop on the tied-back curtains. I'd like to look out, but I was told to sit. I'm used to sitting. It's what I do.

It's getting gloomy. I can see a bulb in the ceiling and another above the bed. At least it's warm here. This chair is quite comfortable, but I am getting wet again.

Footsteps pause. The door opens and a light sears my eyes. I shut them tight, but I face the voice from the door. It comes closer. "Hello. I'm Jasmine. Who are you?" I'm as still as stone. "Stay there Dear. I'll get help." Where is my voice? Her footsteps hurry along the corridor until the carpet drowns them.

Four footsteps and the door creaks open. "Here we are then." Matron is hiding her shame. "Jasmine here will sort you out while I unpack your bag. Take her into the bathroom."

My hands are gently held and coaxed upwards to help me stand and walk the few steps. The door creaks and a magic light clicks on. "Can you manage Dear or shall I help?" I push her hand away and pull the soggy clothing down. "That's it. Sit there until we sort you out." I slowly peep down on her. She's tiny, with jet-black hair tied in a bun above a sky-blue uniform and plastic apron that rustles as she expertly removes my sorry mess and drops it all in a bucket. That she's done this many times before is clear and there's no hint of blame from her to me. "Would you like a shower Dear?" I almost nod.

Privacy and warm water, the freedom that it brings, enlivens me. Jasmine returns all too soon, but brings warm towels and a steadying arm. Matron's disappeared. I'm relieved. The roses are spread across one wall now and my entire wardrobe is laid out on the bed. I don each piece with pleasure.

There's a gentle knock on the door, which opens slowly to admit a tall, thin-faced girl, dressed as Jasmine. "Matron's gone home, but said I was to raid the kitchen as our lady here was missed out for dinner." Jasmine nods and the girl pulls in a trolley. "Cup of tea?" She pours from a black jug into a plastic mug and squashes a cap with a spout on to it. I look for the armchair, but it has disappeared. "Why don't you sit on the bed and I'll fetch a chair." She has a kind tone too.

A plastic-covered dining chair comes in, in front of Flo's name badge. "Sit there please." She places a tray of sandwiches with three small tomatoes on the bed beside me. I turn to them, pull off the half triangle and stuff it into my mouth. Each bread portion is devoured, along with the red balls, leaving behind a mangled mess of ham. "Are you vegetarian?" she asks. Jasmine removes the plate and replaces it with two cakes. They vanish in six mouthfuls. I wrench the lid off the mug and look at the ready-milked liquid. I need it, but can my stomach cope? It will have to take its chance.

"We'll just clear these things away," Jasmine says as she ushers Flo outside with the trolley. "Did Matron tell you anything?"

"A bit." They lower their voices, but the door does little to deaden their words. "Social Services brought her in. No names. She's not spoken since she was found, not in hospital or anywhere."

"Where was she found?"

"Sitting in the middle of the Hogsmill."

2   "SIT!"

Mummy comes in and gently tickles me. I giggle and wriggle. She lets in the bright sunshine and pretends to tickle me again. I squirm away. It's a favourite game. "Nice nap, now nappy. Lie still."

"Nice – nappy." I'm proud of my words.

"Good girl. All done. Let's find a dress."

"Dress." I twist off of the bed and stand by the open drawer. "Red." I point and pull.

Mummy helps me into it. "I think you're growing too big for this one." She tickles my tummy and I run out of the door. I twist at the top and climb down the stairs backwards, holding on to the fuzzy carpet that tickles my toes and fingers.

"Careful."

I run into the room where my brother has his toys out. As I grab for a car he calls out, "No Susie. It's mine." My arm knocks into the bricks that he had built into a garage and they come tumbling down. "Mum!"

Mummy has followed me and picks me up. "We say sorry Tom. She didn't mean it. Anyway, it's toys away please. We're going out when you've both had a drink and biscuit. Sit still please Susie while you have your drink." As I drink and eat,

Mummy puts my socks and big girls' shoes on without tickling my toes. I'm proud of my shoes.

"Red shoes."

Tom's toys are put away in a box and hidden in the dark cupboard under the stairs. "Could you bring our coats please Tom in case the sun hides away?" I wish I could help Mummy like my big brother does.

Mummy pushes my pram down the hill while Tom runs ahead to find a stick to make it click on the fences as he runs past. "Stick – tick – stick." He always does that. I love the sounds he makes. I want to try, but I can't run very fast. Tom stops when he comes to a road and waits, holding on to the pram as we cross.

We come this way quite often. At the bottom of the hill is a narrow road without paths. There are giant trees which give dark patterns that make me shiver. Tom disappears and "Boo!" jumps out again. I laugh at him a lot. "Poo!" he says as we pass by a long fence with strange buildings and trees where we cannot go.

"Poo!" I mimic and my brother laughs. He pulls a funny face and holds his nose, so I do too. Mummy pushes me faster.

He runs ahead to the big dark tunnel, hoping for a rumbling monster to shake the air. I listen. "Monster." Mummy pulls me out of the pram and Tom holds my hand. We stand together and wait. It's getting nearer, slowing down, ready to grumble. The clonks and squeals join in until the groans are replaced with heavy slamming noises. A shrill whistle blows and the monster above growls away. We shiver together before we go through the small space at the end of the fence into the warm sun, up a hill and down again.

We walk along the path beside the grass and the sparkling water. "Doggy."

A man is approaching with his pet leading the way. Mummy stands on the grass to let him pass with Tom hiding behind her skirts. "Don't be afraid. He's looks friendly."

I go towards him and his wet nose pushes against my cheek. "Sit!"

The dog and I obey, but as I do, I tumble backwards on the grassy bank and crash into the water.

3   HOSPITAL VISIT

Oh my Susie. Please be alive. My mind is reliving the trauma over and over again.

That split second and she was gone. My scream as I turned towards the stream to see nothing. The man jumping in – deeper than expected – water up to his chest. The barking dog following him in. Tom screeching. The man plunging his head and arms down into the flowing torrent – and coming up again, turning and ducking down. How many times? The dog swimming away, tail like a rudder enjoying the fun. Fun? And the red material in his jaws.

"Look!" I yelled at the man, pointing to the dress.

"Fetch!" he ordered. The dog pulled the clothes to his master. He lifted them into the air, but slipped back into the water as he struggled with her lifeless body towards the bank. "Good boy."

Susie's lain out on the grass, my mind searching through my mental manual. Holger-Neilson – the latest technique. I knelt behind my precious daughter and put both her hands beneath her chin. I pushed on her back, either side of her spine, with just two fingers. She's so tiny. I lifted her elbows and lowered them. Back, elbows, lift, lower, repeat. Not too quick, not too slow. Come on Susie, splutter for me. Get the water out and the air back in.

I hear Sister's footsteps approaching. Instinctively I brace myself before cuddling Tom nearer as she sits beside us. "She's breathing more normally now. Well done Nurse Robertson. An excellent job. She's sleeping, but you can see her for a few minutes. No noise young man." I've rarely seen that gentle smile before.

She leads us into a small room, familiar to me of course, but unreal. I want to pick her up, but know better. "Sister Susie's sleepy," Tom whispers. I can't answer.

Too soon Sister holds my arm and takes us out. "Come back in the morning after ten. Doctor will talk to you then."

The air has chilled as we walk out of the building. Tom and I catch the bus into Kingston and wait outside the station for a 65. We're both shivering as we walk home up the hill. Alf is out in the street as we turn the corner and runs to engulf us in his embrace. "How is she?"

"Alive," is all I can manage as I carry Tom inside. "Give him some food please, Alf," I say as I disappear to the bathroom to shed my tears in private. When I emerge, they are snuggled on the settee with Tom's favourite story. I collapse into the armchair, lost in thought until Tom climbs on to my lap and puts his arms around my neck. I cuddle him close before carrying him up to his bed and settling him down with another short story.

"You need to eat," Alf says as I come down. He waits so patiently until I'm finished. "Can you bear to tell me yet?"

We sit together, his arm around me, and it all spills out. "How did you find out?" I ask as I finish.

"Mr Penrose, the man with the dog, sent a message through to work and they sent me home. He brought the pram back for you and waited till I got here. He told me what you did to get her breathing again. You were marvelous. I'm so proud of you Lily."

"He was the hero. We couldn't see her. He jumped in and searched under the water. His dog did too. It was the dog who grabbed her dress and pulled her up. Mr Penrose brought her to me. I just did my nursey thing – it's my job." There's a long silence. "I must have told him where we live. I don't remember. The ambulance seemed to take forever. I don't know. I just kept working and praying."

4 SITTING DUCKS

I sit still, lost in my own black thoughts. Tom and poor Lily witnessing it. Our Susie. Underwater. Lifeless.

Trauma returns in vivid colour – back to the terrors of war. Retreat after weeks of fighting, attacked from land and air, bodies falling around me. Mud. I saw the fear in the faces, but know that I'm no different. Follow orders and look out for your comrades. It's simple. Don't think – do.

George was the Lance Corporal, promoted on the field of battle to replace the fallen. But George wasn't NCO material – too kind, a ditherer when decisive orders were needed. But he's my closest friend, a comrade and I had always got his back.

We were holed up in the sand dunes at dusk, sat back-to-back to rest our weary limbs and keep watch in all directions. Some had gone to sleep as night and exhaustion won that battle. But I couldn't. Every wave of aircraft brought new terrors as bullets strafed the sands and shallows. I saw distant boats bobbing on the water, like ducks at the fair, ready to be hooked. Tiny craft were plying to and fro and ants were pulled aboard.

A bloodied Lieutenant ran whilst crouched as low as possible amongst us. "Move down the beach at the whistle," he ordered and passed on to the next ragged group.

I moved onto my knees in readiness, but George hadn't. His face shone as white as the moon above. "George. It's an order."

"I can't."

A single low whistle was followed by, "Move out," from hidden voices. A dozen eyes looked to George, but no-one moved.

"Move out!" I said and grabbed my friend around his waist, pulling him to his feet. "It's our turn so let's not be late." We stumbled through the soft sand until our cover was behind us and felt the tide-washed surface firmly beneath our boots. "Come on George, help me."

The waves were gentle at first, but grew in strength. A whine of bullets came from nowhere as a plane swooped overhead. Too late. We ducked down into the water, but only five heads re-appeared. "Keep going! Head for that boat!" I shouted. The aircraft banked and headed back along the beach towards us. "Down!"

The few inches of water slowed the bullets, lessening the ferocity of their impact, but one less helmet re-surfaced. "Keep going!" There were hands reaching out from our destination, ready to haul men aboard. The first one was rolled like a sack of spuds into the bowels of the dinghy.

"Aircraft!" came a shout as the unmistakable whine filled the sky. We ducked again. The hands had disappeared when we came up for air. I pulled myself up and saw the bodies.

"George. You must help me! It's an order!" A spark registered. We grabbed the nearest soldier and pushed as he scrambled aboard. There was no-one else. "You next!"

As George was half-way-in a plane swooped low and fired. I couldn't let go and dive. The pain seared through me and I collapsed into the sea. George fell forward over the side and twisted to reach for me. It seemed an age before his fingers grasped a scrap of uniform and he pulled with all his might, heaving me into the hell that we must sit upon.

We could see no other soldiers in the water, so grabbed an oar each and pulled away from shore towards the shouts, coming from the larger boats, anchored a short way off. The agonies were overcome by fear as we strained to reach a safer future.

5 SITTING AREA

Tom's nightmares mean we all have had disturbed sleep. I was certain I wouldn't get a wink, but with his little body between us, we all did until the sun penetrated our thin curtains. Alf and I creep out of the bedroom, but our peace is short-lived. "Where's Susie?" How can you explain to a four-year old when you can't process things yourself?

Alf takes hold of him as I try to explain. "She's stayed in the hospital where Mummy works. Daddy's going to take you to Nursery today. Then we both will go to the hospital to see if Susie is ready to come home. I expect she will be playing with her toys when you get here." I turn away to hide my tears.

Alf tells me he will call work from the phone box on the green on his way back from Nursery, so I'm looking for things to do. Washing. The children get through a lot, especially playing outside. Their gardening outfits are shabby, but I can relax when I see the mud being poured from a watering can. Each has planted seeds in that patch, but it's hard to stop them digging them up again. That blackbird is tugging at something. Poor worm. Washing. I fetch the basket and plonk it beside the sink. I hear mother clearly telling me, "Sort the cleanest first and leave the worst till last." I miss Mum. She was only my age.

I'm still lost in thought as the back door opens and Alf returns. "Goodness." Where did the time go? "How was he?"

"Okay, I think. I told Mrs Blake what has happened so she promised to keep a special eye on him. She took him off to the toy chest to see what he would like to choose. Can you guess?"

"Meccano."

"Of course. I'd like to try to get some for his birthday. I'll have a look at work. Have we got any money in the birthday jar?"

"His birthday's not for two months yet. There's time. I can't think about that now." Alf knows this of course. It is just his sweet way of trying to distract me. I scrub at the clothes and drop them into the bucket before rinsing them three times in the cold water. I look at my red hands plunging in the water amongst the clothes. Red. The tears flow as all they see is her dress in the dog's mouth.

I feel an arm around my waist and a gentle breath on my neck. "How can I help?"

"Mangle." Alf pulls the heavy machine away from the wall of our little outside shelter which he built with scraps of timber, gathered from the bomb sites. We work together silently. I pull my peg bag from the cupboard and he passes each item to me to hang on the line. "What's the time?"

It's reality time – time to leave. He holds my hand as we walk, childless for the first time in ages, to the Duke of Buckingham. There's a 265 just up the road so we get into Kingston in no time at all. The connection to the hospital is fast too so we are there with time to spare. I lead the way into a small, secluded garden. "What's this place for?" he asks.

"It's the Nurses' sitting area – if we ever get a break. Sometimes Sister might send someone here for a while if we've lost a patient." I wish I hadn't said that. The flood-gates open again.

15

Alf lets me. He knows I've got to let it out. I've always had to. It's the only way to cope with the job I do. I wish he could sometimes too – with what he's been through.

"Come on then. It must be time. Show me the way."

I lead him through a small side door and towards a flight of stairs. As we turn we see a scruffy man in a brown coat, rummaging in a cupboard. "No visitors until 3 o'clock! Leave."

He seems surprised as I step towards him. "I'm Nurse Robertson and this is my husband. Our daughter was rescued from a river yesterday and Sister told me to come today at ten to speak to Doctor. And you are?"

"Jenkins," he mutters as he scuttles off down the corridor.

Alf gives me a smile. "Definitely Sister material." I give his arm a punch.

My smile disappears as we find our way through the labyrinth of corridors. I raise my hand to Sister as we take a seat in the tiny room just outside the ward. "It's still Doctors' Rounds. It looks as if he'll be finished soon."

Sister follows him in and he sits opposite us. He doesn't recognise me out of uniform, not that he does in it either. Sister hands him a file. "Ah yes. The little girl. She seems very perky. All vital signs are normal." He pauses and I detect the furrowed brow. "Tell me. Has she ever spoken?"

"Miss Chatterbox," Alf says before I can.

"Mm. It's probably just the shock. I expect she'll start again as soon as she sees familiar faces." He looks at us. "Can you look after her at home?"

Sister intervenes. "This is Nurse Robertson, Doctor Clark. I can assure you that she is more than capable."

He peers over his glasses. "Oh yes. Right. Take her home. Lots of rest and liquids, but not to swim in."

None of us think he's funny. Sister rolls her eyes as he leaves. "I'll be as quick as I can." She follows him out.

Alf squeezes my hand and I wipe the tears. "It's good news. She can come home."

6 SIT HERE

"Oh good. You've got yourself dressed, Dear. Did you sleep well?"

I look at another young thing in a pale blue uniform. I've been dressed since yesterday. Does she think I'm incapable? She comes closer and I see Mary's name label pinned to her pocket. She smells of an exotic flower. "It's time to take you to the dining room for breakfast. Do you need the bathroom first?" I rise stiffly from the chair. It's been a long night and I'm desperate.

Mary's opened the roses and tied them in. I stare at the outside world. There's a gentle breeze wafting the leaves of the forsythia just outside where a robin is perched, looking me in the eye. "There's lots to choose from. I expect you're hungry. This way."

She leads me along the corridor. Why is she dawdling? We pass Matron's Office, the Reception Area and front door. Escape, but I'll eat first. I glance left as we pass the kitchen with steam billowing throughout it. Mary takes me through a sea of chairs to the far wall where she indicates a vacant seat. "Sit here."

As I settle, I become aware of a pair of beady eyes studying me. "Hello." She's waiting for a reply. "I'm Sylvie. Who are you?"

Mary rescues me. "Now then Sylvie. Our new friend here hasn't found her voice yet. We're not sure of her name, so don't go pestering her." She points to a trolley. "What would you like?"

I like the look of it all. I point to a bowl of cornflakes which she puts in front of me. As she picks up a jug and starts to pour, my hands instinctively cover the bowl. "That was silly!" she snaps. The milk drenches the tablecloth and the drips from my hands now reach the floor.

"What's the problem, Mary?" a blue-suited, middle-aged lady asks as she approaches. "Get a cloth girl." She turns to me. "Do you like milk?" I shake my head. "Then we'll all try to remember that. Let me dry your hands." She's gentle. She removes the bowl and replaces it with another, along with a spoon that hasn't been splattered. Her label says Assistant Manager. "Can you manage on top of this soggy mess?" I almost smile and tuck in.

I've finished in five mouthfuls and sit waiting. Sylvie tries not to stare, but her eyes keep flicking to mine. I help her by looking elsewhere. There must be thirty people sat in here in various postures; slumped back, slumped forward, dribbling sideways. I realise where I am. I've been put in with old people. I wring my hands, and notice how flabby the scarred skin is around my bones. It's a shock.

The trolley returns with Mary. "I'm sorry about the milk. It won't happen again. Sylvie? Your usual scrambled egg?"

"Lovely. Thank you Mary." A portion is spooned beside a triangle of toast which Mary cuts into small pieces and then does the same with the egg before placing it in front of her.. "That's lovely. Thank you."

I stare as her wizened hand clutches at a spoon and she pushes at the food. A small morsel makes it to her mouth and she savours her success.

"Would you like some too?" I take a moment to regain myself, and nod. "Shall I cut it for you?" I shake my head and grab the knife and fork. I'm surprised at how nice it tastes and try to slow my ravenous instincts, but it is soon gone. Mary is watching from behind. "That went down a treat. Would you like some more?" The helping is more generous and I begin to feel satisfied.

Poor Sylvie. Most of her food is on the cloth. I take another spoon and lean over to take her knife. I manoeuvre a piece of toast and egg onto the spoon and lay the handle towards her. There are tears in her eyes as she lifts it to her mouth. "So kind," she whispers before sucking it in. My eyebrows are asking, 'Again?' and she nods.

Mary and her trolley return with drinks. She gasps, "An empty plate, Sylvie. Well done. Your usual coffee?" Sylvie doesn't answer, but joins my nodding team. A plastic-capped mug with two handles is plonked before her. It reminds me of–

"Coffee for you?" I put one hand above the straight fingers of the other. Mary looks confused.

"She would like tea please," my new friend says, "without milk." I smile at Sylvie, but Mary is more confused.

"It's already in there."

The blue-suit arrives. "Is there a problem?"

Sylvie shakes her head. "Not really Isabel. My friend here would like her tea without milk."

"I'm sure we can get her some. It may just take a little while."

We grin at each other. We'll keep 'em on their toes. My gaze returns to the room as I watch the staff walk and bend, clear and serve, mop up mess and pull their trolleys between the chairs. They are used to the organised chaos I can see. Would they cope with a little more? Or maybe a lot more? Sylvie seems to recognise my intent. "You look as if you're planning something." I touch the side of my nose with one finger and she splutters a giggle. I've recruited my First Lieutenant.

The tea is stewed, but it's warm. People are leaving and Sylvie tries to push her chair away from the table. I'd like to help, but I've been told to sit here. The room has emptied and we sit looking at each other.

"What?" Isabel comes over, a mug of hot chocolate in her hand. "Why are you both still here? I'll have to speak to Mary." She eases the chair backwards to allow Sylvie space and puts an arm under hers to help her up. "Do you need help?" I shake my head. "Then why haven't you moved? You are allowed to you know."

I don't know. I've always obeyed orders, it's what I've done, ever since I can remember. I can remember. I can't. Only coming here and that long, long night, sitting on a chair, staring at roses.

7 SIT STILL

Susie is sitting in her hospital cot watching the comings and goings in the ward as we approach her from behind. Lily's knees buckle at the sight of our precious daughter, so obviously alive. I too have the wobbles, but we must not show Susie any doubt. "Hello darling," Lily whispers.

Susie spins and throws her arms around Lily's neck, threatening to throttle her. I dab my eyes and search the bedside cabinet. There's her red dress and other clothes in a paper carrier bag. Shoes are in the lower drawer. We've brought clean dry things with us and Lily prises off the arms to dress her, ready for home. A staff nurse checks we've everything we need, but leaves us with just a smile.

Our journey home is unnerving. I keep pointing to the things she usually loves, but she seems somehow vacant. On the buses, I sit her on my lap to give Lily's arms a rest. I talk to her incessantly, but although animated in her body, there's no sound. "Here we are, home again. I'll make some soup. You find some toys to play with Susie." I gather many different vegetables and chop them into a saucepan, add a bit of pepper and salt, along with the water."

Susie's playing looks normal as she seems to be chatting to the toys as she moves them. But there are no sounds. We eat, dipping our crusty bread pieces into the hot liquids and cooling them for her. She loves eating the same food as us and smiles as she does.

Lily's washing up so I lie down on the carpet and let Susie climb on board. "Sit still. Sit still!" I bump her into the air and wriggle. "Sit still." She loves this game, but although she smiles, there are still no squeals today.

As Lily sits down to relax, Susie climbs onto her lap and gives her an enormous cuddle, as if she knows what her mother did for her yesterday. I wipe the tears from my eyes as I absorb my view; my two lovely girls sitting pretty, ready for the story that is right beside them.

I'm drawn back to the scene of my own childhood, seeing my young sister climbing onto father's lap as the afternoon closed and her bedtime approached. Not for her the comfort of a mother's arms. No. Mother had given her life for the birth of her daughter. Working wives had no time for rest in their country life. I can only see a faded image of my mother, stepping outside to fetch the eggs for breakfast and hearing her scream. Father had already left the cottage and I was only three years old. I crouched beside her and listened. I followed her instruction to run and summon help from the big house. This is my only memory of my mother; her lying on the path and sending me away.

But father put his whole life into caring for us both. The big house had a nursery and we all ate with the other servants so that father could continue his gamekeeper duties. I grew to be useful too, helping in the kitchen, running errands, polishing boots and silver. But better were the times I spent working with him, learning his skills and values. He taught me to know the ways of animals and birds, to shoot, the weather's vagaries, how the seasons' subtle changes bring different behaviours in all of nature. School was a chore to be endured. Happiness came on release and finally I could take my promised place as second footman in the big house. I was proud to stand tall and greet the guests from their carriages. As silent as the portraits, stood in the dining room, I heard their affectations, their lies, their boasts and aspirations. These were our ruling classes, but we knew we were their betters.

Postman Peter brought an envelope for me. My call-up papers changed everything. It was that mixture of the anticipation of the unknown, excitement and dread. Alice was in tears; father proud yet hiding his concerns with true countryman's grit – and I was off to war.

All of us were treated like dirt; toughened up they called it. The lads from the city were soft compared to us countryfolk and most of the tasks seemed to have little purpose. We were ridiculed for our speech if it didn't suit the NCOs. The officers were those country-house sorts who had idled their lives away until the lure of a rank seemed to suggest soldiering would be a bit of a lark.

But finally, we had rifle training. The corporal dismantled his rifle whilst rattling off the names of all the parts. Then he reassembled it. There were nearly twenty of us watching, so none of us could get a close look. "Stand behind the tables. Right. On my command, take your weapon apart. When you have finished, stand in front of the table." He was waiting for the panic to set in. "Go!"

I took my time to be careful before stepping to the front, looking straight at the corporal. He glanced at his watch. It seemed an age before I sensed anything other than frustrated cursing. "Boom!" he bellowed. "Fall in!" We shuffled forward into our practised positions and stood stiffly. "You're dead!" he glowered. "Useless shower! Watch and learn!" He repeated the demonstration, a little more slowly, before stepping into my line of vision. "Name?"

"Private Robertson, Corporal." He waited. "32695491, Corporal."

"Soldier. Demonstrate." He indicated his weapon so I marched behind his table and picked it up. I took my time to examine it before taking it apart, trying to keep my hands out of way of the pieces as they came on to the table. I stood to attention as I finished. "Re-assemble."

He glared at the men in front of him. "You useless scum would all be dead from a single enemy with a hand grenade. Hopefully Robertson can aim and shoot him for you. Get back to your rifles. Move! Every piece apart – you've thirty seconds."

I remained stationary. Should I stay or return? He glared at those fumbling in the dark, waving his wrist under their eyes. Slowly the soldiers stood to attention and waited. I could see each of their fearful faces. George was last, knocking into the table as he stumbled in front of it.

"Robertson!" he barked without looking.

"Yes Corporal!"

"Demonstrate again." I did so, even more slowly, and then at his nod, re-assembled it. "You could do this with your eyes closed." He took an oily cloth from the table and blindfolded me before placing the rifle in my arms. I checked the table was still there. "Go." How many hundreds of times had I helped father clean his guns, ready for a shooting party on the estate? The corporal was right. Touch was enough.

He removed the blindfold and I glanced at the rifle. Complete. "Robertson. You are dismissed. The rest of you will continue to assemble and take apart until I am satisfied. Is that clear?"

"Yes Corporal!" echoed across the barracks.

I had checked through my kit, polishing and buffing everything, before the first comrade arrived in our hut. He was pleased to be there, but still worried. Others came in slowly and we trooped off to the canteen. The food was basic, but warm. Late comers grabbed some grub and joined us. They were sombre and some sent hostile glances in my direction. We returned to the hut and found George laid out on his bunk next to mine.

He didn't want to talk. I rooted through my locker and pulled out the last of the biscuits cook sent me off to war with. I put them by his nose and he slowly opened his wet eyes. "Thanks." I watched him nibble the first and dispatch the last two. "Thanks."

"We'll practice when we get the chance." I didn't have to say more, but realised how sheltered his life had been, plucked from a grammar school of academic renown without a modicum of practical experience to his name. My education in the woods and fields in all weathers beat his hands down.

"Lights out in five!" was bellowed from the NCO's cosy room at the end of the hut and we scurried to get ready for the pitch-black that would descend. This war wasn't glamourous for us.

8   SITTING WAITING

Where is she? Why hasn't Mummy come. Or Daddy? I'll climb a little higher on the cold tubes to see over the brick wall that surrounds our little playground. When I sit here, I can see Mrs Blake through the window, with her pink hat and fluffy coat on, tidying things into boxes and cupboards. All the other Mummies came, but not mine. Can I climb higher? I never have liked to climb, especially when the rough boys are here, or when the girls are swinging, their legs kicking anyone who's near.

"Tom." I turn my head to see it's Mrs Blake behind me. "Can you come down safely and help me please?" She's too far away. I'm scared. I can't move. Her face is turning white.

I can hear a click and a creak and footsteps before a strong hand holds my leg. "Stay still, Tom. This looks fun."

I'm so pleased to hear that voice and see Daddy's face beside mine. "It's nice up here, but it's time to go home. Hold on to my neck." I feel an arm around my waist as he hugs me tight.

Mrs Blake gives me a cuddle too as we reach the ground. "How is she?" she asks.

Daddy nods in my direction before saying quietly, "Not too bad, all things considered. I must apologise to you Mrs Blake, but we all fell asleep. I only woke up when Susie jumped on me. Come on Tom. Let's go and see what your sister's up to."

We walk along the path past our favourite shop, but Daddy stops and takes me back inside. "Special treat," he says, "I've brought the sweet ration book. Shall we choose something Susie would like?" He looks at my face. "And something for you." He gives the books to the lady and I choose some liquorice laces. Daddy chooses some dolly mixtures for Susie. "Here's the money. Pay the lady please Tom." I reach my hand up to the counter and let go of the silver coin. She gives me a penny back. "You can put that in your piggy bank when we get home."

We say thank you as we leave and I start sucking. It's nice holding Daddy's hand.

"Look," he says, "there's Mr Penrose. He's the man who jumped in the water to rescue Susie. Let's catch him up." Daddy scoops me up and carries me along the path. I hope we don't get too near because that dog is with him.

"Hello Mr Penrose. It's nice to see you again. It's Alf Robertson. We met yesterday when you brought our pram home for us."

"I thought I recognised your voice. How is she?"

"If you've got time, come and meet her. My wife wants to thank you properly too. We're nearly there."

"Daddy? Why does the man have a white stick?"

9 SIT TENNIS

Sylvie slowly guides me around the building, pointing out places and people that I ought to know about. Next to the Reception there's a large room with many armchairs, some of which are occupied by lolling residents. There are some boxes of games, jigsaws and quite a few books for me to read and sort out. The wide windows look out on to a garden. Mm. Another escape route. Through a door there's a stairway which we climb to a craft room. Mm. Useful tools. There are two long corridors stretching out at right angles. "I'm in number 37 along here." She's leading me into a sunny room which looks through the trees to a sparkling stream. That looks tempting. "Which room are you in?" I stretch out the fingers of both hands. Sylvie nods and mouths, "Ten."

We return to the stairway and she points. "This is where the nurses keep all the tablets and drops which most of us need. Do you have to take any medication?" I don't know so I shake my head. She leads me down the stairs again and back to the large room. "I'm supposed to join in as many activities in here as I can, especially those involving movement. Will you join in too?" I nod again and we take a seat in a corner of the room.

A jolly lady with a bright yellow shirt comes in, carrying a dining room chair, followed by two more with Mary and another blue-uniformed helper. They put them in a row and return with more chairs until there are two rows of six facing each other. "Are you all ready for some fun?" she asks brightly, looking at the inmates. None of them move. "Come on Sylvie, lead the way please." Sylvie struggles out of the chair and turns to me to follow. We sit next to each other and are joined by five more bodies. "Just stay there and I'll round up some more."

Some more men and women shuffle in and eleven of the chairs are finally filled. "Let's begin then. All ready?"

"No!" Sylvie calls. "My friend here is new."

"Sorry, dear. What's your name?"

My only response is to give her my stare. "We don't know yet," says Isabel from the doorway. "We're waiting for her voice to return. Do get on with your game, Francie."

"Sorry Dear," she says and pats my arm. "Right. Balloon tennis. One point to the team who can hit the balloon on to the floor behind the other side's line. Ready? Set?"

A muffled response of "Go," emanates from a few lips as Francie lofts the large red balloon into the air between us. It falls exactly in the middle where no-one can reach it. Brilliant. Great game. Francie tries again, but ensures it is nearer to our opponents and a feeble pat spins it towards me. Instinctively I flick it up with my toe and whack it high over the opposition and watch as it sails away and floats gently into the lap of a snoring inmate.

"One to this team," Francie declares.

"That's not fair," grumbles a bearded man, "it didn't touch the floor."

"Don't you start arguing with the referee Ted, or you'll be in the sin bin."

"Again," comes from the rest of his team. I like Ted. He's a rebel and quick assessor of situations. Mm. Maybe another recruit? The balloon goes up and it comes straight to me. Splat. Another point.

"Keep it away from her," says the beard. He's trying, but it twists straight to me. I toy with them, pretending to strike it and tap it to Sylvie who tries to wave her arms quickly, but the movement is difficult for her. The balloon twirls forward and is bashed straight over our heads. The next try lasts much longer, back and forward several times before the beard jumps up to strike it hard to the ceiling. "Take that!" The explosion as it hits the hot light startles the entire room and brings staff running. He stays on his feet and struts out of the room. Oh dear, a bad loser. Perhaps not good for my team. I'll see where he goes.

He marches down the corridor and into a small room at the end. There are two tables set with plates, cups and saucers for four people and he heads to a machine in the corner. I watch him place a cup underneath, press buttons and watch a thick liquid dribble out. He turns with his prize and is startled by my presence in the doorway. A huge grin spreads across his face. "I love causing them headaches. Do you want a cup?"

10 POSITIVE

I'm a big girl now. I can use the potty. I can hear voices. Daddy and Tom are home. Mummy's saying come in to someone else, but it sounds as if she's crying. I want Mummy.

Daddy's come. He picks me up gently. "Good girl. Well done Susie. Let's dry you."

I can dress myself so I push past him to find Mummy. I stop at the door. There's a big man there, being hugged by my Mummy. Why are you crying Mummy? I run and hug her leg. She lets go of the man and picks me up. She's smiling through her wet face and squeezes me tight. "Oh Susie, Susie. This is the lovely man who pulled you out of the water. Can you say thank you?" I bury my face into Mummy's neck. "She's shy Mr Penfold. Please. Let's all sit down. Alf! Could you put the kettle on?"

It's all gone quiet. I can hear lots of breathing. I hear Daddy filling the kettle. One day I'll be big enough to do that. I hear the whoomph of the gas catching alight. Daddy comes back in and sits beside Mummy and I feel him stroke my hair. I like that. I feel safe. "Mr. Penrose," Daddy says, "we will never be able to thank you enough. We are forever in your debt and I want to say that if I, we, can help you in any way, you only have to ask."

I hear his kind voice. "I only did what anyone else would do."

"But you are not anyone! You are –"

"Blind." The man laughs. "You can say it. I am not ashamed of what I am. I used to be, but not any more. And that is down to my own little girl."

"You have a daughter too?" Mummy asks as she gives me another squeeze.

"Yes. Darling Rachel. She rescued me – from depression I suppose. She made me realise that I had to be positive – that life still had a purpose. She brought laughter back to my world where I was wallowing in darkness."

Daddy gets up as we hear the kettle start its whistle. "Tea, Mr Penrose?"

"Thank you. That would be nice, but no milk for me."

He's bringing me a drink in my special cup with a spout. I like this taste. As I pull away from Mummy's neck, I sneak a glance at the man. He has dark glasses on.

I can see Daddy has put a tray on the table with the big fluffy cosy. It's hot. Tom put it on my head once and Mummy shouted at him. Very hot.

"Most people want to ask me about my eyes. I don't mind now. It saves awkward silences which I am well-used to hearing." The man has a deep, but soft voice. I can see his face now.

"If you'd like to tell us, then we'd be honoured to hear," Daddy said as he poured the tea into three cups. "This is still hot." He placed one on the little table just in front of the man and held his hand to the cup's handle.

"Thank you. You are obviously a very thoughtful person, Mr Robertson."

"Alf please – and Lily."

33

"I'm honoured, as well as being Cyril to my friends, which I already feel you are," the man says. "I wear these glasses mainly because I'm not quite sure what effect I would have on people if they could see what's behind them. I get enough pity from the do-gooders. I was in the Third Army Corps just north of the Somme in 1918. We were part of what was later called the Battle of Amiens and we moved silently through the thick fog on the 8th August. We caught the Gerries asleep and we had captured a lot of ground before they fired a shot. But fire they did. We had some small tanks with us and a bullet bounced off one and across my face." He's having a sip of his drink. "I must have blacked out immediately and don't remember how I got back to England. There was nothing the doctors could do to save my sight and I had to accept my lot."

The grown-ups are all drinking their tea and saying nothing. Where's Tom? I haven't seen him. I wonder if he's hiding. I slip out of Mummy's arms and look around the room. Kitchen? No. Toilet? No. He must be in here with the others. I look under the chairs and see something very yellow by the man's feet. As I go nearer, two large eyes open and a head lifts from the floor. "Doggy!"

11   GRIM SITUATIONS

She spoke. "Oh my darling. How lovely to hear you." I drop to my knees and cuddle her. Alf's joined me too.

"Would you like to stroke Jason, Susie?" Cyril asks.

Susie looks to us both for reassurance. I'm taking her precious hand in mine and gently place it on the dog's neck. I show her a soft stroke and she's copying me. A little giggle gurgles from her. "Nice doggy."

"Very nice doggy," I agree. I'm losing the fight with my tears again.

Alf puts his hand in front of Jason's nose and receives a lick. Susie chuckles again. "Susie try." I steady her fingers as Jason's pink tongue wraps itself around her. "Tickles." Before I can stop her, she's flinging her arms around the dog and giving him her special hug. "Good doggy."

Jason is excited by the fuss and Cyril calls a halt by calling his name. Immediately his eyes are fixed on his master who takes hold of the harness and stands up. "I think it is time that I got going. Rachel will be back soon."

I watch Alf slip his hand under Cyril's arm and gently guide him to the door. As I follow, I see Tom disappearing up a few more stairs. "Mr Penrose, Cyril, we would love to get to know you better and want you to know there's a warm welcome here at any time."

"You are most kind to say so, Lily." He reaches out his free hand to me and I squeeze it. "If I'm pointing in the direction of Burney Avenue then Jason will take me home. Home Jason. Good dog."

"Good doggy," Susie mimics.

I pull her up to me and give her a big kiss. "Now let's see what your big brother is doing." As we file back indoors, I hear his sobs. "Alf. Take Susie in for a biscuit please."

As I near the top of the stairs I see the blood. "Tom. Where are you?" There's a trail towards the bathroom and the sound of water. I'm there in an instant. "Mummy's here darling."

My little boy is standing on Susie's step-up to hold his arm under the tap. "Oh Tom. Let Mummy see." I've seen far too many wounds in my time, but when it's your own flesh and blood running away down the drain, it's something far worse.

"Good boy for washing it," I tell him as I yank open the wall cupboard, causing its contents to cascade to the floor. I grab a roller bandage and push it against the wound. "Can you hold that for Mummy please Tom?" His whole body is quaking as I sit him on the floor beside me. "Good boy." I start to unravel another bandage and tightly wrap it around the first. The safety pins have scattered everywhere so it's easy to find one. "Alf! I need you here – now!"

Blood drains from his face. "What –"

"Put Susie in the pram and race her up to the phone box. 999. Ambulance. Artery bleed. Go."

I wrap Tom in the largest towel I can see. His tiny frame is shaking as shock kicks in. I pick him up and carry him downstairs, whispering to him as I go. We sit quietly waiting. Here's the tell-tale bell clanging. I take my precious bundle outside and see Alf rushing to get to us. At least Susie looks pleased to be riding in a speeding chariot.

As soon as the back doors open, I carry him in and sit him on my lap. The doors close and we are soon on our way. I brief the attendant and we look at the seepage through the bandages. It's not as bad as I feared. "Leave it bound, I think," I say to him.

"Because?"

I look at him. "Sorry. I'm his Mum and a nurse at Kingston Hospital. I've packed the wound and bound it tightly."

"Then we'll leave it as is. Can I take his blood pressure?"

"It's alright Tom. This kind man is helping Mummy get you better." I free his other arm from the blanket.

"Mm. Has he lost a lot of blood?"

"Quite a bit. He was over the sink with running water when I got to him. The trail there wasn't too bad." I stroke his tangled mop of hair. "This is an adventure again, isn't it? Yesterday it was Susie and today it's you. We're getting used to the bells ringing, aren't we?" I see the flicker of a smile.

We're straight in and Doctor Clark pulls the curtain closed as he enters the bay. "What's he done?"

"Puncture to left ulnar artery, Doctor," I answer before the ambulance crew can.

"We'll see." He takes the wraps off and a squirt hits his glasses. "Blast!" Staff Nurse proffers a lint dressing which he uses to mop his face as I place my thumb on the open wound. He takes a clean dressing and applies it over my thumb, which I pull away. I lean back to allow more room to start the packing and bandaging process. "Get some fluids in him!" he says as he dashes out.

Staff smiles at me. "It's a good job we're used to him, isn't it?" She puts several more layers on top and then we lift Tom on to the bed. "I'll send in a drink for him. It won't be long."

"Thanks Staff." I turn back to my treasure and caress his brow.

A nurse breezes in with a beaker with a spout in the lid and two handles. "Ooh. Hello Lily. I didn't know it was you. Doctor's not in a good mood. Here you are young man. Your Mummy will help you. I want you to drink this all up for me. Do you think you can?"

Tom tries to nod and raise his arm. "Keep still Tom. I'll hold it. This should taste nice." He's doing really well. "Good boy. That's it. A little bit more will make you feel better." I'm glad to see the bandages are still white. I pray they stay that way. "Very good, Tom. The nurse will be pleased with you. Have a rest now. A little sleep will do you good. Mummy will sit here beside you." I stroke his brow and slow my rhythm until I know the medicine in the drink has taken him into the land of nod.

I stand up and stretch. I've been on the edge of my seat for a long time and I've realised where I'm numb. I shake my legs and bend up and down before I settle back into the chair. The curtain moves and a mug of tea comes in with Glynis. "I thought you might need one. There's another drink for him when he wakes."

"Thanks so much. Can you stay with him for a moment whilst I powder my nose?" I'm relieved to see Tom still peacefully asleep as I return. "Thanks, friend. I needed that."

I smile as I settle back into the chair and sip my tea. These aren't supplied to 'normal' parents. I hadn't realised how ready for it I was. Perhaps we should consider giving a drink in these sorts of circumstances. Parents are in shock too. Mm. I'll talk to Sister when I'm next on duty.

I watch Tom's breathing, calm and rhythmical. He looks so like his father, just as I first saw him, tucked into a bed in Surbiton Hospital. The Dunkirk evacuees were filling all the beds. Surbiton is small so, as I lived nearby, I was transferred there and detailed to one of the Men's Wards. We had double the usual number of beds squashed in and we had to treat without the use of screens or any privacy. Many were dreadfully wounded; others had been in such grim situations they'd shut down their responses; others just slept through exhaustion.

It was Alf's smile each time I passed by that tugged at me – his thanks for every simple task that I performed. So many men were incapable of responding. It was as if he was a sham – as if he shouldn't be there, taking up a bed. But of course, he should. His injury was just as acute. His blood loss had been horrific. How he survived the channel crossing was due to the skill of a seaman on board. But he was a natural fighter. He fought the pain in his body with his head. He found reasons to be grateful to overcome the gloom. He was a ray of hope amidst the sea of despairing bodies. My heart skipped each time I looked into his eyes.

"Mummy."

"Mummy's here dear." My heart skips again as my little fighter comes back to me.

"Mummy. Can I have a drink please?"

12 DON'T SIT THERE

Lily doesn't usually look that worried. "Let's wave to the ambulance, Susie. Good girl. Now. Let's get you indoors."

"Doggy gone."

"Yes. Doggy's gone with the kind man.

"Kind man."

As I park the pram at the foot of the stairs and lift her out, I know I need to clean up. "Let's find you some toys to play with." I pull the toybox out of the cupboard and leave it in the middle of the hall for her to help herself. Right – think. Cleaning materials from the kitchen, bowl, scrubbing brush. Close all doors. "Susie. I'm going upstairs to do something. I won't be long. Play with the toys."

"Toys." She's already diving into the treasures that Tom guards so carefully.

Our thin stair carpet has some dark red spots. The landing lino is streaked red. The bathroom floor is covered in debris from the cupboard. The sink is coated with vermillion. Plan of action. Wash your own hand. Pick up everything clean and put it away. Wipe everything else and make a pile.

I creep down a few stairs and watch Susie. All of the cars and lorries are in a traffic jam, just as her brother plays. I hear gentle brms coming from her. I have to smile.

Back to work. Bowl of water, soap and scrubbing brush after I've wiped off the worst. I'm pleased with how it's looking. Carpet next. Soap and scrub. Mop it dry. That's the best I can do. Check Susie. Finish in bathroom. Wash myself again. All done.

I tiptoe past Susie and look at the mantlepiece clock. "It's ten past seven, Susie. Let's find you something to eat and a story before bedtime." Oh good. There's some left-over soup. I cut us some bread into soldiers as it heats and spoon some into her bowl before it becomes too hot. Susie is by my side to be lifted into her highchair. "Thank you Susie. Here is your soup." I test it with a finger and "Mm."

"Soupa soupa."

I turn off the gas and pour a bowl full. I need this. "Super soup." She giggles as she eats. She's become so good with her spoon so quickly. There's not much splashing down her dress. "Bib?" Oh dear. I'll wash that too. I find her a small bowl of custard in the larder which has set quite hard from two days ago. I chop it into chunks for her. Her smile shows what she thinks of it. A bottle of warm milk to wash it all down and into a clean nappy and pyjamas. "Shall we find a story to take to bed?" I know what she'll choose.

"Doggy story."

She's clutching our well-thumbed copy of 'Rover the Sheepdog', climbing up to the little bedroom. She tucks down under the covers in anticipation. I've only got to the third page. I tiptoe out and pull the door to leave just a crack.

I'd better check on Tom's room. The light helps. I can't see any marks here. Oh. By the bedpost. There's a tight circular band of black laces that have been cut across their width. I gaze across the floor and spot a handle, covered in blood. "Oh no." It's my fault. I left my razor out this morning.

I'll finish my meal and wash through her clothes before Lily comes home. I wonder how he is? No. I've got to be patient so stay active. Less thinking time. Come on Alf. Stay strong.

I've checked everywhere is tidy – twice. I've got to look after myself as well. I'll make myself a cuppa. Mm. I need this.

Nearly as good as that first cup that Lily ever made me in hospital. My she's beautiful. I remember thinking that as soon as she appeared in the ward. She seemed to have more time than others for every soldier; to say a few words or plump a pillow; even those who couldn't respond. Too often a bed would be empty and stripped before it was filled again by another unfortunate. My, I was lucky. Good bed, good food, good view of the sky and trees – and Nurse Crowther to look forward to each day.

But then the doctor decreed I should be sent to rehabilitation. I couldn't argue. It was decided. But I didn't want to leave her. Would she be on duty before I went tomorrow? I remember that night so clearly, wondering, worrying.

I felt such relief as breakfast came round, delivered by my angel. She knew I was going. She had a special smile for me as she pressed a small piece of paper into my hand and moved on with the next tray. I slipped it under the covers as Matron appeared in the doorway, marched through inspecting every bed with eagle eyes before striding on in search of her prey. I gave my best salute and spilt the tea over the bed. I had to laugh, and so did those awake enough to do so. Sister was not amused. "Nurse! Strip this!" Did she mean me? It was the bedclothes that were grabbed and bundled on to the trolley. "Get dressed. You're leaving soon anyway!"

I couldn't find it. It wasn't on the floor. I sat disconsolately on the corner of the bed to finish the food. It was soggy with tea, but still was ten times better than what we were used to over there. "Don't sit there!" Sister barked. "What would

Matron think? Not in my ward! There's a chair in the corridor. Move! Clear that tray Crowther!"

I watched her go and turned to give a wave to my comrades. "Good luck, chaps. Remember who we're fighting! There's a war on!" I gave a salute in the direction of Sister and marched out to the sound of a few feeble cheers.

13 SIT ANYWHERE

I like the look of Ted. He seems a kindred spirit and certainly would have more muscle power than either Sylvie or me. I ease past him to the machine and study it. Mm. Hot chocolate sounds nice. I press the button and he laughs. I wonder why. I look back and see the steaming liquid pouring through the wire mesh. Oops. I take a cup off of the table and catch a few drips before pressing the same button. Better. I take a wrapped pair of biscuits from the basket before I turn and sit at the other table, directly facing Ted.

He sips his drink. He stares past me. "Great tits." What can he mean? My lack of response amuses him. "Out there. On the feeders. They're quite regular visitors about this time." He drinks again and I rip the packaging apart to devour a crunchy biscuit. Nice. The chocolate isn't. Very gritty and milky. I should have known better. I try to cleanse my throat with the other biscuit. I turn to watch the birds.

The clatter of a trolley scatters them. "I hope you aren't leading our new lady astray, Ted," says a yellow uniformed girl.

"Cynthia. How could you think such thoughts of me?"

"Because I know you." She looks at my cup. "Not very nice, is it." She takes it away, replaces the cups and adds some spares to the side table. "Now Ted. Have you forgotten who's coming to see you today?" He looks unsure, and I detect a chink in his defences. "It's half term so she's here again. Your favourite singer."

Ted's face beams. "Come on. She's brilliant!"

I follow to the main room where quite a crowd has already gathered. There are just two chairs left. "Sit anywhere," he says, plonking himself on one.

Luckily the other vacancy is next to Sylvie. "I wondered where you'd got to." I gesture with my hands, waving them along the corridor and left. "Sh. You'll like this."

I focus on the very young girl sat at the corner of the room on a dining room chair. She has kind eyes and a lovely smile as she stands. There's a hush in the room. "It's really nice to be back here with you. Thank you for allowing me to come. As I parked my bicycle there was a bird singing in the bushes and it brought back a favourite song to me. Will you all join in?" She smiles around the room at the nods. "When ... the ... red, red robin comes bob, bob, bobbin' along, along–"

My arm is held by a hand and I am encouraged to stand and follow. "There'll be no more sobbin' when he starts–"

Isabel takes me gently through the Reception Area and along a short corridor to a brown door. She knocks, listens, and then we go in. "Here she is Doctor. If you just sit there Dear and I'll be just here. The Doctor needs to check you over so we know if there is anything else we should be doing to help you." I sit stiffly.

He's looking at me intensely over half-framed spectacles. "Mm. Hello. I'm Doctor Whittle. We'll just do some simple tests shall we? What name shall I call you?" I won't flicker an eyelid until he's averted his gaze to write in his file. He stands and walks round to my side to take my wrist and thrust a thermometer under my tongue. I feel my pulse quickening under his grip. He leans across the desk to record the numbers. He unwinds the stethoscope from his neck and fills his ears.

45

"May I?" Do I have a choice? The metal end is cold on my skin and I shiver, as if I'm plunged into a river. "Mm." He notes everything. "Eyes next. Look up please. Down. Left. Right. And now this eye." He returns to his seat and writes before putting his face into a smile. "That all looks good. Let's look in your throat next." He brings a metal strip and holds down my tongue. "Say Ah." I don't. "Try for me." I don't. "Mm." He feels either side of my neck, pressing firmly until tears well in my eyes. I gulp. "Good. Thank you." He's writing a novel. "Height and weight next please. Just slip your shoes off and stand under here." I do and slouch a little. "Push the slider up with your head." I do. "Let's try again please, without standing on tiptoes. Good. Weight here please." I'm going to wait here as long as I can. He's writing and hasn't noticed. As he looks up, I see a puzzled frown spread across his brow.

Isabel's standing beside me. "Doctor wants you to be weighed here, Dear, not wait there." I can see her eyes sparkling.

He comes and fiddles with the sliding bar weights until it settles at horizontal. "I see." He studies me. "Mm. You can sit down again." He writes chapter two.

"I think that will be all for today, thank you. You can take her away now. It must be lunchtime. Give me ten minutes before coming back for a discussion about her." He gives me his practised smile before turning back to his papers. I want to tip his desk up on top of him. "I think I'll stay for a lunch today if you'll inform chef?" I think I've won a few victories in this skirmish.

14 SITTING TARGET

That Corporal. He delighted in the wake-up din he could create with his spoon and billy-can as he stomped the central aisle of our hut. Those nearest the lavs got there quickly before the scrum developed. A shave is a nightmare amongst elbows and hands. "Inspection in five!"

"Stand by your beds!" The spotty Lieutenant marched in, swagger stick under his arm, to the salute of the NCO. We were stiff as he prodded at blankets and opened an occasional locker.

I daren't look at his face as the fluff he was trying to grow on his upper lip was a regular source of ribald comments amongst the lads. "What's this, Corporal?" He waved his stick under my nose, wiping an oily rag across my face.

"Robertson. Latrine duty. Move!"

The Corporal's boots brought mud in as he inspected my work. His prints were the only fault he could find. "Clean this floor! Rifle Range in ten!"

"Yes Corporal!" I replied from my hands and knees.

I was last to arrive having sprinted to the furthest corner of the camp. The Lieutenant was there, all pomp and no credibility; Public School fast track no doubt. "D squad!" bellowed the Corporal. "Tallest on the right, shortest on the left, single rank, size!" We shuffled past each other, each pretending we had grown taller since yesterday's drill, apart from George who sloped to the left. "By the right, number!" Each called out the next number in ascending order. "Odd numbers, one pace step forward, even numbers one step backwards. March!" Oh dear. Some were still at sixes and sevens. "You horrible shower! What will the Officer think of you?" He turned and saluted before puffing out his chest and marching to the rear.

"Well chaps. I think we could do better. There's no time to lose if we're going to sort out the Huns, so get stuck in and try your best." He turned to a huge moustached figure that had arrived unnoticed and waved a limp salute. "Carry on Sergeant."

"Thank you, Sir!" He waited till the officer was out of earshot. "You are the only defence that your mothers and sweethearts have got from the marauding enemy who will sweep you aside like swine unless you, yes you, learn how to shoot 'em first." He walked menacingly between the ranks. Have they all passed rifle assembly, Corporal?"

"Yes Sergeant!"

"I heard there was a star performer in your squad."

"Yes Sergeant!"

"Name?"

"Robertson Sergeant!" I gulped in a lungful.

"Robertson! Three steps forward!" I obeyed and swayed a little as I halted. His eyes penetrated every fibre. "Have you used a rifle?"

"Yes Sergeant!"

"Take Position One." He indicated a small card affixed to a very low fence to which I marched. "At ease soldier." He placed a rifle in my hands. "Watch carefully!" he bellowed at the squad. I examined the Lee-Enfield point-two-two single shot under his gaze. "Load!" I took a cartridge from the box attached to the fence and loaded it. "Ready. Aim. Fire!" The kick was lighter than I was used to. "Reload. Kneeling position." I bent my right knee to the duckboard. "Ready. Aim. Fire!" The small white target twenty yards away buckled. "Prone position!" I laid stretched out with my left elbow bracing the rifle. "Ready. Aim. Fire!" I was confident of my aim. "On your feet!" He held out his hands for the rifle as I stood, back at attention.

He examined me again. "What did you think soldier?"

"Sergeant. The first shot was a little to the left as this is a little lighter than I'm used to. The other two seemed satisfactory Sergeant."

He received the target from a scurrying orderly and frowned. "Mm. Two holes. One left and one centre." He put it in his pocket. "Corporal. First six."

"Sergeant! Numbers one to six will take those places. Seven to twelve will stand behind with thirteen onwards behind them. Squad – fall out."

Each soldier took six shots, two from each position, before their numbered targets were delivered to the Sergeant who put each man into groups according to their results. "Poor," he said to the first group, "very poor," to the second and "diabolical!" to the last. "Corporal, we'll have to think what is appropriate for anyone who still cannot hit the target three times."

"Yes Sergeant! One to six to your positions."

The morning continued and the pressure to succeed increased with each round. Finally, the Sergeant seemed satisfied. "Robertson!"

"Yes Sergeant!"

"Position thirteen!" I marched to the fence and looked towards the target. Mm. The paper human silhouette was about fifty yards away. "Prone position. Load. On my order, fire at – left hand. Reload. Right knee. Reload, left ear – right ankle. Cease fire. On my command, rapid fire, six shots, alternate head and chest. Understood?"

"Yes Sergeant!"

"Fire!" I enjoyed letting rip at speed and seeing the paper pierced in the distance. "At ease soldier." He turned to the assembled group. "That is how you might survive this conflict. Every single one of you needs to be a crack shot." He held his hand out for the target as the orderly approached and held it to the men. There was an audible intake of air as they realised the holes I'd created matched his orders.

"Corporal. Dismiss the squad – except Robertson."

"Yes Sergeant!"

As the men drifted away, he looked me in the eye. "Background?"

"Father taught me years ago. He's a gamekeeper, Sergeant."

"I thought so. Right. You are our representative in the company shooting contest, tomorrow. Now. Get to the canteen for lunch. You've a ten-mile run in full kit this afternoon."

"Yes Sergeant!"

"And get a good night's sleep tonight."

"Yes Sergeant!" I was going to need it. And sleep I did.

15 SITUATION CONFUSED

I didn't mean to sleep. My arm is numb from resting across the edge of the bed, ready for Tom's gentlest touch. He's so peaceful with the softest of breaths.

I hear the curtain move behind me. "I've brought you another cuppa. Go and freshen up. I'll stay with him."

"You're a treasure, Glynis." It's good to move. The first hint of dawn is showing itself in the east and an enormous shudder of relief floods through me. I make it into the toilet and breathe silently. The warm water splashed on my face revives my skin and I'm ready to face the day.

"Here's Mummy, Tom. I said she'd be right here." He puts out both arms for a cuddle and I melt into him. "What a good boy you've been for us Tom. Now, I have to have a quick look at your arm so, while I get my trolley, how about you and Mummy both have a drink?"

Tom is just as keen as I am and he manages the beaker with his strong arm. Staff Nurse comes in as the trolley returns and smiles. "Tea for two is it? Good idea." She takes Tom's wrist and watches her brooch watch, just as we all do. "Pulse is great Nurse," she says to both of us. "Now we've got to ask Mummy to move a little further away for us to see how that arm is. That's fine there, Mummy." I've changed too many dressings to count, but now is the worst, just watching as the white turns to pale vermillion and many shades of crimson.

"Gently now Tom. This bit is stuck so I'm going to cut the rest off."

Tom flinches, but doesn't cry out. He's my brave soldier. Just like his Dad. I hope he has coped with Susie. "Well done Tom."

Staff smiles at him too. "We'll ask Doctor to come and look. He won't be long."

I sit back beside him and we both finish our drinks. I can see his eyelids drooping as the drug takes effect again. His breathing slows as he drifts off and I settle back into the chair. I do miss his chatter, but his body needs to recover. His tousled locks remind me so much of his father.

Alf was such a character and my heart went out to him. When I learnt he was to be moved on I didn't know what to do. I could only think that he would write if I gave him my address. I thought he liked me, but he never made any contact. I couldn't bear to look at the bed he'd occupied and was so relieved when the numbers dwindled and I could return to Kingston where every day was busy. I kept looking as I walked home or into town; perhaps I'd catch a glimpse of him one day.

And I did. A reflection in a shop window caught my eye and I spun round to see him disappearing along a narrow street, barely wide enough for a cart. I wanted to call out, but my mouth was dry. He turned at the end into the fruit and veg market, full of traders shouting their wares. I lost sight of him and my heart sank, but no, there he was, bent over some oranges. I couldn't wait. I touched him on the shoulder. "Hello there. Surprise!"

He turned, but he wasn't Alf. "Well, hello. How lovely," he said and offered his hand. In my embarrassment I stretched mine out and he took it and raised it gently to his lips. He almost had that same cheeky grin that I had found so endearing. "And what may I do for you, young lady?" The stallholder made a coarse remark. "We'd better move away from here, I think. May I buy you a cup of tea or something and you can tell me who you think I am?" He led me back to a small café and ordered a pot of tea for two. Two large mugs of steaming brew arrived.

I didn't know where to start, other than apologise for mistaking him for a lost friend. He listened attentively as I blurted out a little of my story. When I paused to sip the cooling liquid, he said, "I'm Rod. What's your name?"

I coloured. "Sorry… Lily."

"Well, it's lovely to meet you Sorry Lily." I blushed even more. I didn't know what to say. "Where are you supposed to be going?"

I took another gulp. "Just popping into Woolies."

We stayed silent and drank our tea. "Shall we go?" he asked. We walked together until we reached the swing doors. "May I ask you to accompany me to the cinema tomorrow evening?"

I was taken aback. "Er. Yes. Er. Which one?"

"Good question. Have you seen the new one, The Holiday Inn? It's a musical with Fred Astaire and Bing Crosby. I hear it's quite good. Shall we say the Odeon at seven? I'll see you there."

He'd disappeared before I could change my mind. What had I done?

"What have we here?" asks Doctor Brisket as he enters, "Sleeping Beauty?"

"Tom Robertson, Doctor. Admitted last night with punctured Ulna Artery. This is his mother, Nurse Robertson," says the Staff Nurse.

He glances towards me. "Sorry, I didn't recognise you. Let's just look. Mm. How long ago did you expose to here?"

"Forty minutes, Doctor."

"Excellent. No seepage. Well. Mummy Nurse. If we give you the dressings you'll need, do you think he'd be happier at home?"

"Yes Doctor. Thank you. There's just one snag. I don't think I can carry him to the bus stop."

"That's a good point. Could you sort an ambulance please Staff?"

"I'll try, Doctor," Staff says to his back. "Stay there until he's finished his round."

She's back in ten minutes with her coat on and a wheelchair. "I was due off an hour ago. We'll push him to my car Lily and I'll pop you both home. You might have to wait hours for an ambulance."

16 SITUATION VACANT

Is that the front door? My I'm stiff. "Hello darling." I mustn't ask the obvious in front of Tom. "Have you come home in a car?"

"Yes Daddy. I've not been in a car before. It was lovely and noisy. I'm hungry. Can I have some breakfast please?"

Lily looks drawn as she gives me a quick hug before climbing the stairs to check on our other treasure. "Shall we start with some porridge? Here's some bread while I cook it. Have you been good for Mummy?"

He nods with his mouth full. His bandaged arm seems to be working well. I feared he'd end up like me.

"She's still sleeping. Well done – upstairs." She motions cleaning and I smile a little.

"Porridge for us all, coming up."

"And then you must get ready for work. You missed yesterday and part of the day before. We need you to keep your job." She reaches across and gives my hand a gentle caress. "Not that I want you to go. We'll manage, won't we Tom?"

"Can I go digging in the garden as it's sunny?"

"No Tom. Remember what Staff Nurse said. That arm must stay clean and I've got to be the Nurse-in-charge or I will be in trouble."

The kettle whistles and I make a pot of tea. "I'll go up to wash and change while it brews."

Yes, she's still sleeping. My face looks terrible. As I lather up and take up my razor from the shelf my hand shakes, picturing it in Tom's. Get on with it. Steady under fire, Alf. That's better. Clean shaven and smartly suited.

It's a cut above my army-issue-on-discharge suit. That had clothed me well for some interviews, although all were dismissive of my ability to do their job. My digs in Thames Ditton were rather dilapidated, but cheap. One morning I'd found my landlady tut-tutting over a story in the Surrey Comet about the thefts from the large store in Kingston. "They need catching," she said. "Those flibberty-jibbet girls in there wouldn't be able to. It needs a man to stand up to thieves."

With no other plans for the day, I made my way along the embankment and through the open-air market until the impressive façade of Bentalls filled the scene. I'd nothing to lose and nothing to spend, so I just went in to see what the place was like. The floors were huge with displays of what to spend your rations on. There were wide, double staircases going up and down and lists of what to find on each level. Now, I wondered, if I were a thief, where would I be heading?

I went right to the top and found an almost empty bedding department. Down a floor, most of staff were chatting whilst a few were re-arranging displays. There were two brown-coated ladies, each carrying a large cardboard box. It was their furtive glances that caught my attention. I followed their progress, visiting any stand that was unoccupied. One delivered a box behind the counter whilst the other rested her's on top, positioning herself between her friend and the nearest assistant. The first returned, still with her box and they progressed around the floor, making three more stops before entering a staff service lift.

I descended the stairs and soon spotted them repeating their activity. Sometimes a box was not fully closed and I saw the handles of carrier bags protruding. I left them to it and made my way to the ground floor. The lift was away from the exit and so I approached the most senior-looking lady who was addressing two junior workers. "Excuse me please for interrupting. I understand that your store has been losing merchandise to thieves. I think that two ladies will shortly come out of the staff lift and make their way to the door with carrier bags of goods from several departments."

The face of the senior was plastered with make-up and her expression told me that her domain was no place for a man. The lift door opened and two elegantly dressed ladies stepped out, each carrying several Bentalls carrier bags. "There they are."

"Don't be ridiculous. They couldn't possibly." She stood watching them walk directly towards the exit.

"Excuse me!" I called as I ran towards them.

They bolted. The second one saw I was gaining and swung her bags at my head. As I ducked, I lost my footing on the polished floor and demolished a display of gloves. The carriers' handles broke and scattered contents over customers and the floor. The thief used the confusion to escape onto the pavement and away.

"Girls. Clear up this mess!" Miss Crusty ordered. Other staff joined in and I was soon surrounded by chattering females.

"Miss Swanscombe. What is going on? Who is responsible?"

"He is, Mr Frobisher."

He looked at me over his spectacles. "You'd better come to my office." His tone reminded me of a corporal at basic training. "I don't want any trouble."

From experience I knew this was not the place to argue so walked at his side through a passage to an office with a window that looked out over much of the floor area. "Sit there." Mm. Ex-military from the first time. He sat behind a large desk and looked me over. "Well?"

"Yes. Fine thank you." He didn't look pleased. "Do you want me to tell you what happened?" He opened his palms and sat back. I recounted my observations and encounter with Miss Crusty. "But she seemed to think I was deluded."

"Why did you demolish that display?"

"One of the two thieves swung the bags at me and I lost my footing on your polished floor. The stolen goods were scattered everywhere."

"Why didn't you stop this thief if you were sure she was one?"

"I have no authority to do so." He looked dubious. "Perhaps the young ladies who picked up the goods could confirm they were stolen. Perhaps the two who were with Miss Duckdown will confirm that I informed her before the lift opened."

"Miss Swanscombe will be giving a full report. Ah. Here she comes now." The flustered senior assistant knocked. "Come!" I stood to allow her the seat which made her even more uncomfortable. Thankfully she was full of remorse that she had not taken me seriously. "Thank you. Please return to your post." She lowered her head so as not to make eye contact as she scuttled out.

I re-seated myself as he put his fingers to his chin. "What can I say? You acted responsibly and Bentalls thanks you for that. Is there anything we can do for you?"

"Thank you. I came here today because I had heard about thieves operating and I thought you needed a pair of trained eyes. I'll be totally honest. I need a job."

"Why are you not in the forces?" I pulled the sleeve of my jacket out of my pocket and extracted the stuffed football sock.

"Smashed arm in the sea off Dunkirk. Life saved on a boat across the channel and in hospitals here. Honourable discharge, but no job since."

He kept staring at my football sock. Finally, he asked, "What were you?"

"In the army I was the company sharp-shooter, a sniper. Before that, I'd been raised by my gamekeeper father on an Esher estate and I served as a footman in the house."

"What job do you think you would be able to manage?"

"With only one arm? Most things. I can't cut my own fingernails with scissors. Really. I'm fit and strong, trained in self-defence. My attention to detailed observation I learnt at my father's side. I know how to attend to guests like we had in the big house and how to assess each one. I think you need me in this store. In just one half-hour visit I have seen so many opportunities for theft. If I had had an official position as a member of staff, neither of those ladies would have left the store. They would be here in your office and then in the hands of the constabulary."

"You assess people eh? What do you know about me?"

Careful Alf. "You have the bearing of a war veteran, used to command. I should say you were a captain as you are still aware of others above when you consider making an important decision. You have a logical mind, weighing up the fors and againsts. However, you have, like me, seen horrific things, so have a sympathy for those for whom you are responsible and that earns you their respect."

"Lieutenant. I didn't go to the right school." We sat in silence. "Okay. Come with me please. Sorry. I didn't ask your name."

"Alf Robertson, Sir." I picked up my sock and re-stuffed my sleeve before following him out of the door.

He led the way to the staff lift and up to the top floor where he knocked on the General Manager's door and waited. "Enter!" The carpet was thick and the room hung with stern portraits. A Brigadier-type sat behind a huge desk with his back to an imposing window overlooking the Thames towards Hampton. He let his monocle drop as he inspected me. "Well?"

"Sir. I believe that I may have found a solution to our problem."

"Be succinct man! Which problem?"

"Theft Sir. As a visitor to this store, Mr Robertson here identified two thieves in action, alerted staff who, I'm ashamed to say, did nothing, so he attempted to delay their departure and managed to save at least a quarter of the store's property."

The Manager rose and brought his considerable frame for closer scrutiny. "Have you seen service?"

"Yes Sir. Sniper until smashed arm on the beach at Dunkirk."

"Good man. Mm. Sniper. Excellent eye for detail. Steady under pressure. Cool head in any situation." He stood three paces behind me. "Observations?"

"You are holding up three fingers on your left hand to your cheek. You have also pulled your red handkerchief further out of your top pocket."

He returned to his seat. "How did Robertson know that, Frobisher?"

"I have no idea Sir."

"His eyes followed my reflection in the window. Why did you bring him to me?"

Frobisher took a large gulp. "He is offering to become an employee of ours. I would welcome his skills on my floor, but it is your choice if we extend his role to all areas of the store."

The Manager rose, so we did too. "Give your contact details to Dawn, my Secretary. We will contact your regiment and previous employer for their comments. If everything is as I expect them to be, we will formally offer you the job on Monday next. Report to Frobisher at eight and he will have arranged all that is necessary." He held out his hand and gave mine a hearty shake before settling back to his files.

"Alf! You'll be late! What are you doing up there?" Susie is grinning at me from her cot so I gather her on my way down.

"Sorry dear." I gulp a mouthful of tea. "Be very good for Mummy. Have a lovely day."

17 SIT DOWN

Lunch is pleasant enough and Sylvie appreciates any small pieces of help I can give her. She chatters after each course, telling me about the lovely singer who they all adore. I know she's itching to ask why I'd been taken away, but can see I'm not upset so doesn't.

After three courses, the usual trolley brings drinks and silver-foil-wrapped mint chocolates. Sylvie slips hers into her handbag. My eyebrows ask the question. "I like to have plenty in case I get any visitors. My grandchildren love them." I push mine across the table under my serviette and it joins her collection.

"What's going on here?"

"Sorry Matron. My new friend was kindly covering over the mess I've made on the tablecloth."

"I see. Come with me please." Sylvie looks worried as she tries to stand. "No. Not you, Sylvie. Mary will help you up soon. Come on, Dear. My office."

"You'll be sent to the naughty step!" I don't have to turn to realise who it is.

"Thank you, Ted. That's quite enough of your nonsense." Matron leads the way and I follow. She unlocks her door, hangs the key on its hook and ushers me inside. For some reason being alone with her causes an uneasy feeling. "Sit down, here, Dear." The chair is behind the desk alongside her swiveling one which squeaks as if in perpetual protest as she descends. "Now. Where is it?"

As she rummages amongst the files, I survey her lair. Cluttered. Shelves of books in a muddled mess, with box files amongst them, the large key shape with dangled bunches and labelled individuals, cardboard boxes stacked precariously, two old filing cabinets with buckled doors and certificates at jaunty angles.

"Ah. Here we are." She's thrusting a tattered copy of 'Suitable Names for Baby' at me. "I sent a girl to the charity shop for us. Can you find your name in there for me?" I don't know what I should be called. I'll take my time as if I'm struggling to read.

Alexandria, Andrea, Athelia. Mm. Definitely not Bathsheba or Belinda. Can I spin this out till teatime? Am I a fragrantly flowered Camelia or Delphine – or even Fuchsia? Oh, I'm fed up with this. I'll open a page at random. Something short. Ah yes. Got it. Ted's friend Joe needs a sidekick to add confusion.

I point the book under Matron's eyeline. "Jo. Not Joan, Joanna, Jolene or Josephine? Jo. Good." She writes the two letters on the outside of a file and opens it. "Now Jo. Doctor this morning could find nothing physically wrong with you. He says you are underweight, which is unlike some of our residents who eat like horses." A pot and a black kettle whizz through my mind. "You did puzzle him though. You seem fine after your – cold bath – but he thinks his friend Mr Galbraith should see you. He's a specialist in how the mind works. It's important to keep your mind and body active so please join in as much as you can. We have lots of fun activities every day. You can go now, Jo."

I rise carefully and head out. "Oh, and Jo, I want you to know that my door is always open to you."

Excellent. That's just what I want to hear. My hand brushes through the key rack as I leave. I potter along to number ten and find it spotlessly clean and tidy. Someone has placed a folded nightdress on the pillow. I look into the wardrobe and drawers to find a good variety of clothes. Isabel taps on the door. "Ah good. You're back. Matron's finished with you. I hope the clothes we've brought all fit. Let me know if they don't. Your ones are with the laundry so you should get them tomorrow. Now shoes."

We both look towards the floor. "Sit yourself down and we'll see if these slippers have a size in them." I do and they do. "Well they seem to fit you fine so I'll try to find you some shoes so you can get some fresh air and enjoy the gardens."

Escape is possible and encouraged. Puzzling. I'm drawn to the chattering sparrows in the tree above my window. I am allowed to stand and walk about. I know I can. Come on brain – get these muscles under your own control.

There's another tap on the door and Sylvie shuffles in. "There's a quiz starting in a few minutes in the day room. If you'd like to sit next to me, perhaps you might be able to help. Sometimes we can win a bar of chocolate. Please come."

I smile and stand and try to show my pleasure at having a friend. It's taking her a while to get along the corridor and Francie is delivering the instructions as we sit down. "Today we're going to work together in pairs, rather than some people shouting out the answers before others have had time to think. I'm giving you a piece of paper with the numbers one to fifteen for your answers so I want one of each pair to manage to write just the one letter for each answer." There's some commotion as couples form, but some feel discarded and get up to leave. "Join in together." Too late; they've muttered off.

"It's going well so far."

"Thank you, Ted. Now, here's your answer sheet and a pencil. I'll want them back at the end so no slipping them into your handbags."

"I wouldn't dream of it, Francie."

"Is that 'cos you've forgotten yours, Ted?" They laugh. "Okay. For every question, just write one letter of the alphabet as your answer. Not too much writing. Okay?"

"That's two letters – O K."

They laugh again, but then there's a hush as deaf-aids are tuned in. They obviously like their quizzes here. "Oh. Put your name at the top of the page."

"Ready? Question One. Which one letter is a hot drink?" I write my answer and Sylvie nods vigorously. We smile and wait patiently whilst the question is repeated for several pairs. Question Two. Which insect pollinates flowers?"

I've lots of time to look at the other inmates as they make light or heavy work of the questions. I chuckle as some are shouting letters at their partners who nearly always respond with "A?"

"And the last question is – Which letter is missing from the Christmas alphabet?" There's a general hub-bub and shuffling. "Good. Well done everyone. Now I want you to pass your paper to your right, ready for marking the answers. No, Myrtle, the other right. Has everyone now got another pair's paper?

65

Sorry, Joe. You haven't got one? That's because Ted's got yours. You don't get one each." I have to smile again. A Comedy Club in slow motion. "Ready now? The answers are–"

I feel sorry for Francie. Whatever could go wrong has, or maybe there's more drama to come? Unreadable answers, marked wrong when it's right, added up badly. She collects them all and takes them to a small table to remark them herself. Her flustered face is slowly calming as she sorts the papers into an order and stands to address us. Five have fallen asleep and two wandered off. "Okay everyone. That was fun." She looks, but gets no response so I start clapping. Most join in and we wake up the slumberers. "Thank you. Now. The good news is – there's a bar of chocolate for the winners." Responsive 'oohs' are forthcoming from some to Justine's delight.

"And the bad news is – it's a tie so we've all got to share it!"

"You're nearly right, Ted. We do have a tie between two teams who both scored fourteen points. Let's give Joe and Ted, Sylvie and her friend a clap." They do, although I get the impression Ted is used to winning. "I've got a tie-break question so I want each team to write their answer on their paper, here you are, and hold it up in the air as soon as you have, just in case you are both right. I'll see who is first. Okay?"

I have my pencil poised and grin at Ted, giving him a competitive stare. He responds with an intimidating scowl. "Ready? Which vegetable is the capital of Portugal?" I try to write, but my pencil lead snaps. I scrabble on the floor and find it, but see Ted waving his paper at me. I finish making my mark and raise the paper.

"Joe and Ted were first. They say the answer is Lisbon. Is that a vegetable, chaps?"

"Oh yes. Definitely. It's a variety of spud."

"I've never heard of that one Joe. What have we got over here? The letter P."

"Well done ladies. A pea is a vegetable and Portugal is always written with a capital P. Here's your chocolate. Let's all give them a clap!"

18 TRANSITION

It's going to be a little tricky keeping these two cooped up all day. I think we'd better find a new task which will keep them occupied. What can they both do to help me? "Let's wash up the breakfast things. Can you dry up some spoons for me please Susie? Perhaps you could put them in the drawer, Tom?"

That didn't take long so I add Susie's lid and beaker. "Carefully."

"Susie carefully."

"Yes. You are both doing very well. Could you manage a plate?" She nods enthusiastically and we finish most between us. I wipe the knives and close the drawer before opening the one below and pulling out three dusters. "I have a job to do under the stairs." They both run to the hall. "Careful. Mind that arm, Tom."

I unhook the things hanging on the inside of the door. "Shall we put those by the front door?" My helpers do while I pull the toy box into the living room. "Now. Tom. In the duster drawer there's a torch. Could you find it for me please?" I remove the broom and a large carpet sweeper that seems to shed more than it picks up. "Thank you dear. Oh good. The batteries still work. I wonder what we can see in the cupboard?"

Both peer in as I shine the light above them. "Tins. Lots."

"Good. Now if you two can crawl back out, I can reach them and you could carry one each to the kitchen for me." I dust as I place them on the carpet behind me and they disappear into willing hands. I've forgotten how big my store of tins is. Some have been here quite a while. "Now, where's that torch gone?"

Susie giggles as she finds the 'on' button and waves it into the blackness. "Thank you. Let's see what else might be in here."

"My car!" Tom cries, and before I can stop him, he crawls right in. Susie follows and bangs her head on the underside of a stair.

Her cries are more of shock than pain. She climbs on to my lap, clutching something in her hand. Tom re-emerges with more treasures, but my eyes are drawn to his blackened face and reddened arm. "Oh dear," I say as nonchalantly as I can muster. Look at you two monsters from the black lagoon. Let's visit the bathroom."

We make our way amongst the debris in the hall and upstairs. "Let's just sit you both in the bath whilst I wash my hands and find you some clean clothes." I brush some cobwebs out of my hair as well. I wash and dress Susie before depositing her in the living room with the toy box, pick up a fresh dressing and return to Tom. "I think you need a good wash first, don't you?" I put fresh water in the sink to tackle Tom's arm. "I want you to be very brave for me Tom because I have got to take off this dirty dressing to clean your wound. I'll be as gentle as I can." I dread what I might find under the red bandage, but it's not as bad as I feared. As I get towards the inner dressing I laugh. I moisten it and, a little at a time, ease it off of the wound. "Wow. That's healing very nicely Tom. I am very pleased. You are being brave." I quickly re-cover it with the new dressing and bandage. "All done. I think you deserve a treat. Will you play nicely with Susie until I clear this all up? Good boy."

They're both happy so I'll try to finish the mess. The worst is in the kitchen. A trail from the hall cupboard has left a red line of drips leading to a tin of tomatoes. I put it into a dish. Mm. Soup for starters. I'll open some tins and mix a fruit salad, but first I'll brush out that cupboard and pack things away again. I flash the torch in and see two flat cardboard boxes. I hook them out and dust them off. The larger one has painted wood inside, cut into shapes. I guess it's a toy from Alf's childhood. The second contains some old albums. I'll look at them later.

The cleaning is done and we all deserve a drink and treat. A biscuit is always welcome. As they finish theirs, I carry in the box. "I've found this in the cupboard. I think it must be Daddy's toy from when he was little. Shall we see what it is?" Eager hands pull out each piece and lay them on the floor. "What do you think it is?"

"Daddy's."

"Yes Susie. Can we put these together?" I take a piece that looks like a square tower. There are slots towards its base. "Could we put one of those long pieces into here?" Tom pushes one in and picks up another to do the same to make right-angled walls. Susie tries to copy him.

Another tower is added and Tom pauses. "It's a castle." There are eight towers and eight walls which each have a ledge just below the crenelations.

"And what do you think might be inside this tin?" I rattle it.

"Soldier," Susie says. I'm shocked at her answer, but then see what she found loose under the stairs as she puts her find on top of a tower where he looks out across the carpet.

The tin's rather rusty and won't come apart. I find an old screwdriver in the kitchen drawer and gradually prise it up. It comes off with a pop and shower of rust. The children take a handful each and arrange them on the towers and peering over the walls. Tom lowers the drawbridge in one wall. It's a simple string mechanism which he pulls up and let's down. He finds a horse in the toy box and gallops it inside the castle. I watch them playing happily and sit back to listen to their stories unfolding. It's like they've had new Christmas presents.

That song keeps coming into my head – 'I'm dreaming of a white Christmas'. It was in that film I saw with Rod. He was a charmer. Very attentive, but wouldn't tell me anything important. When I asked what he did, he would tap the side of his nose and just tell me, "Hush-hush, a procurer". I had believed he worked for the government which was why he wasn't in the forces. Sometimes he'd disappear for days, then turn up to take me to a film, for a walk by the river, a boat trip to Hampton Court where we got lost in the maze, a picnic in Richmond Park or a bus ride to marvel at the pagoda in Kew Gardens. He did everything to make me happy. He was an exciting man to know and I found myself dreaming of him. He seemed to be able to find those little things that others found impossible – presents that made the other nurses jealous, but Rod never wanted to meet my friends. Sometimes he'd pull me into an alleyway and give me such a kiss, then walk on as if nothing had happened.

One evening when we'd met beside the river, I was shocked to see his face was bruised, but he just shrugged it off. He told me he'd been walking too near a horse who neighed at a sudden noise. As we watched the sun setting over the water, he became agitated and asked me to go away with him. I didn't know what to say, other than ask to where and when. His answers were away and now. It sounded exciting, but I couldn't just disappear. I had a job I loved and people who relied on me. My refusal seemed to really disappoint him. He gave me a long kiss, said he'd come back for me, and ran off towards the town. Perhaps I was not so important to him after all. I wondered if I would ever see or hear of him again?

"Mummy. I'm hungry." Reality kicks in so quickly. It's great to see Tom back to his cheerful self. Hunger's always a good sign.

19 SITUATION FILLED

Good heavens. It's nine years now that I've been working here. I know everyone by name and we all know the procedures I've put in place if we spot anyone acting suspiciously. I'd persuaded the Manager to appoint a female Assistant Security Officer as my presence was rather putting off the shoppers in some of the more personal departments. Iris is a treasure. She blends in so well. Sometimes she'll wear a headscarf and coat, carry a wicker basket or be a follower of the latest fashion trend – as diverse as our patrons. I'm sure our impact has been noted throughout the underworld too. There are very few times we call in the police.

It was so different in my first week when I knew few people or my way around. After a morning of form filling with the delightful Dawn, and instructions, Miss Swanscombe was detailed to introduce me to each of the buyers and the senior staff of every department. Their reactions were so very different. Some were pleased that they were getting help keeping their stock and not being blamed for missing goods, but others regarded me as a management spy. I realised that my task was going to be far from easy.

We ended back at Miss Swanscombe's department which she introduced as Accoutrements. They looked like handbags, scarves and gloves to me. Her underlings seemed very pleasant, although not encouraged to appear to be enjoying themselves too much. I thought back to the camaraderie of the barrack room, the imposition of dourness from the NCOs and their deference to the Officers' ranks, rather than to the person inside the uniform. There were exceptions, of course. The squaddies who disliked me because of my abilities with guns with their tricks to belittle my standards. The NCOs who recognised ability as an asset rather than a threat. The officers who valued their men above their own status. As a newcomer flown into the middle ranks of this store, I needed to earn respect from both directions, and giving it seemed to me to be the best way forward.

I started again at the counters nearest to each exit. These were the key workers – the ones I hoped would block the doors to fleeing thieves. "How can I help you keep your stock secure?" was a well-received question. Their answers were many and varied. I needed to put thinking time into my working day or I'd be working on strategies all night.

The large clock was approaching the end of the shopping day and assistants were scurrying to pack away. A few customers lingered, looking and completing purchases. One young man caught my attention as he wandered amongst the counters. He was quick. He leant over and flicked a purse into his other hand and into his jacket pocket. He sauntered on and a pair of gloves accompanied him from under Miss Swanscombe's nose. As I approached from behind him, I caught sight of Mr Frobisher standing by his window and beckoned to him. By the time he was on the floor a silk handkerchief had been secreted.

"Excuse me Sir. As a valued customer, the Floor Manager here would like to ask you a few questions about our store. Would you be so kind as to step into his office?" I pointed the way, "It shouldn't take long."

The man smiled charmingly. "This way?"

He took two steps forward and then twisted off to the left. I had expected something of the sort and my foot swung into his legs and sent him crashing to the ground. I put a knee on him and twisted his right arm behind his back. "Would you please send for a Constable, Sir?" There was quite a crowd gathered. "Miss Swanscombe. I believe there may be some items missing from 'Accoutrements'. Would you be so kind as to check your stock before the police arrive?"

I kept the man on the floor until the bobby appeared. Mr Frobisher took charge. "Thank you for being prompt, Constable. This is Mr Robertson who works here. He has a strong opinion that the other gentleman has taken items from our store without paying for them." The constable handcuffed the suspect before I resumed an upright position. "My office please. Okay everyone else. Finish tidying and clock off. Miss Swanscombe please."

The five of us almost filled the space. The policeman sat at the desk, facing the suspect, pencil and notepad at the ready. "And your name is?"

"I don't have to give it. I'm innocent."

"Right. Okay. You first then please. Full name."

"Alfred Robertson, Security Officer, since this morning." I recounted my evidence.

"I'll just have a look in your pockets then, sir." There was quite a pile, more than I had seen. "I haven't found any receipts, sir. Perhaps you could explain why you have these in your possession?"

The man looked over at me. "He put 'em there. Wants to make a name for himself as a hero on his first day."

The policeman wrote every word into his notebook. He looked towards the Manager and his assistant. "Is that possible?"

"No Sir! He was in full view of us."

"May I ask you how I managed that whilst holding your arm behind your back?"

"With your other hand. You've got two, ain't ya!" I moved to where he could see clearly and pulled out the sock.

That had been a baptism of fire for my first day, but by the next morning, every single member of staff knew who I was. Mr Frobisher called me into his office. "We must be careful not to bring violence into the store. Mr Bentall would not like that – and nor would our refined customers. Whilst it was very commendable to apprehend the villain, your methods were a little extreme. We must work on other techniques to give customers the knowledge that they are safe whenever they shop. There. I've passed on what I was supposed to." He paused and lowered his voice. "He got what he deserved."

"Thank you, Sir."

"Now. Next matter. I notice that you have been wearing the same suit each time we've met and then after yesterday it had a knee tear. Whilst your army darning skills are good, we need you to match our store's image of the well-dressed man about town, even though there's rationing. That gives us a little problem, but one we hope we can solve, with your agreement." He looked for re-assurance. "On rare occasions, a customer returns garments to us for any one of a variety of reasons. There may have been a small fault in manufacture or it just didn't fit correctly for his size or shape. We though, cannot return such items to the sales floor, so therefore have a small store room of clothing which may be purchased at a significant discount by members of staff who need articles as part of their employment here. You are such a person as you might feel more able to mingle unobtrusively in summer months in smart, casual clothing and in a suit or even overcoat as winter comes. Shall we take a look?"

With a landlady to pay and my first pay packet some way off, I had very little to spend at present, but this would certainly help into the future, so I followed with a light step. A treasure trove was revealed. "The General Manager, when he heard about the arrest, suggested you have a five pounds bonus credit to spend here in this room with immediate effect. Each garment has a price tag. Take what you select to Dawn who looks after the key. She will tot up the bill and lock up. Any questions?"

"No. That's really generous. Oh yes, one thing. Where can I put things until I go home?"

"Dawn will keep them safe. That reminds me of the other piece of good news for you. Next door to my office is a small store room that hasn't been used since the war. Inside are our 1938 Christmas decorations and not much else. The porters have been asked to clear it so that it can have a clean and be ready for you to use as your office from tomorrow. Okay? I'll leave you to have a rummage in here. Good man. I'm so glad to have you working with us."

My own office to sit and think and pin plans of every floor of the store on the walls. The 'behind the scenes' links were intriguing, giving departments access to their storage areas, but gave me the ability to appear as if from nowhere or watch from a hidden viewpoint. I found several ladies trying to acquire extra goods, but they all were dealt with by the floor managers who gave them the option of having the police called or being paraded to the staff as I escorted them from the premises. They all chose the latter. Our thinking was that they would be either mortified and never try to steal from us again, or at least spread the word to their fraternity that Bentalls now had many more eyes open.

My call to the courtroom came a few weeks after I had started. I had my best football sock stuffed into a blue suit pocket as I reported to the Clerk. "The waiting room is just there." I waited. Hours dragged by. Finally, the Clerk told me that our case was up next. Ten minutes elapsed and he came back in with the Police Constable. "The defendant hasn't appeared."

"He's done a runner!"

20 INQUISITIVE

Everything seems very quiet. I've tidied that messy shelf and hidden a book under my pillow for later. No-one will notice. The Reception Area clock is ticking, but there's been no-one around since we had our evening meal. I'm pretending to read today's newspaper, but really, I'm watching. All's clear. I've been told I'm allowed to stand up and move about. I've been told I'm welcome and the door's always open to me.

But Matron's door is closed, not open. It's a good job I have a key in my pocket. I slip inside and turn on the light. Now. Where shall I start? The desk. Yes. I sit silently in her chair and enjoy its gentle swing from side-to-side. These papers are untidy so I put them together in one neat pile. Lots of files. They should be in the filing cabinet. I carry them there, but it's locked. Put them back in another neat pile. I've seen this one before. It says 'Jo' on the outside. Why Jo? Mm. I'll leave it on top for now in case I remember.

Those books need to be straight. I'll sort them out. What will look nicest? I know. I'll put all of the red ones together on this shelf. There are a lot of them. Not quite right. Darkest red on the left, lightest on the right. Much better. What comes next? Orange. There are only three so I'll pretend the brown ones are dark orange. Richard of York. Yellow. I'm enjoying this.

A tap on the door interrupts me. "Matron. Are you in there?" Well, I'm not going to answer. A louder knock. "Are you alright?" Yes, I'm fine. "I think she's just left the light on. It won't hurt till morning." I listen to the footsteps padding down the corridor.

I look at the neater room, but there's still a lot to do. Sit on the swingy chair. That top file draws me to it. What's inside? Papers with two holes through which are two metal prongs, bent over to keep the papers straight. That's good. 'She was shown a book of names and identified herself as Jo.' Oh yes. So I did. Clever. Next paper. 'Dr Whittle examined patient X and found her to be physically sound. Her weight for her height was low so recommends generous helpings of food at regular meals. Her lack of speech is puzzling as her throat shows no signs of damage or past procedures. At times she displays a lack of understanding of simple instructions, but at others seems very capable. I recommend she is seen by Mr Galbraith as soon as possible and a referral to an ENT consultant should be considered.' I like the sound of patient X. She sounds fun.

What does the next paper say? 'Social Services brought patient X to us for respite and evaluation. She was discovered sitting in the middle of the Hogsmill River and has not uttered a word. She had no personal possessions or identification with her. She is not known to the police, Missing Persons or to any of the County's services. She seems amiable and has displayed no violent tendencies. Social Services will continue to make enquiries to find her origins and wish to keep their budgetary commitment to a minimum.'

'Sitting in the middle of a river.' I can picture tumbling water over stepping stone boulders. But girls are not allowed. I laugh at the big boys, jumping them with ease; two feet together in kangaroo hops. But the water doesn't notice. It keeps tumbling on for ever.

I am sitting in the water. I know I have to get out. But how? Look for a rainbow. There's always a brighter side. Yes. There on the shelf – it's starting. Good. I can. I move, leaving my wetness behind. I unlock and lock the door before making my way back to Downing Street for a change. Warm water wash and clean clothes for a good night's sleep.

21 SIT ON HIM

The first working day of the month is always likely to find me in my office. Iris and I sit together and compare our notebooks with the diary chart on the wall. We've recorded every incident by date and time, which department, which staff, items recovered or not, names of perpetrators, actions taken, prosecutions and outcomes. I pull down the large ledger and we start to enter our information into the columns that have blossomed over the years.

A knock and the door bursting open, startles us. "Toys!" is all the breathless girl can get out.

Alice takes the behind-the-scenes route whilst I take the public staircase to the basement. I can hear uproar as I descend. I retrace to the nearest counter and hail the assistant, "Manager! Police!"

As I reach the lower floor, I hear Iris's soprano voice above the crowd. "That's enough! The police have been summoned! Stay exactly where you are." A large teddy bear is flung at her head. Innocent shoppers are cowering by the walls. There are toys strewn in all directions.

My hand goes to my jacket pocket and I pull out my Acme Thunderer. It's piercing blast creates the shock waves I need as I stride towards the epi-centre of the mayhem. "To whom do we owe this carnage?" The staff indicate just two people. I turn to the customers. "Ladies and gentlemen! I can only apologise on behalf of the management of Bentalls that your shopping experience has not been first class this afternoon. Our staff will be working tirelessly to restore everything to normality as soon as the police have gathered whatever evidence they need. As some of you may have useful information, I would ask you to give your names and addresses to this young lady before you leave the department. I would be grateful if you would then vacate this area whilst we restore order. Thank you for your cooperation and I repeat my apologies."

I turn back to the two suspects. One is a large, elderly lady sporting a feathered hat and a mink coat. She has seated herself on a display bench and is inhaling from a pungent bottle which she has extracted from her cavernous bag. The other is a wizened gentleman who is looking round in all directions. As he hears a deep voice from the stairwell, "Down here?", he makes off towards the 'staff only' door. Iris is pushed aside, but in doing so his foot makes contact with a fire engine and down he tumbles.

"Sit on him, Iris!" I call as I go to her aide. "I suggest Sir that you stop struggling."

The policeman has his handcuffs at the ready and we soon seat the villain opposite the bench. "Give me the story from the start please." His pencil is poised so I indicate to the department head to speak.

"Miss Alder was serving this lady and Miss Grimms this gentleman. Unbeknown to either of them, both customers were purchasing our centrepiece, the hand-crafted, sit-in racing car. As I took it from the display with the help of Miss Davis, both claimed it. Neither would yield and they both lost their tempers with each other and the staff who were only doing their best. They grabbed the nearest things to hand and threw them at each other. Other customers were in danger and the staff were powerless to restrain them. I dispatched Miss Davis to fetch Mr Robertson and he, with Miss Reynold's assistance, calmed the incident until the gentleman heard your approach and tried to escape."

"Thank you. I think I have that clear. Was anyone injured?" Heads indicate not so he turns to the lady. "Do you dispute any of the evidence?" She shakes her head. "And you Sir?"

"She started it!"

"Enough!" The bobby gives him a very old-fashioned look. "I'll take that as a no, shall I Sir?"

"Yes."

"Mr Robertson. What is your intention with regard to this matter?"

We have had many such conversations before and I am expecting his question. "There were many witnesses from the general public whose names we have taken should they be required to give evidence. I believe these two persons have probably damaged a number of toys which will no longer be saleable to our discerning customers, thus causing a financial loss to the store. Reluctantly, I believe we must ask for the law to take its due course."

"No." The lady is in tears. "I can't. It mustn't. No. There must be another way."

"And what might that be, Madam?" the constable asks.

"I'll pay for all of the damage." She's fumbling for her cheque book. "How much would it be?"

I look to the policeman for guidance. He turns to the other miscreant. "What would you have to say about that Sir?"

"If she wants to pay, that suits me. She–" He realises that silence is often the better option.

The assistants have been gathering up the toys and have quickly sorted those suffering damage on to a separate counter to the others. After some totting up on a notepad a figure of twenty-seven pounds, eighteen and ninepence is shown to me. I pass it on.

"Very well. I believe you are both very fortunate to be treated this lightly. If you agree to this financial settlement, I will record both of your names and addresses and caution you as to your future conduct. A record of this will remain on file and if you come to our notice again, evidence of today's incident will be given. Is that clear?" Both heads are nodding, the cheque is written and handed to the Head of Department who checks it carefully. "I think we had better escort these two to your office for the formalities so that your workers can get back to normality, and then we'll escort them both off of the premises."

"But I want to buy that car!"

"Move! I think I'll leave the cuffs on this one."

When we finally rid ourselves of them, the constable joins us in the office for a cup of tea. He looks serious, before his face cracks. "You do know who she is, don't you?" Iris and I both shake our heads. "Judge Ringold's wife! Wait till I tell 'em back at the nick. No wonder she was keen to pay. We should have added a bit to the bill."

"Really Ernie? I'm shocked." We laugh, but Iris is looking very serious. "Don't look so worried, Iris. It's his little joke!" As we sip our tea, I pull open a drawer to find what remains of a packet of ginger nuts. "These are his favourites."

Iris still looks a little uncomfortable after the policeman has gone. "He really is one of the good guys, pillar of the church and very well-respected. I've known him for donkey's years. He's often on duty around the town centre so is quite likely to be the first to arrive. He's very good at sitting on prisoners too."

She has to smile. "I suppose I'll have to take your word for it. Is it okay if I go down and see how the toys are behaving before doing the rounds?"

I give her the thumbs up as I remember Ernie astride his first victim. It was soon after I'd started the job and I heard such a commotion from the basement. I crept down and rushed back up to get the police summoned. There were several youths throwing toys about, threatening the staff and customers. A swift blow dealt with the first who got to his feet and ran after his fleeing mate. Another two were kicking and punching a policeman. I let out a primeval scream as I launched my head into the midriff of the bigger and swiped a fist to the side of the head of the other. The latter staggered away and up the stairs whilst the former writhed on the floor.

It was over in seconds. Only then did I notice the constable was seated on top of a fifth man, pinned under a not inconsiderable weight. Mr Frobisher and two more policemen arrived, handcuffs and truncheons at the ready. Next came an ambulance crew, closely followed by a reporter and photographer from the Surrey Comet office just across the road.

The prisoners were sat against a wall whilst the policeman and I were checked by the medics. One bobby was taking witness statements from the staff and the other the customers when the sergeant arrived. "All peaceful here then." His injured officer was interviewed in detail before he turned to me. "I understand you are the new Security Officer. Is that correct?"

"Yes Sergeant. Alfred Robertson."

"My constable there said you saw off three others before ensuring this one couldn't attack him any more. I'm going to ask you to make a formal statement shortly, but for now, well done." The crackle of a flash bulb reminded him that members of the press were in attendance so he turned away to usher them out. I wondered how the store's hierarchy would view a second bout of violence. The staff on the floor were obviously pleased with my efforts.

Under the headline, 'Fight the enemy, not our bobbies', the Comet published a very brief account of the skirmish, along with a picture of the two handcuffed men slumped against the wall. It ended by giving the date for their trial in the following week.

22   SITTING IN JUDGEMENT

A Mother's routines are very much like those of a nurse. Potties and bedpans have their charms for some of course, but dressing and undressing, listening to tales of woe, feeding those unable to do so for themselves, smoothing away pains with gentle words and showing in deeds that you care, are fundamentals of both jobs. Both of my little ones have been through traumas yet here they are, seemingly unaffected. Susie's chattering away to every soldier who she marches along the ramparts. Tom one-handedly opens the drawbridge for each passing motor car and closes it behind them. Observation is a key aspect of both jobs, seeing what might happen before it does. Yes. Tea for them and bed. We'll miss out the bath as I don't want that bandage getting soggy.

Tom makes no argument when I suggest he goes up at the same time as Susie. By the time I've finished reading 'Rover the Sheepdog' to her, the left-over drugs in his system have kicked in and he is peacefully asleep.

I prepare a simple meal for myself and Alf when he gets home, pick up the local paper and settle down on the settee. I stifle a yawn. I've not had much sleep recently.

I was used to being tired. Those night shifts did seem to drag on when there were no dramas. We should have been grateful that no-one else was ill, of course, but an occasional walk along the ward to the rhythmic snores and wheezes hardly helped keep me awake. I felt alone, even with Staff Nurse in the next-door ward and Glynis further along the corridor. The Night Sister was always likely to pop up at any time so I had to remain alert. The bright full moon and its eerie light cast deep shadows across the beds and their ghostly occupants.

I perambulated again and listened closely to each man's breathing. Some were so shallow; some so slow they appeared to an untrained ear to have stopped altogether. Mr Carlyle needed close monitoring so I bent over him. "Ooh-er!" he snorted in my ear and flung an arm out of his covers. I stepped back and caught my heel on his bedside locker. It wobbled, upsetting the water glass where he had immersed his teeth. The liquid ran in all directions, but mainly soaked into his newspaper. I fetched a cloth to mop up the remains, dry the locker and refill his glass. Were there one set of dentures or two? After I'd checked the floor with my little torch, I took the paper back to my desk and opened it out to dry.

I heard the door behind me open and soft footsteps approach. They were unhurried so probably Sister's. I rose to greet her. I was wrong. Before me was a little lady in a pink dressing gown, not fastened symmetrically. "Hello dear. Are you lost? I think you need to come this way," I whispered. As I led her back through the door and along to Staff's domain, I felt sure there was a dark silhouette just further along the corridor. "One of yours, Staff?"

"No. Probably Glynis's."

We about-turned again, but moonlight filled the space as we shuffled towards the next ward where Glynis was dealing with two other ladies out of bed. "Oh, thank goodness. These two were arguing that she'd been sent home and not said goodbye properly. Let's get you into bed dear. Thanks Lily!"

I walked quickly back to my ward, but even before I opened the door, I could hear shouting. "Nurse!"

The moonlight highlighted four figures in pyjamas remonstrating with each other. "Bed! Now!" I ordered. They obeyed, much to my relief. "What will Sister say?"

"Quite a lot, Nurse." Oh dear. She'd followed me in.

She'd have to wait. I went to each of the four men in turn. They were incensed because Mr Carlyle has mislaid his paper and accused them in turn of stealing it. "I've got it. It was damp so I'm drying it for him. Now go to sleep. I'm in enough trouble with Sister because of your noise."

"Sorry Nurse."

I turned back towards the desk where Sister was sat, sitting in judgement, and took some deep breaths as I approached her. She kept me waiting. "Why had you left your ward unattended?"

I explained about returning the wandering lady. "And for how long were you absent?"

"Perhaps two minutes, or three, Sister."

"And how did this newspaper become wet?"

"I was checking Mr Carlyle's breathing as Doctor has requested when he flung out his arm and knocked me into his locker."

"I see." Sister turned some of the pages of the Surrey Comet. "Disgraceful."

My heart sank. "I'm very sorry Sister."

"No, girl. Not you. You've been doing your duty correctly and you showed good authority over the rabble we have to put up with in Men's Wards nowadays. It's this story in the paper. Have you read it?"

"No Sister."

"Right. Carry on." That was as near to praise as I'd ever had from her before. I crept along the lines of beds once more and was relieved to find all occupied and seemingly in the land of nod.

On my return to the desk, I looked at what had caught her attention. 'Fight the enemy, not our bobbies'. The moonlight played across the picture beneath. "Rod?" The text beneath was quite short, but gave details of a court appearance in two days' time.

I'd not been in a courthouse before. It was unnerving. I felt guilty just walking through the doors. A smartly-dressed old gentleman asked if he could be of assistance. "I – I am here to watch a case," I explained.

"Which one?"

"I don't know what it's called. It involved a scuffle in Bentalls."

"Oh yes. There's been quite a lot of interest in that one. Through that door, up the stairs, turn right and find 'Visitors' Gallery Three'." He turned to the person behind me and I followed his instructions. A large policeman inside the door showed me that there was just room for me to squeeze on to the end of a row, next to a rather gangly youth who could have done with a good wash.

The proceedings got under way with two unrelated cases. It was fascinating trying to judge them from behind and above, and I was misled by the heart-felt stories told by the defendants on both occasions. A few people left after each case and so we were able to spread out a little. My heart skipped a beat as Rod and another younger man were led in, in handcuffs, by policemen. There were mutterings in the gallery. We were told to stand as the three magistrates came in and sat in their high chairs.

The formalities of names were inaudible to me. The statement of the prosecuting counsel emphasised how there was a session of wanton vandalism in the toy department of the store. When a police officer was called, the accused began an unprovoked attack on him. The intervention of the store's Security Officer brought the disruption to a halt and the two defendants were detained until further officers appeared.

The Magistrates had a discussion and the two outer ones nodded. The centrally seated one asked the two lawyers to approach the bench, said something to them before sending them back to their seats. "The serious nature of the charges means that we are minded to refer this to the Crown Court." He paused. The defence lawyer rose and asked for bail for his clients.

The prosecutor jumped to his feet. "With regard to the defendant known as Brown we object. As well as the seriousness of assaulting a police officer, he has a proven record of flight, having been summoned to appear in this place on a similar charge and failing to attend." Another discussion concluded that the other man be bailed, but Rod be held in custody. There must be a mistake. Rod has always been kind and considerate.

23   SIT STILL AND LISTEN

I'm going to big school. Mummy says I can go on Wednesday. I've been waiting a long time for today. Is today Wednesday? I think it is. I wanted to go weeks ago. Mummy said I couldn't because I was spotty. I had to stay in bed and play with toys there. She gave me some big, grown-up tablets to swallow. They hurt my throat. Mummy gave me lots of warm drinks.

I'm holding on to Mummy's hand as she pushes a big heavy gate and go inside to a large playground. We walk to the far end and down a slope. There's a low building with a door in the middle. My legs don't want to move anymore. I grip Mummy's hand tightly as she turns the handle and pulls me inside. It's so gloomy. There are lots of coats on hooks. They loom over me as we wait.

Here comes a big lady. Mummy talks to her while I look around. There's a slope up to another room. I expect that's where the lady goes to bed. I can hear lots of children, but there are wooden walls with big windows all around this room. "Tom. Tom. There's a peg here for you. Can you see what this word is?"

I see my name, but I don't want to say it out loud. I nod. Mummy puts my coat on the hook, takes my hand and leads me to a door which the lady is holding open. We go in and I hide behind Mummy's skirt. "Children!" Another lady has a loud voice. "To your chairs please. Sit still and listen." I peep out and see them all sit down.

The first lady beckons to Mummy and she is walking forward. I'm hanging on. "Good morning children," the first lady says.

"Good morning Mrs Ashton. Good morning everybody."

"I'm very pleased to see such smiley children Miss Stenson. Well done Class One. Now boys and girls. This is Tom and his Mummy. Tom wasn't very well so has come for his first day today. Is this the chair for Tom? Good. Come on Tom. Sit here."

Mummy picks me up and swings me onto a chair next to the lady called Miss Stenson. She's smiling at me. "Now children, it's time for a story so sit still and listen." She's holding a really big book and I can see a funny looking mouse. "Who can remember what our mouse is called?" Lots of children push their hands up into the air, wanting to be chosen to answer. One boy with black hair shouts out. Miss Stenson puts her finger to her lips and points with the other hand to a chair at the side of the room. The boy looks sad as he goes and sits, furthest from the book. I'm the nearest. I'm special.

The story is fun. It's about a mouse who has an adventure. But it's a short story. Miss Stenson stands up and walks away. I look for Mummy. She's not there. She's gone away and left me here with all these strangers. Daddy says I must be a brave soldier and try hard not to cry. I'll try.

I'm given a whole bottle of milk with a straw in it. I watch the other children who are all sitting sucking. I'll try. I don't like milk much. I stop. Miss Stenson notices. "Drink it all up, Tom. It's good for you." I try again as she is smiley. Mummy says we all like smiley people. I see some children stand up and put their bottle in a metal basket on the floor. I watch them stand in a line by the door. "Hurry up and finish, slow coaches.

The train needs to leave the station." I look, but I can't see a train. I'm the only one sitting. I've tried.

Miss Stenson has her coat on. "We'll finish this later, Tom. Come on." She takes my hand and leads me to the door. "Can you find your coat, Tom?" It's where I left it. "Well done."

"Are we going home now?"

"Not yet, Tom. It's playtime. Come on. This will be fun." She takes me out to the playground where there are lots of boys and girls running and skipping and shouting and chasing a ball. I hold on tight. They all look bigger than me.

We walk around the edges with our backs to the walls. Miss Stenson knows everyone's names and sometimes shouts or shakes her head. "Sam!" she calls. A boy, even smaller than me comes over to us. "Sam, I'd like you to take Tom to show him where the toilets are. Will you do that for me please?"

"Yes, Miss Stenson. Come on." Sam takes my hand and leads me to a brick wall. We go past it and find a gap behind where there is a very smelly shiny wall and a gutter. "You can wee there or there's some toilets along here with doors if you need to poo." Sam sniggers and holds his nose.

We escape. I look around, but Miss Stenson has changed into a stern old lady who shouts a lot. Sam and I stand in a corner. "Do you like football?" he asks.

"Yes, but the big boys down our road don't let me play with them and my little sister plays with dolls."

"You could come to my house after school and play with me. I don't have any sisters, or brothers." Sam seems kind. I like him.

There's a loud clanging noise. The children have been put under a spell by the wicked witch. Only an old rubber ball rolls across the ground. The slope brings it to me so I kick it to show Sam what a good player I am. It flies back up the slope to the witch who's holding a large brass bell. "That boy! Come here!"

All eyes are on me. "Come on," Sam whispers. "I'll take you." Close up, she's rather large. "I'm very sorry Mrs Gaskett. This is Tom's first day at school. He doesn't know any of the rules."

"And who are you?"

"Sam, Mrs Gaskett."

"Then, Sam, you'd better teach them to him quickly." She turns away and bellows, "Lines!" Sam marches me to where the smaller children are stood, one behind the other, stiff and silent. "Class One!"

The front moves and we all follow, arms swinging and backs straight, until we're out of her evil eye. Coats are shed and hung on pegs and I follow through the wood-and-glass door back to the large room where the children are doing all sorts of different things. I stand in the middle with my eyes open wide. Smack! The flailing arms of a human helicopter batters my nose and blood gushes. Screams fill the room. "Class One. Sit still please!" A strong arm plucks me from the scene, past the coats and stands me in front of a sink, into which my scarlet drops drip with regular momentum. "Help please!" Miss Stenson's voice calls from behind me.

Footsteps approach at speed and a firm voice responds, "I'll take over. See to your class please." I watch the droplets descending and instinctively turn on a tap, washing my hands and splattering the cold liquid over my damaged face. "You've done this before, young man. Well done." A hand appears and soaks a wodge of cotton wool. "Let's put this on your poor nose, shall we? Let's sit you down here." She pulls a small wooden chair beside the sink and I sit. My whole body is shaking. She takes the red wodge and rinses it before returning it to its place. "That's looking a bit better already." I shiver. "Let's see now." I look up into kind eyes over a reassuring smile. She's drying my face with more cotton wool. "Oh look in the mirror," she laughs, "some of it has stuck to your chin. You're not Father Christmas, are you?"

"No."

"Oh good, because I'm not sure that I've been good all year." She dries my hands on a towel and then very gently wipes around my face and down my neck where dribbles have run. "That's all stopped. So, young man. If you're not Father Christmas, what is your name?"

"I'm Tom Robertson."

"Well Tom, I'm very pleased to meet you. Now. You have had an accident so I want you to come along with me. I work here in this office and I've got a special comfy bed for you to rest on. We'll find you a nice book to look at to let your poor nose feel better." It's just like the beds we had at Nursery School, but I don't want to argue with this kind lady that I am a big boy and don't need a lie down in the daytime like the little ones do.

24 SITTING SILENTLY

It feels so strange leaving Tom at the school. With Susie now at Nursery, I'm not sure what to do with myself when I'm not on duty. All those chores I've been putting off, I suppose. Mending their gardening clothes, cleaning out the cupboards. Do some window shopping?

I recognise that man. "Hello Cyril. It's Lily Robertson. How are you? We haven't seen you for a while."

"Hello Lily. No. I've not been out much. Rachel's had the German Measles so we stayed indoors. She's only been back at school since yesterday."

"Our Tom's had it too. I've just taken him in for his first day. I hope he's having lots of fun."

"I expect he's loving it."

"What are you doing now, Cyril?"

"I was wondering if I could get some cakes for tea. Would you mind going into Peggy Brown's here and buying six iced buns for me? They sometimes are not happy to allow Jason inside so I have to shout from the doorway."

"Of course I will. You just wait here."

"Here's a florin, I think. That should be plenty."

The cake shop really smells lovely and there are no other customers. "Mr Penrose would like six iced buns please."

The assistant smiles as she uses tongs to put them into a thin cardboard box. "He's such a gentleman. How he looks after his young daughter beats me. Thruppence each so one and six please. Thanks. Your change. Nice to see you."

"If you're heading home now, Cyril, may I walk with you?"

"To be accompanied by a delightful young lady will set the tongues a-wagging. That sounds lovely." St Marks Hill is quite a climb, but with Jason in charge, Cyril walks at a very brisk pace and I just about manage to keep up. As we enjoy the downward slope of Burney Avenue, Jason seems to increase his speed further. "Sorry if we're rather fast, Lily. Jason knows there's a treat whenever we get home safely. Will you do me the honour of stepping in for a cup of tea?"

The semi-detached house is not what I expect. It is immaculately clean and tidy. "Come through to the kitchen please Lily. We can talk whilst I do the jobs. First let's get Jason sorted out." He takes a tin from a high cupboard and removes a large brown biscuit. The dog is sat at attention on the doormat. Cyril unlocks the back door and places the biscuit outside. Jason does not take his eyes off of Cyril, who bends to release his harness. "Off you go." Jason obeys. Snatching the treat, he races down the garden path and runs three laps round the rose bed before lying down beside a bench in the sunshine to enjoy his reward.

"That's amazing," is all I can say. Such obedience, such controlled energy, such love, one for the other.

"Sorry Lily. I'm forgetting my manners. Please sit down. Yes, there at the end of the table is fine." He pours water into the kettle and fits the whistling cap to the spout before taking the gas pistol from its holster attached to the cooker and brings it towards the pilot light. The sound of ignition tells him to apply it to the gas which he turns on and place the kettle above before returning the pistol to its resting place.

"That is brilliant, Cyril. You are so skilled at using your senses whereas I rely almost entirely on sight."

"Practice and care to have everything in the same place at all times. Rachel helps enormously too, even though she is so young. She automatically puts things away in the right places. I couldn't cope without her."

I see he needs silence so I watch his dog concentrating on every crumb. He doesn't flinch as a train rumbles past the end of the garden. It's funny how, where we live, we never hear them unless there's heavy snow on the ground, yet just a few hundred yards away, they're so close. The kettle summons him and he makes a pot of tea for two. "I'll bring this through to the dining room. First door on your right. You go first."

I go through to the window which also looks out over the garden. I wait till Cyril sits down before joining him. "There are some lovely photographs on your mantlepiece." As soon as the words leave my mouth, I regret them. "Sorry. I didn't mean to pry."

Cyril takes out a handkerchief and dabs at his eyes. "It's silly that the tear ducts work so well when the rest are shot to pieces," he jokes. "I'm glad you can see how beautiful my Sally is. She still is in my heart and mind, just how I remember her in 1913 when we were married. She hasn't changed, nor never will. Do you like the one with Rachel in her arms? I've never seen it. That was taken the week before the bomb dropped in the road?" He pours the tea. "Help yourself to milk and sugar."

"Cyril, this is a lovely cup of tea. Thank you." Should I ask? "Cyril. Do you mean that there was a bomb in Burney Avenue?"

"Yes. They were trying to hit the railway. Its blast cracked many walls over a wide area. Poor Sally never recovered from the shock and blamed herself for what happened to our baby." He sips his tea. "Nearly all of our windows were blown in and the side of Rachel's face was showered with splinters. We'd waited for so many years for a baby, and finally were allowed to adopt our darling girl when her parents died in a raid. Sally lost her mind with worry. All her life she'd wanted a family, but couldn't. No sooner was Rachel here–"

We both sip our tea.

A bark breaks the tension. "It'll be the ginger tom from three doors down. He loves to torment Jason. I'll bring him in."

The tail-wagging bundle of energy is immediately at my side for a fussing. I won't attempt to resist the opportunity. "So calm when he's working in harness – so affectionate in play mode. You're gorgeous Jason. I could do this for hours. But – I have a mountain of jobs that won't do themselves. I must go. Cyril. Thank you for your hospitality and kindness. I hope to return the compliment soon. Maybe I'll see you at the school gate this afternoon."

"It's been a pleasure to have your company, Lily. I've left something in this box for you to take home. I hope you all like sticky buns – Rachel and I do."

25 SITTING READING

I like this quiet time after the evening meal. Most inmates retire to their rooms and I have space to plan. The main escape routes are locked now of course, but there were many opportunities throughout the day.

I enjoy sitting here reading the newspapers. One is left here every day. This one has lots of pictures of floods. People are wading through the water with their bags held above their heads. That man is sweeping a stream out of his kitchen. They don't look too happy. The headline above it says Hell in Hull. This paper says there's to be a Brown Prime Minister. His door has my number on it.

No-one has walked past me since Flo ten minutes ago. I'll go now. My fingers fiddle with the key in my pocket as I check that each corridor is empty before slipping inside Matron's Office and locking the door behind me. There's plenty of light as the curtains haven't been closed so I can sit in the comfy chair and survey the room. I like the neat red and yellow books. I think I did those. That's good. I'll sort out the green ones. Pale ones first, getting darker. There are lots of them. Ooh. There's another orange one I missed, or has she put it back in the wrong place? I hope not.

I'll have a rest. Now, where's that file I was looking at? Jo. Yes, that's what I'm called. This one. There's a new sheet in the front. 'Please record all observations of our guest known as Jo.' I see that they have recorded what I have eaten at every meal, what clothes I've worn and the activities I've joined in. 'Jo teamed up with Sylvie in today's quiz. She enjoyed it.' Where's a pen? Can I copy that writing? Let's have a go. 'They won the bar of chocolate, much to Ted's annoyance.' Yes. That will do.

What's next? I like the look of this big machine on the desk. I wonder how it works? So many buttons as well as a typewriter. Enter. This must be the way in. I hear clicks and a whirring from within and the screen has a small flashing line in the corner. I sit, mesmerised. The picture changes to a word, 'Password'. There's a sentry on duty. Oh dear. I wish I hadn't touched it.

Richard of York gave battle. Blue books. Pale colours first again before we get to indigo. This room is so much better already. It's calming down from its state of frenzy. My arms are feeling tired. Dare I look at the machine again?

I sit and stare at the screen. It's dead. There are no blinking lights from the box. There are no rumblings from its intestines. I've killed it.

A cold sweat covers me. Think. Escape. Key. Unlock quietly and tiptoe away and learn to fight another day. Where did that saying come from? Way back when – when?

26 SIT YOU DOWN

I like Rachel. She talks to me on the playground. None of the other boys or girls from Class Three do. Some of them call me names. There are lots of boys surrounding me and poking me. I want to get away, but they keep chasing me round by the toilet walls. It really hurts and I know I mustn't hit out at them. I try to hide my face so that they can't see me.

"Stop! Immediately!" Mrs Ashton's voice is not to be disobeyed. "Stand there by the wall!" I feel a gentle hand on my arm. "Now who have we got here?"

I look up at her through my bleary eyes. "I'm Tom, Tom Robertson, Mrs Ashton."

"So I can see, Tom." She puts a comforting arm around me. "Let's take you inside and sit you down. You five. One line. Follow me."

Quite a crowd has gathered as I am led to the door, across the cloakroom and into Class Three. There are rows of big desks and a teacher gets up as we file in. "Mrs McCauley, could you find a drink for this young man please? Now Tom, sit you down there."

I sip at the water. The two teachers with stern faces examine the boys. The silence is frightening. I sip again and stare through the liquid at the bottom of the glass.

"Well?" There is no answer. "Has little Tom here done anything to upset any one of you?"

Mrs Ashton looks to each boy for an answer, but none speaks, until the last. "No, Mrs Ashton. We were only playing."

"Playing!" The Head Teacher holds his shoulder and slaps him with her right hand across the back of his knee. She repeats it across his other knee and with every other child in the room, except me. She slumps into the teacher's chair with her hands to her head.

Mrs McCauley steps in front of them. "In all my years as a teacher, I have never been so ashamed of children from my class, ever before." She looks at each boy's tear-stained face. "To bully a little-one from Class One for no reason – it's unbelievable." She walks behind them and they flinch. "I wonder what your parents might think of you?"

There are obvious signs of fear at these words. Mrs Ashton stands up again. "Will any of you be a bully again?"

"No, Mrs Ashton."

"Can Tom be allowed to play safely and happily in this school?"

"Yes, Mrs Ashton."

"You five will sit at your desks now and each write an apology to Tom. You know where the paper is. I will read them so make sure your handwriting is beautiful and your spellings are correct. Do you understand?"

"Yes, Mrs Ashton." The boys take paper, find their pencils from their desks and bury their heads in shame.

Mrs Aston leads me out. "Would you like to stay inside or go out for some fresh air, Tom?"

"I – I think I'd like to go out please, Mrs Ashton." She smiles and watches me nervously open the big door.

As soon as I am outside, I am surrounded. "What happened?"

"Leave him alone!" I recognise Rachel's voice. "Come on, Tom. Let's go and sit on the steps."

Now it's home time, should I tell Mummy straight away? I've a special painting for her that I've made this afternoon. It's almost dry. I can't see her. She's probably at the back of the crowd of parents on the path. "Ouch." That was a hard push.

I stumble and turn round to see two of the boys who attacked me earlier. "You are in big trouble now, kid." As one raises his fist, I hear a deep-throated growl, followed by a loud bark. The boys draw back.

"What's going on? Quiet, Jason!" The growl subsides a little, but the dog's eyes are fixed on my attackers. They freeze for a moment before turning and fleeing. Jason gives a short triumphant bark.

"Are you alright, Tom?" Rachel's voice is so kind. "Dad. Can we go back in, please? Mrs Ashton needs to know about this right now."

"Of course. It sounds as if you've had quite an adventure today, Tom. Don't worry, your Mummy had to stay at home with Susie so Rachel and I will take you home."

"Thank you. And Jason. I think I like him now."

27 BABYSITTING

I can hear voices downstairs. Tom is laughing. "Mummy!" Here come footsteps. I'm ready with my arms up, waiting to be lifted over the gate that Daddy made when I had my big bed. "Toilet first." I trot to the bathroom and step up to the sink afterwards. "All done."

"Good, Susie. Now let's get you dressed. There's a surprise downstairs."

Mummy holds out a new dress for me. It's yellow with an orange ribbon near the neck and around the edges. "Pretty."

I can walk down stairs quite quickly now like my brother does. I hold on to the wooden poles to be safe. I hear voices so I wait in the hall until Mummy comes to hold my hand. "Come and see who brought you this nice dress, Susie."

"Rach!" I run and give the big girl a hug. I like her a lot. I spin round and the dress follows in a circle. "Pretty."

"I'm very pleased you like it Susie. It was one of my favourites, but I can't fit inside it anymore. Would you like to play with Tom and me?"

"Let's put something on your feet and have your drink first please. Rachel and Tom have had theirs." Mummy puts me on her lap and I watch the soldiers march towards the castle. I can manage my own socks, but Mummy is quicker. "Rachel's

Daddy has gone to a meeting so she is going to play with us until he comes back. That will be fun, won't it?"

"Where's Jason?" I can't see him.

"Well done Susie. He's gone to help my Daddy find the way. You know that my Daddy cannot see you, don't you, so he needs help. I'm not allowed to go to this meeting as I'm too young."

"Rachel helps her Daddy in so many ways. She is so good at tidying away when she has finished with toys or books. In fact, tidying everything. Are you good at tidying, Tom?"

"I try to be – sometimes." Tom looks to see which toys have escaped and puts them in the toy box quickly.

I get down and give Rachel a big hug. "Thank you for pretty dress. I like ribbons."

We play nicely until I wobble and knock over the castle walls. "Susie!" Tom shouts.

"Sorry. Accident. Sorry." Rachel looks worried.

"I think it's time to play something different," Mummy says. "Shall we show Rachel where the castle lives?" We are good at tidying today and Mummy is very pleased. "Let's sit at the table and see what else kind Rachel brought with her in this bag."

Rachel pulls out a box and takes off the lid. "This is a game that I used to play with Daddy, but I think it would be better for you to have than me. It's called Ludo."

I watch as she unfolds a board and shows us lots of coloured circles. "I like yellow," I say as I point to the board and my dress.

"Which colour would you like to be Tom?"

"Red." Mummy gives him a look. "Red please."

"The blue is next to you and so I'll be green," Rachel says as she takes coloured circles from the box and puts them in front of us. "How many counters have you got?"

I see Tom use his finger to touch his red ones so I do the same. "Four."

"Four."

"Now we put the dice into this little cup and shake it out." I see a spot on the top and spots around the sides. "That is a one, so if it was my turn, I would move one of my counters one square."

Mummy smiles. "That was very well explained, Rachel, but I think as these two are young, perhaps we should only have one counter each to start with." She puts three of hers and mine into the box, as do Tom and Rachel. "Shall we let the youngest go first?"

I take the cup and shake. The dice jumps out and lands on the table. "How many spots are on the top, Susie?"

"One, two."

"Well done. So, move the counter two spaces. Good. Now pass the cup to Rachel for her turn."

"Three. One, two, three. Your turn Tom."

Tom shakes and there are lots of spots. Mummy waits. Tom looks closely and bursts into tears. He's getting down from his chair and running away. Mummy looks sad. "Why don't you two play together. Is that alright, Rachel?"

Mummy sits Tom on her lap and gives him a cuddle. Rachel and I take turns to shake and move our counter. I like counting the spots. I almost got to seven with my counting. Mummy's asking Tom what the matter is. "I can't count."

"Yes you can, Tom. I've heard you counting the soldiers. You count very well."

"I can count soldiers because they don't jump about."

Rachel touches my arm. "Now Susie. You have been all the way around the board and now you have reached the yellow road so you move along there to reach the finish. Your turn."

"One, two, three, four, five. I'm on the yellow road, Mummy!"

"Really? Well done, Susie. You are playing very nicely. Thank you, Rachel." She turns back to my brother. "What jumps about, Tom?"

"The spots."

"Oh." Mummy cuddles him closely for a long time.

28   CROWN COURT SITTING

Sister wasn't pleased with me. She pulled a disapproving face when I asked for a day off in the middle of the week for 'personal reasons'. But I had to know more. I'd confided in Glynis of course as I knew she wouldn't tell tales. At least living nearby meant I could catch a bus to court if the weather wasn't kind. Sister had re-arranged my shifts for the week so I was on nights instead of days. I suppose that made sense, but I feel uneasy on my own. When everything is silent, I imagine there are eyes watching from the shadows. Sometimes I sense footsteps creeping away when I've gone to check on a groaning patient.

But today all is calm, peaceful, with glimpses of warming sunlight between the buildings and trees. As I make my way over the Hogsmill towards Penrhyn Road, I marvel at the cleanliness of the water, channeled here between the concrete banks protecting the gardens of the large imposing villas. I watch six tiny ducklings negotiate the currents that threaten to sweep them into the mighty Thames, with mother duck pretending to ignore them and the drake sitting in the shade as if his job has been done.

The building is huge and imposing. The county town has to make its statement I suppose. I'd passed it before, but never dreamt of going inside. Thankfully there are clear signs which usher me towards the right section. I recognise a young man loitering outside.

"Hello darling. Have you come to sit next to me again?" I ignore him and sail past with all the confidence I can muster. "It's this way, darling." He knew I was heading in the wrong direction so I have no option other than to follow his loping gait up the wide staircase. "My friends call me Lanky. We're in Two today." Obviously no stranger to courtrooms, he pushes the door open for me and a policeman directs me to a seat at the front of the gallery. The lout follows and I know I am stuck with him.

This room is so much larger than the Magistrate's Court and even we visitors can sit in more comfort. The panelled walls and doors give the feeling of solemnity and solidity. There are men in wigs and gowns with underlings in suits, mountains of papers surrounding them. The gallery is full of chatter, but it suddenly hushes as doors open and the cast members file in to take their allotted places. "All rise!"

A very stern looking judge takes centre stage and the proceedings begin. I hadn't noticed Rod be led into the dock with the other suspect. He looks small and nervous from my position. After introductory formalities the defendants are asked how they plead. "Not guilty."

The first witness is called, a confident-looking lady. Having established that she was in the Toy Department of Bentalls she was asked to describe what she saw relating to the policeman. "I saw the officer attempt to arrest one man."

"Can you see that man in Court today?" She pointed to Rod. "The defendant, Brown. Carry on please."

"As he did so, the other man ran and started punching the policeman. They all fell to the floor. Then the third man started kicking the officer."

The judge looks startled. "Madam. Are you sure there was a third man involved?"

"Yes M'Lord."

"Could you identify this man?"

"Oh yes, M'Lord. He's sitting up there!" She points at me, but it's Lanky who leaps up and rushes to the door, only to be stopped by the strong arm of the law.

The judge declares a recess and a general hubbub breaks out. I'm glad to escape to the facilities before taking my seat again. Two more witnesses gave similar accounts before the prosecution calls the Store Detective to the stand. Before us all stands a smart, suited man who appears to look remarkably similar to Rod. "Alfred Robertson." My heart skips a beat. It is. It's him. Alf. I've found him. But he didn't want me or he'd have written. My tears flow. I can't hear his words. My mind is filled with images of him in agony, yet always gentle and with a kind word. I came here for Rod, but it's still Alf who touches my heart.

I have to escape. I stumble down the stairs and find a bench where I can sob into my soggy handkerchief. I feel a gentle hand on my shoulder. "Are you alright Miss?" I try to focus on a uniformed lady. "I'll fetch you some water."

I find a dry handkerchief in my bag and am grateful for the refreshing drink. She sits beside me. "Can I help?"

"No. Yes. I don't know. I have just seen a witness give evidence who I lost contact with two years ago, but I don't know if he'll want to see me again."

"Well, young lady, if you don't ask him, you'll wonder for ever. Which court was he in?"

"Two."

"Come with me, Dear. The judge has already sent the jury out, so it might not be long. If you sit there, the witnesses will come out of that door and you can take your chance. What's the man's name?"

"Alf. Alf Robertson."

"Ah yes. I remember him. Charming. You pop into the ladies and freshen up. I'll make sure he doesn't escape before you get back. Take your time. You want to make a good impression."

29 SIT DOWN PLEASE

I'm fitting in quite well to this routine. It's a lot friendlier than any other place I've been in, wherever that was. I've got most of them guessing. I think Sylvie knows I'm a sham, but she's not ratting on me to anyone. She loves the cloak of mystery that I'm weaving. She's looking healthier too as I have helped her eat more than a few mouthfuls of each meal. "The hairdresser's coming this afternoon. Will you get yours done?"

I shake my tousled locks, but think. Shall I get it all shaved off? That would be a different look. No. My scars would show only too easily and lead to questions. Why have I got scars? That part of me must stay hidden away. I don't remember why, but it must. I try to smile at her and shake my head.

The mint chocolates disappear into her bag like clockwork. I wonder where she's storing them. She's not had any visitors since I've been here. We sip our drinks and watch the ebb and flow of home life.

"Jo." Isabel's standing beside me. "You've a visitor." I stand up and follow her to the medical room. "There's a Mr. Galbraith to see you. I'll stay with you if you'd like me to." I nod.

A thin, disheveled character is perusing the file which I recognise. He has a large pad of lined paper beside it. He doesn't look up. "Sit down please, er, Jo." Isabel points to the usual chair on the opposite side of the desk and parks herself in the corner by the door. He has bushy eyebrows which seem to twitch as he reads. His tweed jacket has the remains of leaves on it, as if he's fallen through a hedge on the way here. I try to suppress a giggle, but barely succeed. My splutter makes him raise his head and a well-practiced smile spreads across his face. "How nice to meet you, er, Jo. I'm Mr Galbraith and I've been asked to come along and talk to you. Are you able to reply to me?" I stare through him to the window. "No auditory response." I suppose because I do not speak, he thinks I cannot hear his muttered words as he writes, but my hearing has been fine-tuned. There are going to be a lot of pauses.

He stands and looks at me from different angles. He's so gaunt. He wanders behind me and coughs. I don't flinch. He moves a little and claps his hands. I had guessed that was coming. He walks back and records his findings. I look towards Isabel and she gives me a look that says, 'You're playing him along'. I raise my eyebrows and roll my eyes. 'Who me?'

"Now, Jill. I'm going to show you a series of pictures and beside them there are words. I'd like you to point to the word that best describes the picture." He pulls a well-used flip-book out of his battered briefcase and opens it as he turns it to me. Now. How shall I play this? I point to cat as it's a dog. He turns the page. As the cat is cleaning its paws I point to house. I expected he thought I'd choose dog. I'll get the next one right. Door. I've chosen the third answer each time. Yes. That's a good way.

He closes the book after ten pages and writes furiously in a spidery scrawl. The second book is similar. "I'm not sure how far we'll get with this one," he mumbles. "Which word does not, does not, belong on this page?" The picture shows a plate, knife, fork and spoon. I choose table as it is hidden under a tablecloth. "Mm." Next is a hairy leg with sock and shoe. I choose toes. I am enjoying this so I'll get them all right. I gallop through them, faster than he can turn the pages and write down his notes. There are twenty-four in the book, although the numbers say twenty-five. Picture seventeen has been torn out. I wonder why.

He puts the book away and looks at Isabel. She offers nothing. She's playing my game too. His eyebrows are quivering as he stares at my pupils. Intimidation is my game so have a go chum. He holds a pen and moves it sideways. I stare at the blue tit hanging upside down, foraging for caterpillars.

His notes are impossible to read upside down, but I'm not sure they're legible any way up. A third flip book emerges. "Numbers. Which of the numbers at the side would fit into these sequences?" I look blankly at the first page without blinking. "One, three, blank, seven." How shall I play this one? I point to number four. It comes between three and seven so it is right, although he wants five. "Next it's twenty, fifteen, ten." I point to the two in twenty-five. "Okay?" He's trying to convince himself. "Now, what about sixteen, fifteen, thirteen, blank, six?" I pick up his pen, scribble out the zero in the ten before putting a negative sign in front of the five. Let's see if he can work those out.

He puts his fingers to his lips and presses his elbows onto the desk – an owl at prayer, seeking inspiration. He pulls his scribblings from his pad and draws nine spots in a three-by-three grid. "Now, Jean, isn't it? I want you to see if you can draw four straight lines that pass through each of my small circles without taking the pen off of the paper. I'll draw nine more here for your next go. Take your time. This might be a bit tricky." Once you know, you always know, so I'll get it over with in two seconds. That's confused him all the more. Isabel looks puzzled too. He pulls off the sheet and adds it to his notes.

"I – I think we're done here for today." He closes the file. "Thank you, oh, Jo. It's been very interesting to meet you." As Isabel gets up, he seems startled, as if he has forgotten that she was there all the time. "Er, thank you. Could I possibly have a cup of black coffee with two sugars?"

As she closes the door behind us, Isabel bursts into laughter. "Oh, Jo. You are so clever. I've never seen an expert so confused before. Did you enjoy that?" I look bemused. She doubles up again. "I say. Would you like to fluster him some more? Why don't you deliver his coffee?"

30 SITTING ON THE BENCH

It's so frustrating, sitting on the bench in this tiny room, waiting to be called to give evidence. There are old papers to read, but no windows to see that there is a world outside. "Alfred Robertson." I rise and follow along a narrow corridor. "They're ready for you now, Sir." The door opens and an usher shows me to the stand and gives me a Bible to hold. I'd been to the lower courts before and I'd been told about the formalities here by the police, but the enormity of this courtroom is staggering as I place the good book onto its shelf.

I was used to being clear-headed under fire, so I find the questions fairly straightforward. That's a strange one; do I know any of the defendants? "I have only met the one known as Brown as he had been detained by myself in the store on a previous occasion, but failed to appear in the–"

"Thank you! That's enough! Members of the jury will disregard any reference to another case."

Oops. I think it is relevant. I am pleased to be allowed to sit in the courtroom now I've finished to hear what others have to say. The defence seems pathetic so there's no surprise that the judge is scathing in his summing up, saying how they have wasted his time by denying the charges.

The seven jury members are sent out and those of us who have been witnesses are ushered into a slightly pleasanter room. We are hardly sitting down before the usher reappears. "They're coming back." It hasn't taken long to come to their verdicts.

The judge gives the other defendant four years before he turns to Brown and explains exactly why he wishes he could impose more than the maximum sentence of ten years. Brown's face as he is led away is full of hatred.

I join the exodus with the policeman who'd been assaulted as the personnel changes for the next case. He has a slight limp and tells me he is still having treatment for internal bruising. As we reach the foyer, he shakes my hand and makes off towards the gents. I suppose I'd better get back to work.

"Excuse me," says a young lady. "It is Alf, isn't it?"

"Yes." She is very pretty with long dark hair, almost to her waist. Her eyes are sparkling and they make me warm. "Do I know you, but–?"

"Lily. You were in Surbiton Hospital. Nurse Crowther?"

"Lily? I'm so sorry I didn't recognise you without your uniform and, oh my goodness, such beautiful hair. I've dreamt of finding you, but here–"

"I've been searching for you too. You look well, Alf. Are you?"

"Brilliant. Let's get out of here. That is. You're not supposed to be here for a case coming up, are you?"

"No, no. Let's go."

We walk silently towards the river, each lost in our own thoughts. I have so much to say and guess she has too. We

120

spot an empty bench on the towpath and sit, embarrassed, at each end, not knowing which words to use, watching the passing ducks and stealing glances. "Why didn't you write?"

I draw a large breath. "I didn't know where. I hoped you'd given me your address that last morning, but when Matron appeared, I slipped it under the blanket. Then I spilt the tea and you were ordered to clear the bed and your precious note was gone." She's dabbing her eyes. "When I was released from rehab my first place to visit was the hospital, but you had gone and none of the staff would tell me where. I had nowhere else to go so I got digs nearby and wandered the streets in the hope of seeing you."

She is melting before me. "But I thought you didn't care."

"Oh Lily. I've never cared so much in my life." She reaches out for my hand and pulls it to her. As we get nearer her head nestles into my shoulder and our words reverberate through our minds. My breathing falls into the rhythm of hers and the months of loneliness drift away with the flowing Thames.

31 THE OPPOSITION

I'm feeling guilty, but my curiosity is even stronger. I must find out. Surely there would have been a fuss when Matron found out, but she hasn't.

My casual newspaper reading and corridor checks are part of normality after supper. No-one takes any notice of my appetite for news. I slip the key into the lock and myself inside in a practiced, fluid action. The sound of keys turning seems all too familiar.

I peer at the machine and see the blinking lights are back, playing out their patterns. Good. I survey the room from the swinging chair. Almost there. I think those dark books will have to count as indigo. They were probably black before years of sunlight have weathered them. How many shades of black can there be? Great.

So where are the violet ones? Panic. I can't find any. No. That can't be right. I sit and bury my head in my hands, my fingers playing on the scars. All this sorting.

The files are scattered across the desk as always and I soon find mine. I'm getting used to Jo. Good choice. The staff have given up their daily records of everything I do. They've accepted my normality! This top sheet is new. Mr Galbraith's report.

'I met with the lady known as Jo within her normal environment. She is an enigma. She appears on the one hand to lack basic education in reading and writing, yet has excellent spatial awareness. Her lack of reactions to audible stimuli were of concern and might be an indication of long-standing difficulty which should be thoroughly examined. And yet, on occasions, she appeared to understand more complex instructions and act appropriately. Without her medical and mental history, it would be wrong to conclude any diagnosis based on such wildly differing results.

I advise for her to be closely monitored as she may develop unexpected symptoms and show unexpected reactions to situations. I advise an exploration of her audible capabilities. I suspect she may have been mal-nourished for some considerable time so advise a nutritious diet be provided.

I am copying my full report to the Psychiatry and Psychological Teams, as well as ENT at this hospital.'

Oh dear. I seem to have confused him. I've had so many of these tests over the years. Have I? Where did that come from? I do believe I am remembering more. That's good, isn't it?

The door handle moves. There's a tap. "Jo." It's a quiet whisper. "Jo. I know you're in there." Stay calm. Ignore it. "If you don't let me in, I'll fetch Isabel. You've got twenty seconds. I'm counting."

I recognise the voice. He will if I don't, so I unlock, turn the handle and step back. Ted comes in and closes the door silently, pointing to the lock. I drop the key in my confusion, but he does it for me. He studies the key and chuckles. "Where did you get this from?" I point to the dangling bunches. "Brilliant." He looks as if he's going to pocket some more, but he resists the temptation.

I retreat to Matron's swivel chair and wait for him to speak. "What have you been up to?" I give my non-committal look, but he's not going to accept that. I point to the desk of files with mine on top. Ted's eyes light up. He rummages, but can't find his. "I'm locked away I expect." He looks at the shelves of books. "Yeh. I like the colours. This isn't Matron's style." He turns back to me and detects my guilt. "Good job. I like it. Mm. No violets. How about us making some?" I nod. "Perhaps another day. Who are these two silly asses?" I hadn't taken much notice. "She could be a young, slim version of Matron. What do you think?"

I put my finger to my lips and cup the other hand to my ear.

"Yeah. Okay. I think we'd better retreat now in case we're missed."

He unlocks, looks out and waves me to follow. He locks the door and starts to walk away. I catch his arm and pull him back. I hold out my hand. He smiles and dangles the key above it. Will he? "Tomorrow." He drops it and gives me a thumbs-up.

32 EXQUISITE

It's today, the day I never thought would come. I'm sitting on this hard pew feeling numb. Everything about Lily is perfect. And she likes me too. She said yes.

We'd synchronised our times off work to be together for every moment we could. I took her to meet father and my dear sister Alice; to show her my childhood. We ate in the Servants' Hall with them all. It was so lovely catching up with some of the people I grew up with. Even Mr Watkins, the butler, seemed pleased to see me. As we rose to say our goodbyes, he whispered, "The mistress would like to see you both."

Lily looked puzzled as he led us up the back staircase and showed us into the drawing room. "Robertson and Miss Lily Crowther, Madam."

I hardly recognised the girl I grew up with, playing Hide and Seek in the woods and building dens with her two brothers. Yes, she'd grown wild and free before being sent away to boarding schools from which she'd returned for holidays, tamed, yet with a certain twinkle that gave her true feelings away. Yet here was an elegant young woman rising to greet us. "Miss Crowther. I'm delighted to meet you. Do come and sit here beside me and tell me how you've captured him." She beamed her angelic smile in my direction; the one usually reserved for when she was up to no good. "May I call you Lily? Alf can sit there and be embarrassed."

I perched and watched them grow into friends before my eyes. Desdemona was obviously used to socialising, putting people at their ease, asking gentle questions that gave her the answers she wanted. I admired her skills. This awful war had already elevated her through no fault of hers. I knew from father that she was the sole heir to the estate and had married a wealthy officer in the Brigade of Guards. She was also involved in many good works in Esher and the nearby villages. Even so, it was still Lily whom I watched even more intently; how she overcame her feelings of social inadequacy and relaxed into enjoying Desdemona's delightful company. They looked like two sisters, sharing stories and giggling.

The scream of a siren sent shudders through us all. Lily and I followed down the main staircase into the hall where I had greeted so many guests, down again two flights and into the basement where we joined the rest of the household. Everyone had their place, their station underground still rigidly enforced. Desdemona beckoned us to sit with her as she spoke, "Do relax please everyone. We're all in the same boat here." I looked around the company. There were far fewer than in my time on the staff and far fewer men. Dad wasn't there, nor Mr Watkins. Desdemona understood my thoughts. "Fire watching duty. On the roof."

An hour or more is a long time to think in the candlelight. At least I had a lovely hand to hold. 'We're all in the same boat' triggered many memories I had tried so hard to erase.

The 'All-Clear' siren could vaguely be heard and, as we trooped up the stairs, the butler was ready with his reassuring words, "False alarm!" Dad was back on his rounds and we said our farewells. Lily was glowing as we walked to the bus stop and travelled back to Kingston, but she wouldn't tell me why. "Desdemona has sworn me to secrecy. I mustn't tell anyone. There's a war on!"

I'm wondering if she'll tell me today? I'm sitting here in St George's in a pin-striped suit, next to a smartly uniformed

George who has been granted a forty-eight-hour pass, and with twenty or so friends and family. As I look around at them, a pang of guilt sends a shudder through me. I must be the luckiest man alive. Lily has no family, just a few colleagues from the hospital who could be spared. The doctor who was going to give her away has been called back on duty. I wonder how Lily will cope without him.

The vicar motions me from my seat as the organ music begins. Breathe Alf. Steady. She's coming. George squeezes my arm. "Move out, soldier," he says and pulls me to my feet. "As someone once said to me on a beach, it's your turn so let's not be late." I have to smile at this assertive corporal who now is putting fear into raw recruits.

I'm unsteady as I turn to face the heavenly vision walking towards me, lit by a myriad of stained-glass light. I am the luckiest man. Lily is approaching, supported by the strong arm of my own father. Perfection. He looks so proud to be honoured with this task. I can't take my eyes off of her. Her smile radiates from under a veil, which Glynis lifts and tucks back so all may admire my bride. Alice steps forward to collect Lily's bouquet.

Such a whirl of emotion. Such a spreading of joy. Such pleasure in the knowledge that we are at last to be together for ever.

As we exit the church, I see the Rolls Royce I used to polish with envy, with its hood down and door open, beckoning to my wife and I to climb inside. We turn to face the congregation spilling out behind us and I see, under an extravagant hat, a grinning Desdemona, blowing us a kiss.

"So this is the secret," I whisper. Lily is seated when I look back to her, and see the perfection of her dress. "Exquisite." It is. She is. I can't move. I'm totally under her spell.

I feel a strong hand push me and I fall at her feet, to cheers from behind. "That's right Alf. Learn how to grovel!"

Lily offers me her hand and I regain my composure as I thank her with my eyes. We wave to our friends who are all cheering us on our short journey to the church hall. But the chauffeur is passing it and continuing along the road. Lily's laughing at my concern. "Relax and enjoy yourself. They'll be ready for us when we get back. I want to enjoy a ride in a lovely car with my lovely new husband."

"What happened to the old husband?"

"He wouldn't do as he was told. Just look at the trees." I do – reflected in her sparkling eyes.

Our journey turns the heads of many people who all seem cheered to see a beautiful bride in a beautiful car. I know these lanes very well and can point out so many places where I had adventures. We turn into the estate past the gatekeeper's lodge and skirt the lake before joining the main drive up to the imposing front steps of the house where there is a crowd assembled. Lily takes my face in her hands and smiles before kissing me. The car door is open and I finally realise what has been planned behind my back.

George demands attention from the topmost step. "Madam. Ladies and Gentlemen! I am delighted to welcome you to share in the happiness that today has brought to our dear friends. Our generous hostess–" he salutes Desdemona, "– wishes you all to join the happy couple in the dining room where you are invited to help yourself to food and drink. Everyone here is a guest, but please, make room for our guests of honour to lead the way, Mr and Mrs Robertson!"

The cheers are deafening as we climb the steps through the funnel of friends. George bars the way. "Turn back to them and wave." We follow orders, and have to smile all the more as a flashlight explodes.

The photographer calls out. "This time, will all of you please make sure you can see the camera so the camera can see you? Ready? Say… congratulations!"

33 SIT TIGHT

This is even more magical than I could ever have imagined. Alf is so wonderful, kind and thoughtful. We are so lucky that this wretched war has thrown us together and here we are, in a beautiful house, celebrating with his family and our friends. Desdemona has been so generous, lending me her own gown, her home and giving us a banquet. It's been so hard keeping these secrets from Alf, but I know he has appreciated everything too. And now he's mine for ever.

"Lily. I'm just stepping outside with father and Alice for a couple of minutes. They say they've something for us. They've been up to mischief, I think. Love you!"

I'm so glad Desdemona has arranged for all of the staff to be guests rather than waiting on us. They've all worked so hard to get it ready. I'm trying to thank each one of them personally. I think I ought to slip away and change out of this gorgeous gown. I'll need help getting out of it. Where's Glynis? Ah yes. Always a sucker for a uniform. "Sorry George. I need her for a minute."

"Can I come as well?" I'm used to cheeky comments from patients so give him my, 'sorry, I didn't quite hear that' response.

We're using a bedroom as a changing room. It's so luxurious with its own bathroom. Alf doesn't know it's ours for tonight as well. It was such a shame that Staff Nurse had to be back on duty so quickly, but at least she came to the church. "What do you think, Glynis? I've this new frock thanks to Alf's discount scheme at work. He got a secretary to help him choose it."

"Let's see it on you. Oh yes. Good choice. Perfect. And a jacket. Smart and practical. He'll be pleased to see you–" The wail of the siren in the town freezes our thoughts. "Action stations, Nurse! Where's the shelter?"

"Follow me."

Most of the guests are already making their way down to the basement as we descend the grand staircase. Mr Watkins beckons to us to follow. "Most are already down there, Madam. I will proceed to my duty post on the roof."

"Please stay safe and remember we are both nurses if we are needed." He smiles and gives his butler's bow of the head before turning and ascending the stairway. "Down two flights, Glynis."

The basement is quiet. Desdemona is busy checking who is present. We sit near a silent George, rocking on the bench by the doorway, conscious of still being the centre of attention. Desdemona returns to us. "Four unaccounted for at present. Alf, his father and sister, and Watkins."

"Watkins said he was going to the roof. Alf went outside with his family to see what they had been up to, just before I went up to change."

"At least they're together. I wonder if Watkins needs someone else up there with him?"

"Probably. I expect Alf's father will go up."

A tremendous crash fills the air. We hold our breath. "Sit tight, everyone!" Desdemona is definitely Matron material. A loud rumble is followed by another series of thuds. I see the horror on George's face, just as I saw in the beds in Surbiton. His white knuckles are gripping the edge of the bench.

It's no good. I've got to find him. I run back up the stairs and emerge into the hall. Despite it still being the afternoon, the air is dark with dust. There's glass over the floor too as I head for the door which isn't there. Debris litters the steps as I pick my way down. "Alf!" I listen. "Alf!" There's no reply. Which way? I turn to my left and head towards the servants' part of the building. "Alf!" My footsteps crunch as I run on the gravel. "Alf!" There's a huddle of bodies. "No!"

As I reach them, I see rubble. I roll a huge chimney pot aside and pull at the top suit to free it from the chaos. Shattered bricks fall on to my feet. I hear more footsteps on the stones and recognise Glynis's strong arms. "Together. On three. Two. Three!" We heave on the jacket and Alf's father rolls over towards us. His glazed eyes tell us what we didn't want to know. "I'm sorry. Come on. Move to the next patient Nurse Crowther."

A groan from the pile gives us hope. We roll Alf's lighter frame from on top of Alice, who opens her eyes to us. "Thank you. See to them first."

I listen to Alf's breathing and am glad to hear some. I look for blood. There are small patches where cuts have broken through the dirt. I take his wrist and look for my uniform watch. "Stupid girl."

"No. Beautiful wife." I kiss his cheek, tasting the grime, but I don't care. "How are the others?"

"Let me check you over first. Can you move your legs for me please? Good. Arm? Well done. Are there any really painful places?"

"Only where I've lost my heart." I kiss him again. "Just lie quietly or I'll send for Matron." I turn to Glynis who has her thumb firmly pressed on Alice's thigh. She nods in my direction. "Right. I'm going to take over here from Glynis who is going to go back to the house and ring for an ambulance. You Alf are not going to do anything except stay still and quiet. Do you understand?"

"Yes, Nurse Robertson. Whatever you say."

The 'All-clear' is loud and many footsteps approach us fast. Desdemona carries a box of bandages and dressings. "Perfect." Alice is drifting in and out of consciousness with her blood-loss and I see danger signs of shock. "She needs blankets."

"George has them. They're here. Some for Alf too – and his father." I turn to see her lovingly cover his body from the world without comment. George is in a trance. Alf has stayed silent. Am I ignoring him too much? He's in shock too.

Glynis takes my hand away and observes the wound. "Nearly stopped. Well done. No phone at the house. One of the maids has cycled to fetch help. See to your husband." With in-built skill, she applies the dressings.

I turn to Alf whose eyes are closed. My heart freezes. I bend to feel his breath on my cheek. It's there. Relief. He's in a sleeping shock-shut-down. Good. Best thing for him. I turn him gently into the prone position. "Ouch." My mind focusses on my knees. I've spent all this time on them, pressing stones to my bones.

As I struggle to my feet, Desdemona takes my arm. "Can you come with me? They've found Watkins." I want to stay, but a patient in need must be attended to. I look at George, but realise he'll be of no use. My legs gradually move more quickly as I'm led back through the house, and up ever-decreasing staircase widths until we climb out on to what is left of a roof. Three lanterns tell me we are not alone. "Light the way. Nurse coming through."

I find an ugly scene. Watkins lies crumpled under slates and timbers, splintered and twisted. I feel for his jugular, but there's no pulse there. "Clear the debris and we'll turn him. Quickly please. Ready? Towards me. Turn." I hear the gasps and even under flickering light, they know he is beyond hope. I check for any signs of life, but are none. "I'm sorry."

Desdemona is in shock. Her natural poise has evaporated with the sight of the rock of the household who had guided her since birth. She turns and flees. I draw a long breath and summon my courage. "There is no point leaving Mr Watkins here. With your help, I'd like to take him to his own room. I'm sure you know where that is." We manage to grip his overcoat and lift him clear before inching our way to the stairs. We stumble, but do not fall as we take this proud man to his resting place.

I leave them to grieve and rush back to my husband's side. He's sitting up with eyes wide open. I hear an ambulance bell drawing closer.

The crew carry Alf's father in first, then Alice, to the two beds. We sit Alf and George on the floor between them. Glynis sits beside the driver to make enough room for me to tend them too. Alf is staring up at me. "Is this the happiest day of your life?"

34 SITTING NONCHALANTLY

I've let myself into the office early. That picture on the wall has been flashing in my mind and bugging me all day. What was it Ted said, "Who are these two silly asses?" I'd only laughed at that. "She could be a young, slim version of Matron."

Up close I can feel that I've met her before. The look on her face gives me the shivers. Sitting on a donkey on the beach should be a happy time, but she's more menacing than merry. It makes my scalp creep. I pull my fingers through my hair as if I'm caressing away troubles as a caring parent would for a fretful child. Yet my fingertips touch the raw nerves of the scars that haunt me.

The ghostly tapping is repeating. I unlock and let in my accomplice. "That was close. I could hear a trolley approaching."

Ted pulls half a dozen felt pens out of his pocket and removes four cream-coloured books from the shelves. "These are the best violet ones I could liberate from the craft room. Scrap paper trial, I think." He's rummaging in the bin. "This'll do."

All are different shades. He takes a book and colours the spine before replacing it on a shelf. I give him a silent clap and join in with relish as he brings back another batch. Colouring is very therapeutic, especially when it's naughty too. I feel good having a partner-in-crime.

I take charge of arranging my rainbow collection. I feel that it brings a calming reassurance, one that heralds a brighter future beyond the storms of the past.

"What's next?" Ted tries the filing cabinets, but they will not yield. "Where would she keep the keys?" He's drawn to the doorway hanging collection. I pull at the desk drawers. Locked, except the lowest which glides open. A glass bottle rolls to the front, clinking as it does so. I pull it out and see Ted's eyes light up. I've not seen him move that quickly before. "Well, well. A little drop of medicinal by the look of it. Do you want a sample?" I shake my head. He smiles as he unscrews the top and takes a gulp. I watch his face contort as he collapses into the chair.

It seems an age before he wipes his eyes on the sleeve of his cardigan. "By gum. That's a good drop. It's the first I've had in years." I move the bottle out of his reach and replace the cap. Returning to the drawer, my finger catches on metal. Ah. Small keys on a small ring.

Ted snatches them from me and heads for the cabinets. They do not fit so he throws them across the desk as if it's my fault. "Useless." I try the desk locks and pull open the top drawer. Paper, envelopes, pens and pencils. The second one is a surprise. Neatly stacked are old tobacco tins. I prise off lids to discover drawing pins, paper clips, rubber bands, rubbers. Some rattle. Mm. This sounds promising. Ted grabs the keys again and is delighted with his success. The drawers creak as they are pulled forward, revealing their filed treasures.

A screeching alarm fills the air. We both freeze, wide-eyed. Don't panic. Stay calm. Reverse everything. Lock files, key to tin, tins stacked, drawers locked, keys away. Bottle. Nearly forgot it. Felt pens. Scrap paper. Deep breath. Listen at door. Footsteps running past. I turn the key gingerly and let Ted go first. The commotion is to the left so he makes off to the right, leaving me to relock.

I follow the noise. As I reach the Reception Area, I see a huddle of overalls bending over a prostrate resident. Sitting nonchalantly, I pick up the paper from the side table and pretend to be interested in the latest fashion trends. The nurse is making reassuring noises, but I hear alarm in the support staff. Jasmine detaches herself from the group and walks swiftly to the telephone. "Ambulance please." She rattles off the Home's address and phone number. "Sylvie Watson. Seventy-three. Nurse suspects a broken hip."

35 THIS SITE

Funerals are always difficult and now during war, doubly so. Poor Alf is struggling. He seems to be elsewhere. But here we are, just a few days into marriage. Poor Alice isn't well enough to say goodbye to her father. Her leg was badly broken beneath the artery bleed. Desdemona has been splendid and has arranged everything for both of her workers, despite being so badly affected herself. She is hoping that her husband might arrive in time on compassionate leave.

We all feel we're going through the motions of living, realising that life can be cut short so swiftly. And that is what the vicar of St Georges is trying to say, although having married us here with smiles, he too is fighting back the tears. I keep feeling that strong man's arm as he walked me down the aisle. I never really got to thank him enough.

We travel back to the big house in cars, but the extent of the damage is obvious as soon as we get to the site entrance. The cavalcade plays follow-my-leader to the tradesmen's entrance where we are ushered into the Servants' Hall. There is another spread laid out on the table with the chairs pushed to line the walls. A tall, moustached figure is standing with his arm around Desdemona. It's good to see he's here for her now. "Ladies and Gentlemen." He has a commanding voice without it needing to be raised. "Please accept my apologies for not making it to the service. If you would like to find yourself a seat, my wife and I would like to say a few words."

She looks so vulnerable and yet, his arm around her has brought her the strength to speak. "Thank you all for being here at this sad time. We have had to say goodbye to two dear rocks; two stalwarts I have known all of my life and whose gaping holes will never be filled." We share her tears.

He sits her down before continuing. "My wife has kept me informed over the telephone system as to how every one of you has rallied to her aid, and I will always be grateful to you for that. There is however, the immediate future to sort out and inform you of. Much of this house is in a dangerous condition and this site must be made safe. Until it is, the main house will be boarded up. We have yet to organise who will be asked to carry out which tasks, but hope that you will find yourself able to be flexible in the work we undertake together to bring us through this terrible time."

Desdemona touches his arm. "But enough of the future. The present is with us now. We are able to use this wing so those whose beds are above are safe to stay here. For those who had a room in the house, we'll find a room here or on the estate. Those of you on the staff, please meet with us here at nine in the morning. That's all, so now, please have a really good feed as this last week has taught us, we never know what tomorrow brings."

I squeeze Alf's arm and pull him to his feet. "Set a good example, Alf. Let's get some of this delicious food inside us." He obeys and we sit back to put in some fuel without savouring cook's best efforts.

As our plates empty, Desdemona squats beside us. "Can we have a quick chat outside?" We leave our plates on the seats and follow her lead.

There's a gentle breeze wafting in some country fragrances as we crunch over the gravel path without speaking. She takes us to the steps from where the estate stretches away to the copse beyond Keepers Cottage. She raises her face to feel the air on her cheeks. I watch as Alf mimics her and a smile flickers momentarily across him. "Isn't it refreshing?"

"Yes."

"I'm glad you think so because I have an enormous favour to ask." She searches our faces. "I have a duty to look after the people as well as the buildings and land. Charles has to return to barracks by noon tomorrow so I am faced with a mammoth task alone." Again, she seeks a reaction. "I am hoping that my oldest friend and his wonderful wife would help me for a few days get things into a routine."

I look into Alf's eyes for an answer, but he seems slow at processing his thoughts. "How could we? We both have work of our own."

"Yes." Desdemona turns away a little to take a long breath. "I've been selfish and done something naughty."

I feel Alf's grip tighten on my fingers. "Not for the first time."

The tension breaks as if glass has splintered and I see genuine smiles at this simple rekindling. She throws her arms around him and laughs aloud without embarrassment. "What a lovely man!"

Happiness wells inside me as I welcome him back. "Perhaps you'd better tell us what and how it involves us."

"Sorry Lily. Yes." She takes a deep breath. "Grandfather used to be on the board of Bentalls so I used that information when I telephoned and asked to speak to Mr Bentall himself." Alf's eyes are dancing. "He said that he would be willing to grant his Security Officer a three-week leave-of-absence to help rescue a damsel in distress."

"I'm sure those weren't his words."

"Well nearly, Alf. I then telephoned the hospital to which father has been a generous donor in the past and asked for a similar release for a nursing angel." I had to chuckle with them both.

"So what is your plan for us?" Alf turns towards the wreck of the house. "I'm not much use a builder's labourer."

"Without Charles, I need people I can talk over ideas with, to help organise the workers we have left, to find suitable people to run things. I realise it's a big ask, but you are the only ones I can truly trust." I wonder what is racing through his mind. He's looking into the distance. "Is it too painful to be here?"

She knows him well. He gives that resigned smile that tells me he's summoning up his courage. "Of course. If Keepers Cottage is too painful for you, I'm sure there is somewhere else you can stay. I'll go back inside now and leave you to talk it through."

Alf takes my hand and we stroll silently along the path. I can see where we are heading. He pauses at the door and gulps in the air. "I'm here with you." He pushes the door open and we tiptoe in. The kitchen table looks as if his father has just walked out to work. Alf slumps into the chair and puts his head in his hands.

The old clock on the wall tick-tocks away and regulates the rhythms of our breath as I sit as close as I can and hold his hand. "I can't." I watch his tears flow without comment. "I can't."

My mind is translating these two words. What does my brave soldier mean? I can't ask. I've got to let him interpret it for himself first. A flutter of wings distracts my gaze to the open door. A blackbird has hopped onto the mat and is turning the leaves and gravel our feet have provided, searching for a tit-bit. I turn back to Alf and see his smile. He silently pulls at the drawer handle, hidden at the table edge, and takes a pinch of bread crumbs and seed. Slowly he stretches out his arm and drops the grains. The bird's head tilts to one side and our eyes meet. He makes the decision. He can. He can trust us. With a grateful squawk he lifts on to the table and grabs an orange beak-full before disappearing out of the door. I look at Alf. He puts his finger to his lips and keeps focused on the opening. I turn back as the wings return for second-helpings. He stays longer and is joined by a brown look-alike. They stay until the food is gone. "Wonderful."

"Generations of blackbirds have been coming since I can remember. They bring their broods each year because they feel safe here. I do too, but I can't–" I squeeze his hand "– I can't sleep here without Dad. I want to help Desdemona. I know I – we – can. I've got to get this cottage ready for another keeper. I'm the only one. Can I ask you to help her too?"

"Oh my dearest. Of course I want to. She has welcomed me from the moment we met and taken to me as a long-lost friend. And I agree. Anywhere for us, as long as we're together." We close the door behind us, wave to the chortling birds in the bushes, and return to the wake.

36   BOMB SITE

Our three weeks has been exhausting. The Dower House had been empty since before the war, but with Desdemona offering to share it with us, we have had a safe home away from the turmoil that is the rest of the site. Lily has been a treasure, taking to the domestic life so easily. Of course, with her training, she is used to clearing away mess and seeing to people's needs before they realise what they want. But most of all, we have all learnt to appreciate what we have, how to laugh without guilt and use our energy with wisdom to make a real difference.

There were just ten of us assembled in the Servants' Hall by nine o'clock. Charles had arranged the chairs around the huge table and we all sat together as a united team. "I am certain you are all wondering what the future will bring, but I'm afraid none of us can predict that. I must do my duty for King and Country by returning to my regiment this morning. In my absence, I am delighted that my dear wife has been on a recruitment drive and secured the services of a trusted Lieutenant whom most of you know well. So, other than assure you of my continuing thanks to you all, I leave you in their capable hands as I hear the approach of a taxicab to take me to the station."

Desdemona followed him out to the doorway and we knew their embrace would have been heartfelt. "Then there were nine," she joked on her return. "Alf and Lily have kindly agreed to spend the next three weeks helping us all. They and I will be living in the Dower House, but we are all going to work together each day after breakfast, have a cold luncheon at half past noon and our main meal at seven, after which I hope you will fill your evenings with pleasurable things. Mrs Grant will be charged with providing the meals, as she has done now for many years, but I'm afraid it will be without assistance in the kitchen. Each one of you has a room of your own so you will be responsible for its cleanliness. Young Martha, as scullery maid, has been used to the basic tasks, so I am putting the hygiene of the stairs, shared rooms and facilities in your capable hands. I expect those tasks to take the morning hours, so we will have your labour in the afternoons. Now for everyone else, we are going to take a walk and assess what is needed."

We stepped out into the sunshine and looked around us. "Do we all know what happens in each of these buildings?"

"I used to, but I'm sure Lily doesn't at all." Lily had a notebook and pencil poised. She was going to be Desdemona's helper in everything, but by recording all decisions and needs, they would get done. My short time in middle-management was useful for assessing the people and situations, as well as proposing solutions where I could.

The gardener was dispatched to shut the gates or blockade all of the entrances except the one nearest the town. He was also a handyman and had suggested his father might be willing to come out of retirement for some free food on some days. Keeping the kitchen supplied was an important task. 'Dig for Victory!' was his motto too.

Desdemona had long since renounced the need for a Lady's Maid despite her status as a county trend-setter so all of the female staff were used to being tasked with varied roles as and when the need arose. This gave them the confidence to make suggestions. One reminded us of the little-used staircase at the far end which was designed for taking young children to and from the grounds and Nursery without disturbing the main flow of household activity. It gave us a wonderful access to the roof from where we could assess the damage.

Desdemona couldn't fight back the tears as the three of us looked across to the hole. "Thank God it was a small bomb."

I led the way around the front parapet, checking every footstep was sound before progressing. The majority of the slates were intact, the initial hit creating the hole and the explosion creating its carnage internally. "Tarpaulin needed Lily with ropes to lash it in place. That should be possible from here and round the back parapet."

As she looked up from her notes she pointed. There were Watkins's binoculars, flung across the void to just a few steps away. Through my tears, I retrieved them and handed them to Desdemona. No words were needed. They would be treasured.

And so the days had continued. We explored each floor of the house via the Nursery staircase, repairing the superficial, but as the wrecked end was approached, erecting stout barriers. Our teams worked brilliantly, sawing, hammering, sewing and even painting when we could find a tin that matched. We were all tired, but happy in a job well done.

One task I had to do with Lily's help. Keepers Cottage had been Dad's home for over thirty years. And it had to be cleared, ready to show any applicant for the advertised Gamekeeper's job. We started with the hardest task, the bedrooms. "Anything you want to keep is fine by me." I had to smile. She already knew me so well.

"Keep nearest the head end, offer to others in need on the bed, burn on the floor." It sounded simple when I said it, but it was far from that, especially when I found things father had kept of my mothers. That had finished me for that evening.

I had to take Lily to the stable where Alice and Father had fatefully led me on our wedding day. There under a horse blanket were the two hand-crafted boxes made with loving care from the trees of our woodland. The one was for my tools and the other, beautifully lined, was a workbox for Lily. Our tears flowed, but they were such treasures.

We filled boxes with books and even found some old toys. "They might come in handy, one day." Lily was blushing as she said those words, but our cuddle showed how much they meant. Our sorted belongings were moved from the cottage to a bonfire, an old stable or taken to the vicarage for the needy. It was a mammoth task, but necessary. Alice was able to join in with the sorting out when she returned on crutches from her convalescence by the seaside.

But our three weeks were almost over. Desdemona insisted that we take a ride in the car away from the bomb site for a little relaxation. She was an excellent driver. We passed over the Thames and admired Hampton Court before following the road to Kingston Bridge and passing by Bentalls. "I thought we'd better check it was still standing without you!" she called to us, enjoying the back seat as we had on our last outing in the Rolls. We made our way through the town and along Villiers Road. As we were climbing the hill Desdemona turned off left and soon pulled up in a suburban street. "What do you think?"

We looked at each other with puzzled frowns. "Well," she said as she got out. "I owe you wages for your work over the last weeks, but I'd rather spend it on a present." She had her impish-child look on. "If you agree, then I would like to give you the deposit to buy this house. Would you like to look inside to see if you like it?"

We did and we did. The solicitor was expecting us as we walked in and signatures were all that was required. "Your references have already been taken. They were excellent and so I am delighted to hand over the keys to your new home."

37 OPPOSITE

I feel quite grown up now I'm seven. My little sister Susie is only four, even though she says she's six. We usually play well together, but sometimes I wish I could go and play with some of the big boys without her. They have lots of adventures. The old bomb sites are great to climb in and you can find real treasure. That's what they say. There's a field at the end of the allotments and if you wiggle the rails you can squeeze through the fence. The grass is long, but it's a good place to play football. I've only been once. They said I was too small to play so I could only sit and watch, but it was an adventure.

They always have good adventures in our story books. Five on a Treasure Island is one of my favourites that Mummy and Daddy read to me at bedtime. I'm going to have my own adventure today. The big boy who lives across the road told me that at the bottom of the hill they're building a space station. It's true. Last night, I woke up when it was dark and looked out of the window. There were lots of different coloured lights. Some of them kept flashing. I know how to get there too.

I've had my dinner and I go out into the garden to play. I go through the little gate, past the chicken house where the noisy birds squabble for the maggoty loganberries I flick through the wire wall. At the end of the path there's a huge heap of manure that Daddy spreads to help the garden grow. I didn't like falling into the heap and having to have an extra bath. It's sunny today so it's extra smelly. The wide path now is crunchy and there's the big gate at the end for the people to come in from the road. Someone's left it open. Good. I can keep going on my adventure.

I walk down the road and turn along the lane. It's where Mummy takes us sometimes. I can smell the spaceships. There are big gates with a huge padlock, but I can't squeeze under. I can't climb over the high fences. They have prickly spikes at the top to keep the aliens in. I stand and stare, hoping to see one.

A slimy wetness grabs my hand. "Eurgh!" I scream. I daren't look.

"Tom. Why you scream?" It's Susie. She must have followed me. "What are you doing?"

"I'm having an adventure – on my own."

"Susie come to see the monster. Come on." She's running along the lane. The aliens will have to wait. I've got to follow her. She's standing in our tunnel. "Listen, Tom. A monster's coming."

I hold her hands as Mummy does. "Mumble, tumble, hear him rumble, monster now will squeal and grumble!" It's our rhyme that Mummy made up. Susie loves it.

As the monster moves away, Susie lets go and dodges through the gap as we do with Mummy. "Susie. I think we should go back home now."

"This way," she calls as she follows our usual route up the hill and down again towards the river. I hesitate, but follow. She finds the bench and sits on it. "Drink please."

"We haven't got one here." I sit next to her and watch some boys climbing and jumping on the boulders. Two are having a wrestle on the top and both jump into the water which splashes up and over their wellies. They laugh. It's fun. Now they're kicking water at each other.

"Oi! Go home!" The boys are scattering in all directions. The Park Keeper's waiting until they've disappeared before going back into his hut.

Susie's jumps down and stands on the first stepping stone. "Susie. No. Come back." She goes forward to the next, and next, until she's in the middle. One big boy was hiding, but now he's coming over. I must get in front of her. I jump to the boulder beside her. I've not jumped high enough and my sandal slips, pitching me –

38 SITTING ON THE BANK

"Tom!" He's in the water. Is he playing a game? I don't think so. I get close to him. "Tom!" I can't see his face. I pull at his shirt. "Tom!"

A big hand pulls Tom out. His leg knocks me off the stone and I sit in the water. I can hear tumbling splashes over the boulders. I watch the keeper put Tom on the bank and slap his back hard. Tom coughs and splutters as he gasps for breath. He starts to cry. The man pulls me out too before climbing on to the bank. He swings us both up on to the seat where we cling to each other in tears.

The man looks angry. He wants to shout at us, but he can see how upset we are. There are other people coming round, but I'm not looking at them.

"It's a disgrace."

"That young. They shouldn't be out."

"Where's their mother?"

"Now then. What's going on here?"

"Thank goodness, Officer. I heard the screams and pulled them out of the stream."

"Thank you, Sir. Well done. I'll get to you in a moment. Now then young man." A large policeman stoops over us and holds Tom's hand. "What's your name?"

"Tom."

"And is this your sister? What's her name?"

"Sister Susie."

"And where do you live, Tom?"

"That way." Tom points back towards the monster's tunnel and I look the way he's pointing. I slip off the bench and run.

"Come back, Susie!"

I don't listen. I run straight into Mummy's arms. She cuddles me tight and runs back to the crowd where she sits and cradles Tom as well.

"Do I take it that you are the mother of these two little children?" the policeman asks.

"Yes, Constable. Why are you both wet?"

"That's fairly obvious, Madam. I wish to know why they are away from home without an adult."

Mummy looks up at him. "As soon as I realised that they were both quiet, I looked for them in the garden. I found that someone has left the gate open at the end of the allotments. It's about half a mile away, so I had to check all the way to here. This is somewhere we have often come to walk and see the trains."

"That's all very well, Madam, but young children shouldn't be able to get out to roam the streets. We'll get them checked out to see if they are well enough to go home."

"I am a nurse. I can assure you I will be checking them thoroughly. I'll just get them home for a warm bath and dry clothes."

"I'll accompany you. I'll come back and take your statement afterwards, Mr Park Keeper."

Mummy picks me up into her arms and holds Tom's hand as we go through the tunnel. My mind is full of the gurgling water over the stepping stones, the big splash – that bully boy who jumped in front of my brother and made him slip, tumbling so slowly, over and under the water. The laughter. The silence. The screams. But the water keeps tumbling on for ever.

I hear a rumbling noise, much gentler than the monster. It's Tom. He's being sick, all over the policeman's boots.

39 SITTING ANXIOUSLY

I'm sitting anxiously in my room before breakfast when Isabel taps on the door. "I've got some news for you." My mind has been churning all night. It's all my fault. I stole the key. I embroiled Ted in our escapade in Matron's Office. If I hadn't found the next keys, if he hadn't opened the filing cabinets and set off the alarms, if Sylvie hadn't been so scared, she wouldn't have fallen, if – "I think you know that Sylvie was taken off to Kingston Hospital last night." I nod. "Yes, Jasmine said she'd seen you. Well. It's not as bad as Nurse feared. She'd twisted her hip out of position, but it's not broken. It's amazing, her being so frail and eating like a sparrow, although, since you've come, she's been putting on weight each time she's been checked. She's enjoying eating again, and that's all down to you, so well done Jo." I take a deep breath. "She's being kept in now for a few days to monitor her progress and then they'll decide what should happen next."

I stand up and gaze out of the window. There's a gentle breeze dancing through the leaves and two male blackbirds are strutting their stuff on the well-groomed lawn. I check the reflection. She's gone so I can wipe the tears away. Poor Sylvie. How can I make it up to her?

I sit through breakfast alone and go to the quiz session, but it's always been Sylvie who's enjoyed it the most. I perch in the back corner to observe and think in peace. Francie has mustered the usual suspects and is about to start when we are graced with an appearance by Matron no less. "Friends!" Her voice penetrates even to those who've turned their aids to minimum. "Friends. I've just been on the telephone to the hospital to check up on dear Sylvie. She has had a peaceful night and has eaten some porridge for breakfast. We know how she loves her quizzes as they help to keep our brains on fire. I'm sure you wanted to know she is doing very well."

I watch her go. The backside of a donkey comes to mind. Then she's on top of it, turned with that scowl towards the watcher. She's the one. She's the one who keeps my brain on fire.

I run from the room to my sanctuary and slam the door. I'd lock it if there were a key. I barricade the door with the back of the chair under the handle and fling myself into the bedcovers. Instinctively, I finger the scars from the frying of my brain and the horrors return. I do have memories. I do. Her face is the worst. I see her now in starched uniform in the stark room where I've been strapped to the bed. The dome is lowering, its coiled wires stretching ever up into the distant void. The sudden pulse of pain as the first shock is thrust through me and every muscle convulses against the leather thongs that bind me.

I come back into the present with a loud knocking at the door. "Jo." I'm soaked in sweat and tears. So is the pillow and the bedclothes. I've been on fire. "Jo. I'm worried about you. Will you please let me in?"

I have a lot of time for Isabel. I know she won't go away. I pull at the chair and stand in front of her. "Oh." She takes in the scene in an instant. "How about a nice warm bath?"

It has helped calm me, being immersed in water, with bubbles frothing over me. Yet a vague image of another bath has been awakened. I dress and sit on the chair awaiting the questions. "Mary and I have made the bed and taken your things to the laundry." Her smile expresses kindness, not condemnation. "After lunch, I would like to try something new and am hoping that you might help me. It would be good to have a man try it as well. I'll have to see who might be willing to have a go."

It's a good roast lunch. They've all been told I need feeding up and I'm surprised at how much of an appetite I'm developing. Two helpings of rhubarb crumble go down well too and a hot cup of tea with a chocolate mint to follow. I think I'll try it today to see what it's like. Mm. There are gritty bits which must get under dentures, but it's tasty.

Isabel's hovering as I finish. "Okay? We'll hide away upstairs." She leads the way and I follow into the craft room where Ted is staring out of the window. "Come and sit at these tables, where I've put the chairs." I watch Ted turn and his usual brash demeanour has disappeared. As he realises it's me as well it becomes a puzzled frown. "That's it. Good. Now please relax. I'm trying out an experiment and I know that both of you have your brains switched on, but sometimes find communication less easy to achieve, so you are the ideal candidates to help me. This isn't compulsory so you can choose to stop at any time, but I hope you won't as I truly believe this might help." Our backs are to each other so we can't see what the other is doing. "On the table I've put lots of pens, pencils and ten sheets of paper. I want you to draw or write whatever first comes into your mind. I've put a number one on the first sheet. Any questions?"

She knows I won't speak, but neither does Ted. "Right. I'm going to give you just a couple of minutes to draw or write before I go on to sheet two. Okay?" I nod and have a pencil ready in my hand. "Right. Draw or write about your favourite food." I write 'crusty cheese roll and fresh salad.' "Moving on to sheet two. What makes you happy?" I swap to pens and draw a rainbow, adding a laughing mouth beneath it. "Three. What makes you angry?" I've got a dark pencil and draw a circular dome with wires coming from it, hanging over a body. "Four. By being in this home, what are you missing?" I carry on with my drawing, tying the body onto a bed and then put a question mark on the next sheet. "Half-way five. Where's the place you most dislike?" 'In my head.'

Ted's making grunting noises. Isabel isn't looking, she just seems to be clock watching. "Six. What was the best job you ever did?" 'Helping Sylvie eat.' "Seven. Which of your skills should you use more?" 'Writing and thinking.' "Not many more. Eight. What's your favourite animal?" 'Dog.' "Nine. "What makes you laugh out loud?" 'When Ted doesn't win.' "And the last one. What are your hopes and dreams?" 'My dreams are nightmares. I don't know what is true and what is a dream.' I cross them out. I doodle a man's face. I write, 'Sylvie gets better.'

Isabel is all smiles as she gathers the paper from us both. "Thank you so much. You are both stars. I've asked chef to put aside two large sticky iced buns with your names on them to go with your afternoon tea as a thank you. You've really helped me." Ted is still in his chair, facing the window. "Are you both going to Bingo? It's about to start." I walk round to face him and see the tears flowing into his beard. I reach out and take his hand, but he recoils and leaps to his feet before storming off to his room. Well, at least I know I've not said anything to upset him.

40 DIFFICULT SITUATION

"This is the entrance to the allotments, Officer." I lead the way, but the sliding bolt is across and the padlock closed. "There's no way they should be able to get out unless one of the allotment holders has not bothered to close it behind them."

The policeman rattles the gate, but it will not open. He's looking either side for any holes, but there are none. "I agree. I expect someone just popped in for a few minutes to gather some crops for tea."

"I need to get these two home." I walk away, knowing he'll follow. We carry on to the top of the road and turn left. As we do, I see a man closing our gate. "Cyril! We are here! Come inside everyone."

"Doggy!" Susie squirms out of my arms to give Jason a cuddle. He doesn't mind her damp clothes and hair, lapping up her attention as Cyril releases him from his harness.

"Cyril. We've got a policeman with us who wants to check out the allotments from our garden. Please sit yourself down and I'll sort these two out before we can all have a cup of tea. Is that okay, Officer?"

"Yes. This way, is it?"

I open the back door and see him out before taking two soggy children upstairs. They are well-trained enough from muddy gardening to help get ready for a quick bath and dressed again. The kettle has the magic power to summon the police.

"I have a serious request. Whilst I appreciate the convenience of ease of access through that gap to the chickens and allotment, these two need to be kept in the garden unless you are out there with them. If your gate had a high bolt, that should be sufficient. Hopefully by the time the young man is strong enough to open it, he will also be trustworthy enough. Do you think you could get that done?"

"My husband will be seeing to it immediately."

"I have to record this incident as we need to ensure young children are safe and to make sure this sort of accident doesn't happen more than once. There are parents who treat their children very badly."

"I understand."

"Good. This is a very nice cup of tea."

Cyril has been silent since he'd arrived. "May I make a comment, please, Constable?"

"Of course, Sir."

"Lily and Alf are the most kind and caring people you could wish to meet. I have a daughter of my own and I would not hesitate to leave her in their capable hands. In fact, that was the purpose of my visit today." Cyril takes a sip of his tea before continuing. "I was hoping that I might ask if Rachel could spend the afternoon with you tomorrow. I have to have my annual session at the eye hospital and Mrs Jones, my neighbour, has her rather boisterous nephew with her for the week and Rachel is rather nervous of him."

"Cyril, we'd be pleased to see Rachel tomorrow. What time?"

"Jason will take me to the ten past two bus so we'll be in plenty of time for the appointment at half past three. I should be back here before five, but you never know what delays there could be. If you can help, I'll bring her at about quarter to two."

"Well, Tom. Do you think you'd like to have Rachel round to play?"

"Yes Mummy." He's still a little nervous of Jason, but whenever we've walked back from school with Rachel they have got on well. Susie adores her too.

The constable finishes his tea and stands to go. "I'll go and talk to the park keeper now." He turns to the two children. "And I don't want to see you near that river, ever again. Do you understand?" Tom nods and clings to my skirt. Susie says nothing. "Good. Make sure you do."

41 SIT YOURSELF DOWN

Wednesday afternoons are precious. Kingston shops close at lunchtime and we all get a chance for relaxation. Some choose the opposite. The Wednesday football league has started up again and our team is winning most of their matches. I took my turn to support them, but I've never seen the point of all that running, jumping, falling over and getting covered in mud. We had enough of that in the trenches.

At least digging this trench and getting covered in mud has a purpose. I'll fill it with all the food scraps we can't feed the chickens for the next few months and then grow some great runner beans next year. With Susie and Tom both shooting up so quickly, we need all the food we can produce.

That meal we had with Desdemona and Claude on Friday was something else. It took me back to before the war when I helped serve at those dinner parties, but there we were, Lily and I as the only guests. Despite the grandeur of the repaired dining room, we were in a new smaller side area which was decorated to Desdemona's modern taste. Claude was so different from his military-persona and was the perfect host.

As the meal finished, he explained that he must 'borrow me' for a few minutes. He led me through another newly furnished area into his den. He proffered a drink and poured himself a large brandy. "Sit yourself down Alf." He looked nervous as he dropped into his leather chair behind his desk. "Are you sure I can't get you one?"

I raised my hand and gently shook my head. I was intrigued.

"I'll get straight to the point, Alf. You may know that I'm on the board of several companies in the city." He waited for my reaction, but I had none to give. "One of them has just acquired one of the largest department stores in the West End." He took a gulp. "Our board are delighted, of course, with the prestige that this brings, but there are many changes that are going to have to be made, alterations and problems to solve – and – I'm hoping you may be able to help enormously with one of them."

My mind was immediately back to the last time I was helping Claude, and Desdemona. "I'm surely not qualified to help re-build a department store. Organising the workers and materials we had to make this place waterproof was one thing, but–"

Claude nearly choked as he laughed out loud. "Sorry. I wasn't clear. That's so funny. How rude of me. I apologise Alf." He drew a long breath and took a small sip. "I'll try again. The store we have bought has some rather large holes in its expected profits. There are many theories as to why and even more suspicions. In strictest confidence, of course, we believe that some of the management has been less than scrupulous. There seems to be a lax attitude to all levels of checking of staff, the merchandise, money handling and accountancy of every department. This pervades onto the shop floors and so we think pilfering is accepted as normality."

I realised where he might be heading, but a cool head was needed. "I'm not sure what you are asking of me yet, but I will say, up front, I would not make any decision without the full knowledge – and agreement – of Lily."

"Oh, my dear chap. That goes without saying. Of course. But I felt it only proper to sound you out first. If there was a definite negative reaction from you then we would not have had to involve the ladies at all."

"So what are you thinking I could help with?"

"I have been asked by the board to head up the team to oversee security within this whole company, beginning with especial emphasis on this store. I have many contacts throughout the city so can easily find a trustworthy accountant to scrutinise the finances, but the real need is an insider who knows how stores run from the management down through every level. You, Alf, have transformed Bentalls in your time there and I believe you are the only man I can put absolute faith in to see, and deal with, whatever is thrown at you."

His words were very good to hear, but were they just buttering the parsnips? What were the ramifications? "I think you need to tell me a little more of what you think I would do."

"As soon as you say yes, assuming you do, you would become a salaried member of our company with the title 'Head of Security'. You would give the notice necessary to your present employer. I believe you have trained an excellent deputy who we could also use, but I do not believe that would be fair to Bentalls. How you go about your work would be up to you, but I would guess that you would make a series of visits to the store to gather discreet impressions of the present situation. I'm sure you can blend into any department."

"I might have to enlist Lily's help in some."

"Of course. Men do rather stick out if alone there. There would be an office and secretarial assistance in our Headquarters and you would have clearance to examine any information we have. My team will be kept to a minimum, each individually responsible for their own area of expertise and we will have regular meetings to update each other on our findings. One small discovery in one area might unlock a wide avenue in another."

"Might I take you up on your offer – of a soft drink, please. A tonic water would be fine. Thank you."

"I realise there's a lot to digest. Let's hope this helps."

I sat and sipped the drink in silence. I loved my job and the security it brought our family. It was an easy bike ride away from home. It was an easy job now as we had a well-oiled machine in place. Easy. How long have I been coasting along Easy Street? Am I staying there until I retire? Am I ready to leap into the breach to face unknown problems? Have I lost my analytical prowess? Have I the courage to say yes?

Claude was shuffling papers in a file, pretending to read them, when I startled him. "I am ready to talk about this with Lily."

An almighty squawk shatters the peace and my fork showers damp soil into the top of my welly. "Blast. What on earth has upset the chickens?"

42   SITTING EXAMS

The children are growing up so quickly. Primary School has flashed by and I'm doubting whether Tom will cope in the cauldron of the grammar school system. Perhaps it won't be the right place for him? Exam sitting might be a nightmare for him. His teacher has explained how well he performs in the classroom and in the practice tests they have been taking, but he is still rather shy whenever there's something new. His confidence in maths has certainly improved. But pressure still seems to bring on those headaches and we've never been able to sort those out satisfactorily. Why are decisions so hard?

And now Alf has a difficult one to make. He tells me he wants and respects my opinion, but I have a different one each day. I know Claude would like an answer quickly too, and that makes things even more tricky. If Alf says yes then his hours will be much longer and I will have to switch to a short midday-only role at the hospital, or permanent nights. I don't fancy that much. But the money he would earn is probably twice what we both bring home now and Tom is shooting up and will need so many new things wherever he goes to school. Do I want to give up any thought of promotion, but if not, how would I study for the necessary exams? I think he'll regret it forever if he doesn't. Should I deny him that chance for my own small ambition?

"Nurse." The call from the far bed cannot be ignored. I take an empty bed-pan with me as I know this patient's needs.

It's been a long day and I'm stuck here until the night-shift take over, no matter how late they might be. The screens do deaden the bowel movements, but do nothing to cheer my spirits. The medication he's on certainly causes a unique aroma that they don't sell in Bentalls' Perfumery. I walk with care at arm's length to sluice away the stench and scrub my hands meticulously again. They do get red so quickly.

As I slide back through the ward door, I can see a shadowy figure crouched beside the second bed. Who's got out? I see that the top drawer of the cabinet is open and a hand is pocketing the contents. Do I summon help or challenge? I block the gap between the beds and gently cough. "Excuse me."

"What the–!" I recognise the face as Jenkins twists and stands to his full height.

"May I ask what the problem is?" The surrounding patients are now all wide awake and staring at us both. "Well?"

"I – I – I was asked to check that the bedside tables were all secure and safe for the men to open and close."

"Really? You were asked to do so when they were all asleep for what reason?"

"It was on my list for today and the other jobs all took longer than expected. I was being very quiet until you frightened me, Nurse."

"I'm sorry if I'm frightening, Jenkins, but I am not convinced that you are telling the truth."

"What's going on here?" Sister's voice wakes up the rest of the ward. "If there's any frightening to do then I'll do it!"

"I am very sorry to say, Sister, that I believe that Jenkins here has items in his possession that are not his."

"Turn out your pockets."

"You can't make me. I know my rights. All the stuff in my pockets is mine!"

"Really. Whose word is law on this ward, Nurse?"

"Yours, Sister."

"Perhaps you would prefer a strip-search here in front of everyone?"

Jenkins looks around the sea of men's faces that have gathered around the nearest beds. "That won't be necessary, Sister." He pulls out a wallet from the left pocket of his overall, puts it on the bed in front of him and steps back.

"And the rest?" His eyes are firing arrows at me. Four watches, cuff links, three pens, another two wallets are accompanied by a cascade of loose coins. "Do men usually need that many watches?"

The surrounding mass of masculinity seem intent on a lynching until Sister orders, "Back to your beds. You will all check your lockers after breakfast tomorrow. These items will be taken into safe keeping and I will speak to anyone tomorrow morning who believes he has lost anything. Now!"

No-one dares defy Sister's tone and they scurry away like scalded rabbits. "Nurse Robertson will bring the items to my office where you will stay until you are properly dealt with. You know where it is. Move!" The door swings open and a flustered night-shift nurse hurries in. "You're late. I won't tolerate tardiness either." As the scalded nurse steps into the shadows, Jenkins makes a bolt down the corridor and away into the dark bowels of the hospital.

43 SO SENSITIVE

I hope it's not my fault. Mum and Dad seem to have been having a lot of problems. I keep hearing them when I'm trying to go to sleep. The floor isn't very good at stopping their voices carrying up. I hear words like, "Exams, security, money, children, decisions." What do they mean?

Rupert at school hasn't got a Dad at home. He told me he has gone to live somewhere else. He doesn't see him any more. He thinks it was because he got lost once and when a policeman brought him home, the trouble started. There was a lot of shouting after he had been sent to bed and the next morning his Dad had gone. Gloria says he's dead and Ethel says he's in prison. They are so nasty when they say those things to Rupert. He's so sensitive and I try to cheer him up with a silly joke like one Dad told me. 'What did the lift attendant say to the customer? Life's full of ups and downs.' I've told him that one lots of times, but he knows I am his friend. He smiles.

I don't want Dad to leave us. Should I say that I don't want to take the exam to go to a grammar school? I know that would cost a lot of money. I do polish my shoes so they last a bit longer than when I used to play football all the time in the playground, before I hit my head on the wall when Simon foul-barged me and it cut open. I don't like bullies. I'd rather play marbles now up in the corner where we can draw a chalk circle and fire to knock them out to keep. I usually win a few more than I lose, but I don't mind if I don't. I only play with my not-so-good ones.

Mum looks worried too. I don't think she's sleeping well. I think she has a lot of difficult decisions to make when she's at the hospital. Maybe she should give it up. But perhaps that is why they are worried about money. I try to do jobs around the house and in the allotment. I do take my turn to feed the chickens, but they still seem to want to peck my bare legs even when I pretend they are footballs. I can dig up some of the vegetables that Dad grows and as I get stronger, I will help more. What else can I do?

Susie doesn't seem to notice. She's always cheerful, singing silly songs or telling stories that sound as if they're true. She has a terrific memory. Schoolwork comes so easily to her. She'll pass the Eleven Plus for sure and join up with Rachel there. I miss Rachel. She has a lot of homework and jobs to do for her Dad. They've just had a new guide dog called Jasper as Jason was getting too old. The two dogs seem to have fun together when we're invited round to visit. Jason looks sad when Jasper gets put into the harness. Perhaps he feels useless like I do sometimes. I do hope it's not all my fault.

44 SIT ON THE POUFFE

The wind's blowing the weeping willows down by the stream and the birds are huddling in the bushes, but it's warm and safe beside my roses. I'm quite content here, except I miss the company of the only two inmates I've got to know and trust. Sylvie hasn't re-appeared. I hope she's alright. Ted's not been in the Dining Room or Lounge for any of the activities for days now. No one else seems to miss him. I suppose they are used to people suddenly disappearing and new people arriving. His room is at the end of the upstairs corridor so I can't just walk by and listen. I can't ask anyone. I wonder if that test Isabel gave us has upset him more than she realised.

Can I remember what the questions were? Can I remember what I answered? If I can then perhaps I might understand what Ted might have written or drawn. Come to think of it, Isabel has been away all week too. Perhaps they've run away together. The very idea of it makes me chuckle.

"Well. That's good to hear. I think that's the very first time I've heard you make any noise." I see Isabel framed in the doorway with a huge smile on her face. "May I come in, please?" I nod and feel my cheeks burning. Where did that sound emanate from? She puts her arm around my shoulder, giving it a gentle squeeze. No-one's done that since my mother. I wish I could remember her. It feels nice, warm and comforting. She squats down beside my chair and is grinning.

"I want you to come next door and meet the person who has moved in there."

Why would anyone want to meet me? I stand and follow as Isabel leads the way, giving a light tap before opening the door and ushering me ahead of her. This room is a mirror-image of mine with the same red roses festooned on the curtains, but the high-backed armchair has a trailing cable plugged into the wall socket. My mind sees myself strapped and wired for pain. I shudder uncontrollably.

"Come on, Jo. Sit on the pouffe." Isabel directs me to the front of the chair and I lower myself as instructed. My eyes focus on a pair of fluffy pink slippers.

"It's so lovely to see you again. I've missed you so much." I slowly shift my gaze up to the beaming face of Sylvie. Tears stream down my cheeks.

45 UNHESITATINGLY

It's been agony, debating the benefits and disadvantages, the familiar with the unknown, the changes to our normal lives at a time when our children's lives are changing too. We've slept on it; except we haven't really slept. We've gone to work and looked anew at how we love our jobs; and yet freshly-opened eyes have not found perfection. I have often teased Lily that she was Sister material and only now she has confessed that she has been harbouring some thoughts of seeking promotion. Can we both take on more work?

Oh Lily, you are such a darling. You have nurtured me from that very first day in hospital, understanding my needs and putting aside your own. And now you say you unhesitatingly support me taking on this new adventure. You argue that I will always wonder what might have been if I don't. You say that I will be brilliant at it; that Claude has the inbuilt senior officer's eye for talent and he has chosen me.

The number 12 bus pulls up in Oxford Street where we alight with excitement running through our veins. We window-shop our way along the pavement, jostling with the Saturday crowds. The side road is more like an alley, just wide enough to admit a furniture van or lorry. "Let's look at the back entrance first." The glitz of the frontage gives way to dark, grime-covered walls with barred windows and sealed-up doorways where once there were many smaller shops.

The road widens at the rear, allowing a tight turn into a cavernous loading bay where three trucks are having goods added or subtracted in total confusion. We pause on the opposite side of the road. Men in brown overalls transport boxes and chests hither and thither. A whistle blows and they drop their loads wherever they are and troop through a door. "Tea break?" Lily asks. Two small figures appear from nowhere and make off in a flash, each with a prize as big as themselves. I have to restrain Lily as she moves to give chase.

It's ten minutes later when the whistle sounds again and the workers return. Two scratch their heads and shrug their shoulders before going about their business. Lily and I continue around the block, following the one-way system back to Oxford Street, pausing only to make discreet notes of the alley into which two large boxes have recently disappeared.

The frontage has enormous windows showing complete room scenes, filled with enticing furniture, hangings and populated by glamorously dressed mannequins. The toy display has fabulous working Meccano cranes, removing crates from Hornby trains as they stop on their way around the island of delight for children of all ages. "Don't let ours see this, Alf."

We enter through a glass door, opened for us by a uniformed attendant who smiles as he has done for years. I can't help noticing his jacket sleeve is pinned to his lapel. "Comrades without arms, perhaps?" Lily gives me a punch and we walk slowly through Perfumery to the lift. "Top floor please."

There are six levels to explore, but we have most of the day before us. There are very few staff here, but carpets, wallpaper and curtains are not easily hidden in pockets. Unattended tills are more tempting. The prices I see are rather higher than I'm used to. As we seem to be the only customers, a young youth in a suit he'll grow into, comes forward. "May I be of assistance?"

"Thank you young man. My husband and I are about to move to a much larger house and so we are considering what you have that might be suitable. It would be so convenient if we could find everything in one place. Shopping is so tedious otherwise." I just marvel at Lily's airs and graces.

A supervisor has too and an obsequious man buts in. "That will be all, thank you, Charles. Madam. Sir. I am certain that we can supply all of your needs. For customers like your good selves, I am sure our special services can be arranged. What may I show you first?"

Our escape is one I use when unnecessarily embroiled with a Bentalls customer; a sudden stomach pain. We stop on the stairs and compare thoughts. "That special service scheme sounds unofficial; concocted by himself."

Claude's 'expenses' when I told him we were making a visit, are very generous. I put four five-pound notes into Lily's hand before we head towards the most feminine of departments. "Be a real customer."

"Is there a waiting area for husbands?" Lily asks as she approaches a more mature assistant who indicates a corner area with three small armchairs, all facing the wall. "Wait there!" Lily commands and I gladly obey. As I squat, I pick up a copy of The Times and move the chair to give an overview. Lily is in full flow, with two younger girls fetching all manner of items for her approval, as she sits beside the counter.

There are many women here, customers and staff I presume, but it is not easy to distinguish between them. One catches my eye as she confidently moves around the floor. Most seem to have an area of responsibility, yet this one goes everywhere, taking things to put elsewhere. There seems no purpose to her actions; unless – I watch her gather a pile of garments and transfer them into a box, carry it to another unattended counter and do the same. Like a squirrel, she watches carefully, remembering where she has stored her booty. With her treasures out of sight, she saunters through the centre of the floor and disappears through the double doors marked 'staff only'.

A shadow I recognise falls over me. "I hope your view hasn't been too stressful. Come on. You're buying me lunch."

Lily leads me to a quiet corner where again we can watch and not be overheard. Our meal is over-priced, but delicious. "Well, that was very interesting," she finally says. I know I have to wait. "I think they make up their own prices. A customer in a mink coat was charged more for exactly the same thing that I had already bought. When I queried this, the older woman blamed the junior for getting it wrong, but by the look on her face, I guess it is their common practice. They probably share out the bonuses at the end of each day."

"You say you have bought something. I don't see a bag."

"I'm collecting all of the items when we are ready to leave. You'll have to wait until we get home to see what they are."

46 PROPOSITION

I've really enjoyed today. It has been such a long time since Alf and I have had a day to ourselves. I do hope the children have been good for Cyril. It's a lot to ask, but he was insistent that they would all be fine.

It's a good train service from Waterloo to Surbiton and the walk up St Marks Hill is reminding me how tiring shopping can be. Both of us are used to being on our feet for hours at a time, but acting undercover roles is totally different. I can see why Alf is good at his job as his attention to detail is so well honed. He has been scribbling on his notepad all the way home. I think I now know what his decision will be.

The downward slope leads us to Cyril's door and we pause. I take Alf's face in my hands and give him a kiss. "Accept Claude's proposition."

Barking makes needing to ring the bell unnecessary. Footsteps are running to open the door. "Mum, Dad, we've had a wonderful time. Mr Penrose says you're to come in. The kettle's on. Rachel's got everything ready for your tea."

The dogs are excited to receive our pats before Cyril's voice demands their obedience. I never tire of watching such unquestioning devotion, from man to animals and in reverse. Our young hostess has certainly prepared an array of sandwiches to tempt us. "Susie has helped me enormously whilst Tom has been reading to Dad. She has told me the things you like so we hope we have made them well. While Dad had a rest this afternoon, we took the dogs to the cake shop to buy six iced buns. I hope you still like them. Shall I pour you both a cup of tea?"

47 SUPPOSITION

I promised Angela I would before I thought. I said I could before I'd asked. It's so much harder being in this big school where the other girls all seem to know what to do and what to say. And now tomorrow, I've got to tell Angela I can't and she won't like me any more because I've broken my promise.

It's all Mum and Dad's fault. I explained to Mum when she came home, but she said she didn't think that it was a good idea. She said I'd got to ask Dad. He just said no. It's so unfair.

I tried again at teatime. I explained that Angela was getting tickets for the concert in the Richmond Theatre and it was just the same bus as going to school, only a few stops more and I'd promised her and she'd told her Mum I could go with her so if I can't go, she'll not be able to go and it's on Saturday so not a school day and if I don't, she'll never talk to me again.

Dad looked at Mum and Mum looked at Dad. They seem to have a secret code that I can't break. He said, "I'm sorry, Susie, but we can't allow it." He held his hand up and I knew not to speak. "The concert you are speaking of is not suitable for girls of your age. The music and performances are designed for adults. I know you are disappointed, but I am very surprised that Angela's mother has agreed to her going. That she will pay for you too is a big supposition to make." He poured himself another cup of tea and I knew he wouldn't budge. He's so old-fashioned.

I've been in my room now for about three hours. I can't speak to them. Tom will get a pillow thrown at him if he pokes his nose in. What if I go anyway? What's the worst that can happen? I think Angela's Mum is paying for the tickets. How much have I got left in my piggy? I'll have to remember the bus fare too, both ways.

48 POSITIVITY

Sylvie is back and able to move a little more freely. She tells me that it was a knock on the locked front door that made her fall in the Reception Area. I can't tell her how guilty I've been feeling, but it is a huge weight off of my shoulders. She's been given exercises to do and a physiotherapist is going to visit her weekly to check up on progress. Sylvie wants me to do the exercises with her. She thinks I will be able to motivate her. I've not seen such positivity from my friend before.

Isabel has arranged for Sylvie to move to this ground-floor room. She says Marjie wanted to be upstairs, but by the look on her face during lunch today, I'm not so sure. But I don't care. Part of Sylvie's treatment is to join in the Lounge activities again so we make our way in for Sit Tennis. We are undefeated when I've played, but that empty chair opposite will make it all too easy.

"I hope there's room for me!" booms a voice from the doorway.

Startled sleepers snort before a disbelieving chorus of, "Ted!" rings through the home.

"Has anyone missed me?"

"No!"

"It's been lovely and peaceful."

It's a full ten minutes before the game can begin and Ted is in full flow with energy and guile in abundance. He looks so invigorated. I try to involve Sylvie, conscious of my new role of assistant carer, and have no regrets when our team are heavily defeated.

Sylvie is ready for a rest in her room so I wander off to the tea machine where I'm not surprised to see Ted already consuming biscuits. "Are you well, Jo?" I nod. "Have you been up to any mischief without me?" My innocent expression is matched by his of disbelief. An approaching trolley cuts short our one-way conversation, except for a parting, "See you later!", accompanied by a wrist twist.

"Is that a date with trouble, Jo?" Jasmine asks. I give her the vague look and chuckle at the key-turning signal. I don't think I've ever had a date before.

It's a really great day and Sylvie is eating well, even being more able to feed herself. We both tuck into our food with gusto and she is trying so hard to do her exercises correctly. I'm enjoying being useful; being liked and respected. I can't ever remember being treated kindly; of having people I could call friends. I feel a warmth just thinking about it as I sit and stare at the newspaper in my familiar place where I feel at home.

I've not used the secret key in my pocket for a while, but it still shifts the lock silently as I let myself in. The books aren't right, but I can soon fix them. I quickly answer the tap signal and Ted comes in and plonks himself behind the desk as I relock the door. "Sorry I couldn't tell you why I went away. I made contact with an old workmate of mine who has learnt a lot about these computer things. He's given me a crash course on getting into this one so we can do some digging." I look perplexed, so he adds, "Without a spade."

The lights start flashing as soon as he touches the keyboard and he taps furiously. He's brought a notebook with him and he flicks from page to page. "This is where I wanted to be. Staffing."

I sit beside him, mesmerised by the typed words on the screen. "What's Matron's name?" I pull open a drawer where I have seen letters stored and find it. "Mildred Carter." Ted guffaws. I put my finger to my lips and he stifles his noise. "Oh Mildred, dearest. She doesn't look like a Mildred."

A bang on the door startles us. The handle turns. "Are you alright, Matron. Shall I get Isabel with her key?"

The machine is turned off and we beat a rapid retreat. That was close, but so exciting. Life is fun.

49 PROPOSITIONS

My last Wednesday afternoon off. I'm glad its sunny and I can finish the planting out. I doubt I'll have much time now I'm London bound. Bentalls took it well. I guess they were just grateful for the differences I've made. They advertised for my replacement and I helped sort through the applicants. Some sounded quite reasonable, but I knew who my favourite was.

On Friday, I gave each of the four candidates a guided tour, behind the scenes as well as throughout the shop floor. I was careful to give nothing away as to how I did things; a fresh perspective would be called for by the panel. One man was particularly abrasive, making comments about some of the staff who he considered inferior. Another was forthright about his present employers who had foolishly appointed a woman to head up a department. How naïve they both were to think that my observations would not be passed on through to the interviewers.

It was a long day for all concerned. The panel had taken my comments on board and had two strategies under consideration.

Two candidates were asked to leave after their interviews. The panel explained that they would not fit in the future shape of Bentalls. As I escorted each one to the staff exit, they turned on me, uttering expletives I'd not heard since the trenches. The threats were both to my family as well as myself as both were convinced that I had turned the panel against them. I reported everything to Dawn in accordance with our normal procedure. Their reactions spoke volumes about their characters.

The two men remaining were asked if they would be comfortable with the proposition of accepting the role of Deputy Security Officer. One immediately declined and was shown out. The one that remained was a young man who had been set upon by youths in a nearby town centre when he was a police cadet. He had managed to keep hold of one until a colleague handcuffed him. Sadly, his shoulder was badly dislocated and ligaments permanently damaged making his police career short-lived. The panel felt he was too inexperienced to be in charge and he readily agreed with them, saying that he would have applied to be an assistant rather than head if both had been advertised. Iris will train him well.

Now I'm going to have to train a lot of new staff to change their working habits. Corruption is an ugly word, but there is no doubt it is rife throughout the store. As I saw deeper into the practices, I saw endless opportunities for theft. Some employees must be doubling their wages. Claude's accountant Gerald was equally shocked, immediately recognising the duplicity of the auditors with the Financial Director.

The showdown began as the store was about to close on Monday. Claude made an announcement on the loudspeaker system. "This store will not open for trading tomorrow. Every member of staff will assemble at their normal place of work by 8:30 a.m. and you will be informed as to the changes that are to be implemented. The Directors have been summoned and these instructions apply to every level of employment. That is all. You may clock out, including the evening cleaning staff who will still be paid for this shift. Goodnight."

Our small team had recruited new faces who tomorrow would place posters on the doors announcing the closure 'for staff training' and then be stationed at all exits. But before then, a lightning search was to be made of every part of the shop floor, stores and offices and detailed lists made of any items in unexpected places without disturbing them. As midnight approached all were summoned to the canteen where refreshments were provided and I was shown a cupboard packed with dresses and coats. We split into two teams for four-hour shifts, resting in the staff lounge chairs or continuing our searches. By eight o'clock we were ready.

Each section of the store was instructed to carry out a comprehensive stock-take. This was to be under the direction of each Department Head. The Directors that had been summoned to the Boardroom were each given an envelope, detailing the severance of their Directorships. They were told that as criminal proceedings might be following, their silence was demanded. They were then escorted from the premises.

The Managers were next. Each was spoken to in private. Some were dismissed, some retained under scrutiny. The corridors echoed to departing footsteps.

I made my way to the loading bays with two new employees. We found the workforce in the canteen engaged in heated discussions. Silence fell like a curtain ending a drama. We made our way to the far end and turned into their hostility. "Gentlemen. I need to introduce myself. Alf Robertson. Head of Security." The murmuring was short-lived. "The new Board of Directors will be meeting this afternoon to approve the changes being made to the running of this prestigious store. There will be a new management structure and new working practices. The owners have discovered that criminal activity has been rampant and are determined to stamp it out. Warrants have been issued for the arrest of some staff already. We will root out corruption." I paused to let the message percolate. "I am starting here. I have witnessed theft from the floor of this loading bay because of sloppy practice. I have instigated a reorganisation of your work to ensure such an occurrence cannot be repeated. These two gentlemen are your supervisors. One team will solely operate on goods in whilst the other deals with goods out. Teams will have team leaders who will allocate the specific tasks. All goods will be recorded. Nothing else will enter or leave this area."

"How dare you!" bellowed a huge bearded man in my ear. "I'm in charge here!"

I turned to him. "Mr. McManus I assume. It's good that you are here. The two gentlemen by that door would like you to accompany them to answer their questions." His bluster deflated instantly as he realised the predicament he was in. The workers watched him leave.

"Fair wages for honest work are promised. Hard work will be rewarded. If that does not suit you then you may terminate your employment. Mr. McManus's regime is over. As randomly as we can, we will now split you into two teams. Those whose birthday is in January to June stay in here whilst the July to December group go through to the bay. Your supervisors will introduce themselves and give you today's tasks. This store depends on your efficiency. The owners will be paying bonuses to the best teams. Let's make sure the money comes your way!"

I'd hardly slept for weeks since the propositions were agreed. Finally leaving Bentalls will be sad on Friday, but the changes I'm overseeing are exhilarating. I just hope that the sackings that have happened and the gaps we try to fill will not be too substantial to make achieving our goals impossible. I believe in the possible.

It's possible that I have transplanted too many lettuces, but I suppose I haven't when the slugs have their fill. I'll have to set Tom and Susie a challenge to see how many they can find in a week. My back is complaining. I'll go and have a long soak before Lily gets home. I'll try not to nod off while I'm in there.

50 CONFUSING SITUATION

Another shift complete. These shorter days are suiting me quite well now. I can usually get home at about the same time as Susie and Tom. I like to involve them in the meals as they will need these skills as they grow up. I wish I had been given the chance to learn more.

It's quite a distance from the Men's Wards to the main road. There are always crowds of visitors at this time, walking in all directions, looking bemused. I daren't stop to help or I'd certainly miss the bus. It's a good job there's a porter about to point them in the right direction. That one looks very much like – it is him. Surely not – he wouldn't dare. Should I challenge him on my own? There's Glynis.

"What's the matter, Lily?"

"I'm sure that's Jenkins."

"Where?"

I point. "Oh. He was there a moment ago. I'm certain."

"What do you want to do about it?"

"How can he just have disappeared? It's a confusing situation. Should we alert everyone in case he's back at his old thieving ways, but, if it wasn't him, I'll be wasting everyone's time?"

"You're the one who saw him. You decide."

"I'll tell the Head Porter in the morning. I didn't think Jenkins would ever show his face around here again – ever!"

"Good. I'm off dancing tonight. Fancy a jive? Oh look, Lily. There's your bus. Run!"

I run as fast as I can, but in vain. I swear some conductors ring their bell on purpose when they see us running. I'd better catch my breath before I start walking. It's not worth waiting for the next. It's all his fault, despicable little man. I wouldn't be surprised if he points visitors one way whilst picking their pockets with the other hand. Oh. I shudder at the very thought of him. The quicker I get into town the better. I keep imagining shadows and hearing footsteps getting nearer. That car's slowing down.

"Excuse me, young lady. Can you tell me the road to take to get to Richmond Park?" a woman asks.

As I bend to her open window, a strange smell fills my nostrils as a cloth wraps around my face and a hand holds–

51   SITTING IN THE DARK

Am I so different to everybody else? I used to be very scared of animals, and being alone, and the dark, and sudden noises. There are so many things I can't understand. I suppose that's normal when you're growing up, but others don't seem to worry. Is it just that I'm shy?

Susie isn't. Miss Chatterbox has sailed through primary school, laughing and being the centre of attention. Now she loves her new school and has so many new friends too. She goes there with Rachel every morning. I wish I could walk her to school. I really like Rachel. She's always been my friend, since I was little. She's so kind and gentle to everyone. She's wonderful. One day I'll–

But I do get fed up with these headaches. They come and go more often now. I've had them since I can remember. I don't think the boxing helped. I didn't want to. I'm skinny and tall now, for my age. The prefects said I had to represent the House in the ring like everyone else because I was the right weight. It was a good job I have long arms to keep pushing into my opponent's face to keep him from hitting me. But when it was all over, they said I'd won and had to do it again. They were pleased with me and said I was good. For a few moments I felt good too, being liked by others at school. But the next boy in the ring is in my class and we all know he's aggressive. He came straight at me and knocked my puny arms aside before bashing me until I fell backwards and hit my head on the post at the corner of the ring. Why is a square with four corners called a ring?

I had to lie still for ages after that. Mum was called from work and she took me straight back there. The blackness stayed for hours. I've had lots of tests, but they can't agree what's the matter.

And now I sometimes wake up and the night hasn't gone away. I'm getting used to sitting in the dark, being on my own, thinking. Dad's got his last half-day today. I like early-closing days to give the workers some time off during daylight. He's having a long soak in the bath. He needs it, being on his feet for most of every week. I've heard the back door. I expect it's time Susie was home and she's gone straight up to change out of her uniform. I wonder what's for tea. I can make myself a drink and find the biscuit tin. "Susie! Are you in?"

I hear the footsteps running down the stairs. I hear her breathing, trying to speak. Oh no. She's lost it. She grabs my hand and pulls me up the stairs, across the landing and into the bathroom. "Dad. Dad!" There's no answer. She puts my hand under his arm and I feel her pulling too. We heave together and feel him falling over the side on top of us. I feel for his wrist as I've seen Mum do so many times before. She taught me when I was young. Pulse. Come on. "Stay with him. I'll get help." I feel for the bannisters and descend as fast as I can, open the door, jump the step I know is there and walk towards the gate. "Help!" I'm off-centre and fall into the flower bed. "Blast these eyes."

"Hello Tom. What's the matter?" My angel's voice.

"Rachel. It's Dad. We can't wake him up."

52   SIT WITH THE CHICKENS

Dad. Wake up. I'm screaming inside, but my voice has gone. I grab all the towels I can see and rub him hard. Surely this will make him cough out the water. I wish Mum had taught me how to make him breathe. Why isn't she here when she's needed? I can hear Tom bringing someone up the stairs. It's Rachel. She's gone all white. She's run away. I thought she would help. She's supposed to be our friend. Don't leave us.

Tom bends down beside me and rubs like I am. Tell me what to do, Tom. You can speak.

Our arms are aching and yet Dad still hasn't moved. "We'll turn him over. Help me. Now." Dad is heavy even though he's not fat. His head flops to the side and his tongue sticks out. Tom rubs hard on his back and I join in again. "Keep going Susie. We've got to try."

I hear a bell and footsteps. Rachel's voice tells men where we are. "We'll take over." They're strong and we fall back to the walls as they push and prod our Dad. Tom can't see and I can't look. "I'm sorry. There's nothing we can do." They pull a towel over Dad's face and I get out as quickly as I can.

I've got to escape this hell. I run and sit with the chickens.

53 PAINFUL POSITION

My head hurts. I can't bear to open my eyes. I'm cold. I ache everywhere. My body's in a painful position. What's happening? I listen. Nothing. Where's the ticking clock that Glynis gave us? It sits on our bedside table. Alf wound it on Sunday.

I open my eyes into darkness. I've always left a chink in the curtains since the war, because I can. The gentle moonlight is soothing. But there's no moon tonight. This mattress feels hard. "Alf." I can't hear his breathing. "Alf." I reach out for him. "Ouch." My hand hits a brick wall, scraping skin from my knuckles. I roll away and fall onto a cold, damp floor. "Help!"

My voice echoes. I pull myself back up onto the bed. Pull yourself together Lily. Think. Remember. Leaving hospital, Jenkins, Glynis, the laughing bus conductor, walking, footsteps, car– A horrible taste fills my senses and I want to vomit. Deep breath, slowly in, hold, out. "Blow those fumes away."

I shiver. I'm alone. I'm not at home so where am I? I touch my knuckles and feel loose skin. My hand instinctively retrieves a handkerchief from a pocket to wrap around. Nausea is not far away. Lie down Lily. Recovery position. You mustn't be sick lying on your back. Look after yourself. Help will come.

54 SITTING IN TEARS

"What do you mean – there's nothing you can do?"

"Is he your father?" I nod. "We can see you tried your best, but I'm sorry to say that he was dead before we got here. Was that your sister with you?"

"Yes. Susie. Sometimes when she has a shock, she loses her voice."

"That explains why she was quiet. And you?"

"I'm Tom. I can talk, but have days when my sight goes. I can't see today."

"And your mother?"

"She's a Nurse at Kingston Hospital. Lily Robertson. She should have been home some time ago. Oh Mum."

I feel an arm around my shoulder and hear footsteps going downstairs. The tears flow. As my sobs start to subside, I realise there is light returning. I feel a hand holding mine and see a skirt next to my leg. I turn to the face of my angel, shedding tears with me.

Footsteps returning suddenly make us self-conscious. Rachel moves aside and I try to stand up as a policeman fills the doorway. "Right young man. I think we'd better get you downstairs. You too Miss." We obey.

There are policemen in every room. Rachel sits beside me on the settee. I'm so glad she's here. "Where's Susie?"

"We're looking for her. Do you have any ideas where she might have gone?"

"The garden, or allotment. Not far."

"How long ago did you last see your father?" a man without a uniform asks.

"I don't know. I've not been able to see at all today. Dad did some jobs in the garden this afternoon and told me he was going to have a soak in the bath before Mum came home. I just sit here thinking when my eyes won't work."

"What made you go upstairs?"

"Susie fetched me. She pulled me up and helped me get him out of the bath. We tried. We tried." Rachel squeezed my hand again and shared my tears once more.

"And what about you, Miss. Who are you and what can you tell us?"

"I'm just a friend." I returned her squeeze. "Rachel. Rachel Penrose. I saw Tom run out of the door shouting. When I saw what Susie was trying to do, I ran next door to ask them to ring for an ambulance and waited to show them the way. I wish I could have done more." It's my turn to put my arm around her and pull her close, just like I've seen Dad do to Mum. Oh Mum. Where are you?

"How did Susie know your Dad needed help?"

I don't know that. "I suppose she went in the bathroom when she came home."

"How long had she been home before she fetched you?"

I don't know that either. "I was lost in my thoughts. I heard the door. I called out to her. She didn't answer. Then I heard her running downstairs and she grabbed me."

"We need to find Susie."

55 AWKWARD POSITION

I'm numb. I'm used to collecting the eggs, but I've never tried squatting on top of their roost amongst the straw before. The corrugated roof is very low. It's quite an awkward position, but I can just see out through the wire mesh. The birds squawked a lot at first, but they've forgotten I'm here now. They look quite funny from my perch. That bald patch on Fluff's back is getting worse. She really is hen-pecked. It's been getting bad since we got down to just four birds. Still, they're all laying well.

Those policemen seem to be looking for something. I hope they don't tread on Mum's flowers or Dad's veg. Dad'll get cross if they do.

"Hello. Are you Susie? Can you come out now?" I haven't heard. I'm not here. I look through him. I'm a chicken. He's coming in. Go on girls. Attack. "It looks as if your leg is bleeding. Let's get someone to look at it."

He's holding out his hand. I suppose I've got to. Okay. Ouch. Keep your head down. My legs are stiff. Oh. They are bleeding. How did that happen?

He takes hold of me and carries me out. Fluff spots her chance and legs it. She's always looking for an escape route. I know where she'll head. She loves the loganberries that Tom and I flick through the wires. Two policemen are chasing her. She'll just carry on. I watch them getting nowhere. I wriggle out of his grip and walk slowly along the cinder path. The men stay still. Fluff seizes her chance and perches on the loganberry row. I let her eat three before reaching out and clasping her firmly from behind. She complains, but knows the game is up. The door is opened for me to deposit her back amidst the complaining hens. They can detect the berry juices that they have not tasted. The policeman leads me indoors.

Rachel's here with Tom. They give me a cuddle. Tom doesn't usually do that. I sit beside them on the settee. There's a man in a suit sitting opposite them on Mum's chair. Where's Mum?

"So you are Susie." I don't like the look of his eyes. He is trying to find a smile from his hidden charm training, and failing. "Now Susie. You're not in trouble, but I must ask you some questions. Okay?" The sparrows are enjoying the clematis, rambling over the fence. "What time did you get home?"

Tom puts his arm round me, my protector big brother. "I've already said, she has a problem speaking sometimes. It has happened before after a shock."

"But I have got to know these important details. How do you usually communicate when she stops talking?"

"When she was younger, she would point or mime. Then she would write odd words or draw pictures."

"Then let's get on with a written statement." He thinks that's easy, so he pulls out a pad from his case and a cheap pen.

I give Tom a signal. Rachel puts her hand on his. "I'll go." She's so in-tune with us. I know she is such a good friend. I take the pen and rest the pad on my knee. I draw a chicken fleeing the hen house. Rachel brings me the drink. I smile my thanks to her. The chicken has a man's head on it. His eyes are pure evil. Yes. That's right. I thrust the pad at the policeman and lay my head on Tom's shoulder. That face will haunt me.

56   IMMENSITY

Before my eyes open my memory floods with horror. Instinctively I touch my knuckles and the nurse has to look for damage. My sight adjusts slowly. Slight grazes. Some brick dust probably. Soft old red bricks lie beside this bed. I'm in a corner. I swing my legs off and sit upright, steadying my giddiness. Some light is coming from higher up across the room.

To my right I can see the shape of a door so I stand, and wish I hadn't. Whatever I'd been knocked out with is still in my system. Try again. Door. Where's the handle? There's a hole where the shaft should go. My forefinger fits and I pull. It will not budge. Pushing is equally useless.

Next to me is the foot of a flight of stairs with a turn at the bottom. I hope the treads are sound. There is a handrail fixed to the wall although it doesn't feel totally secure. I tread gingerly, hoping each step will take my weight as I venture ever nearer the light. I can now see a drop into the room on my left and my hand grips tightly as I make my way to the top.

The glass is grimy and my hand soon blackened. The effect is good, though not perfect as there are layers of dust outside. The pane is about a square foot with two vertical metal bars, again outside. There's no handle and the door will not yield to my pushes or pulls.

I peer out. A thick hedge to my right meets a high fence, just visible above a jungle of brambles. Beyond it, I make out a terrace of old houses with a pale blue sky above their roofs. I'm in a basement, probably of a Victorian home.

I turn back into the gloom and inch my way down again. The stairs have been boxed-in, much like ours at home. Why did I think of home? Tears flood my cheeks. "Oh Alf. How will you find me? Tom. Susie. I love you all."

The immensity of my position is sinking in. I allow the tears to subside before I feel along the wooden wall. My hand hits a handle and I push down on it. I'm buoyed by success. Escape. Or is it a trap? Caution.

The doubt in my head does not take long to resolve. A full-sized door creaks open into an even darker space. My foot feels for solid floor and my hands are outstretched. A brick wall. Of course. The width of the stairs. I turn to my left and my knee hits something hard. I feel all round. It's smooth and feels wooden. I lift and it hinges, giving access to another round wooden shape. Oh Lily. Think girl. It's what you're desperate for!

I am relieved. I sit and cry. I feel along the bare walls. I stand and wave until my wrist hits a chain. I pull and a gush descends.

The dim light through the doorway guides me out and I spy a small sink and single tap. The H on its top is a lie, but I'm happy to wash. There's no soap or towel. What would Matron say? Sister too would be holding an inquisition.

Next to the sink is a double cupboard below two drawers, one of which contains just a box of hard toilet paper. Underneath there are two rough blankets, a small towel and a bag of clothes that look as if they've had several previous owners. I can't see very well, but that seems to be all there is.

In the corner is a small table and chair, beside which is a rickety armchair. Will it support me? I sit carefully and my eyes retrace the circuit I have made. As I pass the bottom of the stairs, I make out some unfamiliar shapes that weren't there before. I realise there are two small boxes and a mug containing some lukewarm cocoa. I take these to the table and sniff suspiciously. The boxes have sandwiches and a stale bun inside. I realise how hungry I am. Should I savour or save any? Too late. They're gone in a flash.

Returning to the door, I see a slip of paper. 'Put the empties through the flap or you'll get no more.' What flap? Ah. Near the bottom, just big enough for an arm to reach through, but not a body. There must be someone on the other side. But who?

57 ULTRASENSITIVE

Mildred Carter. The name keeps jumping in and out of my head. Have I heard it before? Carter perhaps; just a surname. Can I hear it being shouted along a long foggy corridor in my memory?

Ted and I meet again in our secret den as soon as evening somnolence sets into the majority. It's when we truly come alive. He's ooing and ahhing as he flashes his fingers over the keys. "That's very interesting. Paper. Pencil or pen." I'm used to being given orders. "I don't usually tell people I was an accountant. These figures are very revealing. Either Matron is totally incompetent – or – she is earning a small fortune." He's scribbling figures furiously, flicking pages of numbers on the screen and tutting as he makes his own records.

Daylight through the window is dwindling. We've been engrossed and not realised how time has disappeared. I realise the evening cocoa will be on its way to our rooms and we'll be missed. I put my hand on Ted's to stop him. He gives me a strange look. I don't know what that means.

I take my hand away and point to the gathering dusk. "Crikey. We'd better pack up." He clicks on the keys and the screen turns blank. We are stiff as we try to stand and fall against each other. He gives a gentle laugh. "Steady on there."

As I go to unlock, he takes hold of my hand. "We've got to talk this through. Not here. Not out there where walls have ears. Tomorrow morning at breakfast, I'll tell Isabel that I am taking you for a short ride in my car. It's about time you had a taste of freedom. She'll agree it's a good idea. You know you must say yes if she asks you if you want to."

And now I'm shuddering. Freedom is a word I've never used. I have no concept of what it means. What does Ted want to tell me? Am I being ultrasensitive?

58 HESITATION

Oh dear. Susie's deep this time. I wish Mum were here. Where is she? The police are having a conference in the hall. It looks as if a senior officer has arrived to take charge. Oh Dad. Why didn't I know you'd fallen asleep? I should have checked.

"Hello. I'm Inspector West. Rachel. There's a man with a dog outside who says he's your father. Would you please speak to him and then come straight back here? Thank you." A policeman takes her away and I watch her go.

"Now then, Tom." He's speaking as he's reading the notes he's been given. "First, I must say how sorry I am for the circumstances we find ourselves in. Is this right that you can't see and your sister can't speak?"

"I have an eyesight problem that means for many hours or days I'm blind, but then things can clear, like they did a short while ago."

"And you can see clearly now, or just a bit?"

"Your moustache has a breadcrumb caught in it."

He wipes his hand across his mouth. "Sorry about that. I missed lunch. So what can you tell us that your sister means by this drawing?" I take the pad.

"Some of our hens do take on personalities, but this is more significant. I would guess Susie means that she saw a man in, or coming out of the hen house as she came up the allotment path. She often comes in that way from school if the gate's been left unlocked. I think the man saw her and ran for it." I'm not telling him Susie's squeezing my hand.

The Inspector motions to three subordinates who disappear at speed. "I'm sorry to have to ask you, but please tell me every scrap of detail you can about this afternoon. We understand that you were sitting here for most of the time, but start from when your father came home."

Before I can do so, Rachel comes back in and the policeman whispers in the Inspector's ear. "Sorry. Excuse me a moment."

"I heard them say the pathologist was about to leave. What does that mean?" Rachel says.

"I don't know. I expect we'll be told." I hadn't noticed that there is a lady officer here until she brings in a tray of drinks and biscuits. She puts it on the small table next to Rachel. I pass a cup on to Susie who sips it. She takes three biscuits as the plate is offered and puts them in her lap. She crumbles one up into the tea and watches the pieces float before pushing at them with her finger. I've never seen her do that before. Her finger is red from the heat, but she doesn't seem to notice. I take her hand away from the cup and kiss her finger better. She withdraws it and drinks the tea soup. Rachel and I also drink in silence. It's unnerving being watched over. "Why isn't Mum home yet?"

"We've been to the hospital. She signed off at two. A porter, Jenkins, said he saw her get into the back seat of a dark car. We spoke to a nurse, Glynis, who said she'd seen her running to catch a bus outside. They can't both be right. Do you know these two people?"

"Glynis has been Mum's friend for years. Jenkins? I think she told Dad some weeks ago about a thief she'd caught in the ward. That might have been his name. Yes. I think it was."

"Did she say she was going anywhere after work?"

"No. She only works short shifts to be at home for us when we get back from school. She knew I was home today and that Dad would be here this afternoon. She would be coming straight home." I must try to bring Susie back to us. "Did she tell you she would be late, Susie?" I squeeze her hand, but get no response.

The Inspector returns. "Sorry again. It's vital you tell us everything." He raises his eyebrows to the woman constable, who seems to understand what that means. She sits back down, facing us with her notebook and poised pencil. "You couldn't see, but you could hear. What mood was your father in when he came home today?"

"He was a bit annoyed that a thief had got away because the assistant stopped the wrong person, but otherwise was his normal self. He worked in the allotment before his bath – sorry – I heard him singing a song from a Gilbert and Sullivan opera." She's writing my words down. "He's been trying to learn the words to a modern major general because it makes us all laugh when he gets in a muddle – did." Both girls squeeze my hands. I'm glad Susie is responding, that's good.

"And then?"

"I'm not sure if I nodded off or was just lost in my thoughts. I heard the floorboards creak. I assumed it was Dad moving about. Then later, I thought it must be Susie home. I called out. She came and dragged me upstairs to try to help Dad. We pulled him out and rubbed him and Rachel came and then the ambulance and they said he was–"

"Okay. Could the creaking floorboards have been caused by someone else?"

I'm not sure what he means. "We know which ones creak so where to walk if we're trying to be quiet, but no-one else would."

"Would you know, Rachel? Or your father?"

"No. I've not been upstairs here until today and you've seen my father. He cannot cope well in different places."

"So, Rachel, how well does Tom here get on with his father?"

She's frowning. "Very well. They all love each other very much. Susie too. It's such a happy family. They make me feel welcome whenever I'm here. And Dad."

"Thank you. I'm sorry I have ask these questions. I believe you." He's flicking through the papers. "Tom. Did your father wear a ring?"

"Yes. It was a wedding ring. He wore it on his only hand."

"Would he have taken it off and put it somewhere safe before he had his bath?"

"No. How could he?"

"Sorry. Of course not. Nearly finished."

I take a deep breath. "Do you know why Mum hasn't come home?"

The Inspector looks at the Constable. "We don't know. We want to speak to her of course. In the meantime, we have to sort out what to do with you now. You can't stay here. Do you have any other relations?"

"Only one. Aunt Alice lives in the big house at Esher."

"Would she take you in for the night?"

"I don't think she could as she only works there and has her own small bedroom."

"Okay then. Here's what's going to happen. Rachel, an officer will take you home to your father. I don't think we will need to talk to you again, but if we do, we know where to come. Okay?"

"Tom and Susie need to collect a few clothes together. You will be taken to a Children's Home in Kingston. There you will be given a bed for the night and then tomorrow we will have to talk to you both some more. There will be police here all night so when your mother returns, she will be told everything. Does that make sense to you?"

I look Susie in the eye. She holds my hand very tightly. She's scared. So am I. "Yes."

59 ANIMOSITY

I don't have enemies, only friends. In nursing we try our best to look after people through kindness. I do recall one man who threatened us all when his brother died. He claimed it was our fault; that we didn't do enough. They had both been drinking in a pub, but when he went to the gents, his brother staggered out into the street, right in front of a car. He suffered multiple fractures and internal bleeding, as well as vomiting most of his week's wages away. The ambulance got him to the hospital in minutes and surgeons tried to stitch him together. He somehow survived enough to come up to the ward, but the shock had kicked in late and his heart suddenly couldn't cope. That was three months ago now. Surely the brother's sobered up enough to realise that drunkenness was the culprit. It was his own guilt that made him lash out at us.

I sit in the armchair for a long time, thinking. Only one name comes to mind. Jenkins. For years he's been around, masquerading as a porter, often on the evening or night shifts. He always seemed able and willing to carry out orderly duties; pushing a trolley or patient in a wheelchair to another ward or for an x-ray. It was only after I caught him rifling through the patient's drawer that we reported him to the Chief Porter. He was perplexed. There had never been a Jenkins employed there to his knowledge, which spread back three decades. His brown coat gave him a plain disguise and licence to go anywhere.

He'd disappeared until today, or yesterday. I'm sure it was him. I can understand his animosity towards me, but this. Is kidnap the right word?

60 INQUISITION

This place stinks. I hate it. I've been given a bunk to sleep on and a tiny cupboard to store my clothes. I remember Dad talking about his army barracks and this is worse. There are girls in here. I don't trust any of them. They surrounded me when I got here, asking questions, demanding answers. We've done the Spanish Inquisition in history. It felt just like that. They thought that I couldn't speak because I was frightened. Of girls? They learnt. I squinted my eyes and moved towards the biggest, the one they called Crystal, baring my teeth and twisting my lips. The silence was overwhelming as they all backed away. I circled them all, like a lioness choosing her victim. It felt great. I changed my face into my sweetest smile as I returned the other way. When I got back to the ring-leader, she was sat on her pillow with her knees drawn up to her chest, expecting an attack. I paused – and walked away.

I've hardly slept. My mind-pictures are of Dad, of Tom and I trying, trying to get him to breathe. My chest is tight, as if I've been under the water with him, fighting for air. It's so vivid. Darkness and water fill what dreams I have, fighting, pain, despair. Waking is worse. Reality.

I dress. I've not brought uniform. For sure, I'm not going there today. The other girls are subdued in theirs, browns and greys, sombre and unflattering, ill-fitting remnants of their lives. This is their normality. It won't be mine.

I follow them into a communal room and see Tom, sat with his back to me amongst the boys. I rush to sit beside him, but a strong arm takes mine and pulls me away. "Girls sit there. Fetch your food." A big woman points to the back of the line. I obey.

I shuffle forward, watching the process those in front go through. Tray, spoon, bowl, plate and cup are collected from stacks. A wizened witch sends a dollop of porridge splattering into my bowl, plonks a piece of blackened, buttered toast on the plate and a gush of grey liquid cascading into the cup and tray. "Manners. Where's your 'Thank you' Missy?" She gets my stare before I turn on my heel.

Despite myself, I have to eat. I don't think I've had anything since school dinner yesterday. That seems a feast to me now. The liquid is disgusting, the porridge would be better as glue and the toast threatens my teeth. I need more. I look around. No-one is getting any seconds. The slices were counted to fit exactly.

"Prayers!" The others stand to attention. I sit until the large woman hauls me to my feet. "Thank you, God, for everything that we receive. Amen!"

"Amen," is muttered under many breaths before the boys file out towards the entrance hall. The girls follow.

A policeman is standing, waiting, with Tom by his side, looking very pale and lonely. I stop beside him. "Is this Susie?" Tom nods and holds my hand. "Good. We'll be off then. You know where we're going, no doubt."

No. Are we going home to Mum?

61 LET'S SIT

I'm petrified, yet mustn't show it. The last time I was in a car was being brought here, so long ago. I was a frightened rabbit in the headlights. Don't remember those bright lights pouring fear into my brain. I shudder at any memory from way, way back when– "Here it is. Get in."

Ted is playing the perfect gentleman. He's put on a clean blue shirt with almost matching tie and I do believe he's trimmed his beard too. I try to sit in elegantly and he closes the door with care. "I hope you like my old gal," he says as he sits behind the wheel. "She's a classic. I found her in a barn and spent three years restoring her. I almost sold her when I moved in here, but I'm glad I didn't. Hold on to your hat. Here we go!"

I'm not wearing a hat, but I hold onto my head as the engine roars and we speed backwards. He swings the wheel with great delight and we career out of the gates and into the wide world. "Where would you like to go? Sorry Jo. Stupid question. I'll park down by the river and we can find a quiet spot."

My knuckles are white when we stop. I feel as if I haven't breathed since I got in. He opens the door and I swing my legs out. I take his proffered hand to stand. "This way." We take ten steps through shrubbery and emerge on a wide pathway beside a flowing river. "I love the Thames. I used to row for my school along here. We were pretty good." I can see the pleasure his memories give him. If only I had some of those.

We walk for a few minutes and I find I'm breathing deeply, savouring the atmosphere, making myself a new memory. "Here's an empty bench. Let's sit, shall we?" He asks rather than tells. My eyes flash across the water to a family, chatting as they stroll, pointing to whatever takes their interest, picking up leaves or treasures until they disturb a brood of ducklings who splash into their safe liquid home. It's safe in the water. That thought fires a doubt through my whole body and I shake. "What's the matter?" He puts a strong arm around my shoulders, but I recoil. I don't know what that means, from him.

We sit in silence until I can face him. 'Sorry,' I mouth. 'Sorry.'

He offers me a chocolate mint. He smiles. "I always keep a supply in hand. They never miss a few at a time." I take it and smile back. 'Thank you.'

We both suck silently. "This is really nice. I'd forgotten how much I miss being out of the home. Oh, don't get me wrong, it's the best place for me, but I love the feel of the breeze across the water." He mimics rowing his boat badly and I laugh without a sound.

"I don't want to spoil our mood, but we do need to discuss what to do about Matron. I stayed up quite late last night, going through my scribblings. There's a name that keeps cropping up, but not of either an inmate or a member of staff. Roderick Cartwright. Around the middle of every month a substantial amount is transferred to an account in that name. It's never the same, so as not to draw attention, but there are no tradesmen who supply food or do jobs called Cartwright." He can see I've followed his train of thought. "So, the money coming in and the money going out are almost the same every month. The wages of the staff and most expenses have not changed for years, yet the fees are regularly increased. The parent company is kept at bay by a small profit which suggests adequate management. But based on what I have seen, there is skulduggery afoot."

I nod wisely. I'm sure he's right. He speaks so commandingly, yet he's treating me as an equal in this quest. Why does he live in this home when he seems so capable at everything? A cascade of water heralds a swan's arrival in front of our noses. We should have smuggled out some bread.

The thoughts of food remind Ted that lunchtime is approaching. "Come on. We can't miss hotpot or the tongues will wag. They'll say I've kidnapped you."

We settle ourselves into our chariot and Ted swings into a quiet road away from the river. We stop at the junction and I stare at the church on the corner. Its stark, square tower and dark stonework trigger something. We pass it and a small school, nestled between rows of terraced houses without front gardens. Familiar? The main road is busy, but Ted swings into a gap and gives a burst through the exhaust to tell them that we're not to be trifled with. Perhaps it will be trifle for pudding today?

62 HYPERSENSITISED

I sit close to Susie in the back of the police car. She holds my hand rather tightly, but I can't reprimand her. The pain is somehow comforting. At least we have each other. I hope he's taking us to Mum.

The car is slowed by the Kingston traffic, but it's always this bad in the centre. We swing past the front of the Victorian police station and turn left again before huge iron gates are opened for us to drive through. As we get out, I look back through them across the road to more iron fencing which keeps the animals penned in on market day every Monday. Today it's just stallholders, shouting their wares. "This way." We follow the policeman's lead into a corridor with doors off in all directions. "Up here."

More rooms beckon. "In here please. Someone will be with you soon." We sit next to each other, facing two empty chairs across a desk. The room is depressingly unwelcoming. We hear footsteps approaching and both of us tense. We stare at the closed door, willing it to open and Mum's warmth engulf us.

The woman PC follows the Inspector in. "Tom, Susie. We met yesterday. I'm Inspector West and this is WPC Myers. Can you see me today, Tom?" I nod. "And have you found your voice, Susie?" Her eyes do not flicker.

"No. I don't think she was very happy last night. Neither of us were. It's a dreadful place. We just want to go home to Mum." Susie gave me her squeeze of agreement. She knows I'll always speak up for her, even though I rarely do for myself.

"Okay. I'm going to ask you some more questions about yesterday. You may think I've asked some of these before, but you may have remembered a small piece of information that will help us. Susie, I think it would be really helpful if you would nod or shake your head. Would you do that for me please?"

I look at Susie, squeeze her hand and nod encouragement. She slowly nods. "Excellent. Do you go to the grammar school on the 65 bus each day?" Susie shakes her head.

"She may take your questions literally. She doesn't go at the weekends and sometimes she catches the 265 bus."

"Sorry. Thank you, Tom. Did you come home from school at the normal time yesterday on the 65 bus?" She nods.

"I'm sorry to interrupt, but we want to know about our mother. Where is she? Why has no-one mentioned her to us?"

The adults give each other resigned looks and the WPC is motioned to speak. "Sorry. We can't tell you anything because no-one has seen her since she left the hospital. She hasn't been home. But don't worry. Every policeman in the area is on the lookout for her."

"That's right. So the best way you can help is to tell us anything that might help us find her more quickly. Okay?" He ignores the tears that we are both shedding. "When you came home from school, Susie, did you come in via the allotment?" Susie nods. "Did you see anyone else near the allotments?"

Another nod. He opens a file and pushes a paper towards us. "Is this what you saw?" Susie nods strongly.

"I think Susie has drawn this to give us a full picture. Am I right?" I get her squeeze. "I think she saw this man hiding in our chicken run, but when he realised that he'd been spotted, he flew away as fast as he could." We can all see Susie's agreement.

"Was he as tall as me? No. Was he taller than Tom? Yes. Fat? No. Thin? No. Get the desk sergeant to circulate the man's head and add medium build and height." The WPC scurries off. "That's a fantastic help, Susie. Well done." He looks through his papers until the WPC returns. "Now Tom. Some difficult questions for you as you are older. Did your parents argue recently?"

Susie shakes her head at me. "Er, no. They have been discussing Dad changing jobs a lot over the last weeks. It has been very difficult for them to know what's best. Mum has gone part-time and so can't get promotion and Dad was upset that this job would make her unhappy because of it. They have spent hours talking ever since Claude offered the job – but – not arguing."

"Who's Claude?"

"Desdemona's husband. He was a senior officer in the army. They live in the biggest house in Esher. Mum and Dad were married there, during the war."

"A soldier. Do either of you make your parents cross?"

I'm not sure what he's asking here. "I try not to. I can only remember one time when Susie asked to go to a concert and Mum and Dad said no, but she went anyway. That made them cross, didn't it?" Susie grips my hand, making me yelp. "They stopped her pocket money. She had to go with them to Angela's house and apologise for lying and leading Angela astray. It made us all tense for quite a long time, but Susie did try her best not to repeat those things again. Mum and Dad have been pleased with her."

He's writing a lot. "Has your father made any enemies?"

That's a difficult one. "You know he is the Security Officer – oh – was." I find my handkerchief. "He caught thieves, but you should know who they were. He's had to go to court quite a lot over the years." He's writing a lot. "I heard Dad telling Mum this week that he had made a lot of people angry because they were losing their jobs up in London. I think they'd been stealing and it was Dad's job to sort them out. Claude should know who they are. I don't."

"You're both doing very well. Now I want to ask you about the neighbours. Are there any people who don't get on with your family?"

"No. We get on with everyone."

"What about the girl and her father?"

"They are our best friends. Rachel is lovely. She helps Susie at school like she did when I was at primary school. She helps her Dad so much too. He's fantastic and so kind. Do you know he saved Susie from the river when she was little?"

"I didn't, no. Okay." He scribbles, shuffles and reads before asking, "Susie, could you please draw what the man was wearing? Oh, and about how old was he?" Susie takes the pencil and her lightening sketch appears, hair first. As I watch, even I am amazed at how exact a copy it is of yesterday's face, as if she is hypersensitised by this memory. A suit, shirt and thin tie are added. Susie writes 'brown' and sends arrows into the groin, sleeve and centre of the chest. The shirt is labelled 'white'. Underneath she writes, 'old – about your age', before turning it round and sliding it back to the detective.

The WPC looks over his shoulder and laughs out loud. He does not look amused. "Thank you, Susie. I'm only thirty-eight. I'm in my prime." The WPC doubles up and gives an enormous smile for us both to share. "I think we'll have a break there. Myers, please take them to the canteen. I'm sure they could find something nice to eat and drink. Stay with them in the lounge afterwards until I send for you."

63 HESITANT

Isabel is awaiting our return, like the mother duck fussing over her brood. "There you are. We were wondering if that old car had broken down."

"Please, Isabel, don't insult my mechanical expertise. Jo and I have had an excellent trip to sit beside the river and watch the real world float by. And, it's given us an appetite for more. Is lunch ready?"

"Very nearly. Jo, Mr Galbraith came this morning to see you. He was surprised you had gone out. He said he'd have a lunch and fit you into his extremely busy schedule afterwards. Shall we go straight in? I'll get you served first."

Jasmine is taking a tray into the small room and gives us a friendly smile. "I see they've all been talking about us, Jo. We'll have to think how we can give them more to gossip about."

"Behave yourself, Ted. You're making Jo blush."

I'm glad it isn't trifle. Sylvie always finds that difficult to control. Solid peach slices, cut up for her, have a much better chance of staying on her spoon. She is really doing well, yet seems a little distant today.

"I'm surprised at you, Jo," she finally blurts out after secreting her mint. I look puzzled. "Going off with that man in

219

a car. Who knows what might have happened to an attractive young woman like you?"

I'm flabbergasted. Attractive? Young? It's not how I feel, although the fresh air certainly has made me feel alive and Ted was very attentive. I mouth 'Sorry' and pop the mint in. It's fresher than the one I had earlier, but that's the one I'm tasting.

"Are you ready?" Isabel motions to me to follow and I sit opposite the tweed jacket whilst she perches in the corner. He's engrossed in his files.

Isabel scrapes her chair along the floor which startles him. "Oh. You're here at last, er, Jo. Good. I've a busy afternoon." He unfolds from his chair and approaches, as if he hasn't seen me before. "Please focus on my left ear. No, the other one. Okay." He walks behind and claps. Has he forgotten how I reacted last time, or rather didn't? I delay a second before leaping to my feet and spinning round. He staggers back, hitting his heal against the weighing scales. "Ouch." He limps back to his chair and picks up his pen whilst I sit without making eye contact with Isabel.

He seems rather hesitant. "Jo. I'm just going to gently touch your head. Is that alright with you?" He comes around the desk again. Is he scared of my next reaction? Well, that will depend on what he actually does. He's standing behind me. I can sense his anxiety. He very gently touches my scalp. I feel his bony fingers creep along the scar lines. I hear him draw a deep breath. It takes all of my self-control, but I remain motionless. He sits.

I stare past him to the wood pigeon high up in the trees, arguing with two rooks who are claiming the berries are theirs. Their raucous protestations sound like a children's playground, whilst a flock of finches feast under their noses. "I – I see from the notes that Jo has made excellent progress with her eating and socialising. That's good. But still no speech. What did E. N. T. say?" Isabel shakes her head. "That's appalling. I'll make a call. How can I do my job when we don't have all the facts. Really. It's not good enough." He bundles the papers into his briefcase and hits his knee on the desk as he rises. "Blast it! That's my afternoon ruined!"

We watch him stumble out of the door. Out of the window we see his erratic journey towards his car. He opens the boot and slings the case inside. "Did you see? Golf clubs. He's such a busy man."

Isabel turns away and leads me towards the lounge. "I think Sylvie could do with some company this afternoon. It's Bingo. I realise it's not your favourite, but she would appreciate you helping her." I can't argue. Isabel is a caring soul. I'm so lucky to have her as a friend too. Ted is conspicuous by his absence, but it does mean there are less interruptions than usual. He'll be hidden away with his figures I expect. At least these numbers will help me pass the time until we meet again.

Our rendezvous comes along on time and I find I'm breathing heavily as I unlock the door at his signal. The computer responds to his deft touch and I watch fascinated. Ted's not aiming for finances this time. "I've got the figures all straight now. Let's see what else is hiding in here." Personnel. There's a file for each category of employee. "Manager." A list of just two names pops up; William Fitzwallis and Mildred Carter.

To my surprise, Ted clicks on the former. A photograph of a middle-aged man appears, along with lines of information. Ted makes the words fly upwards until he reaches the end. "Here we go. Look here Jo. After seventeen years' service, William Fitzwallis was unable to continue in post after a sudden bout of food poisoning. The Assistant Manager was asked to stand in." He flicks to Mildred's entry. "Wow. Lookie here, Jo. Miss Mildred Carter is to be Stand-in Manager until the replacement Manager is appointed. Look at the date, over four years ago. I wonder why the next one never came?"

He goes next to the Assistant Manager list and finds her. Her photograph is rather flattering, but I suppose it was some time ago. "Here's her application form. She joined nearly five years ago. Let's make some notes. Home address. I wonder if she still lives there? Previous employment. Nursing Sister at Epsom Hospital, Assistant Matron of an independent Care Home in Iceland and before that, Senior Carer on the Isle of Mull. They sound impressive, but the dates she gives don't quite make sense. She would have become Senior Carer straight from school at fifteen. I've not heard of a hospital in Epsom other than the Asylum. I wonder if they checked her out?"

My eyes have stayed focused on the image of the younger Matron. I'm certain she's the one. Epsom Hospital. Was that where I was – in the torture chambers?

64 MONSTROSITIES

Yesterday happened. Today feels unreal. The events play over and over in my mind, making little sense. What should I have done differently? How could I have saved Dad? Why all these questions? We want answers.

WPC Myers seemed kind. She kept popping in and out to check that we were alright, bringing us some nice food and drinks. She put some paper and pencils on the table in case I wanted to draw or write. I just wished they'd tell us they've found Mum. What could have happened to her? I wanted to ask Tom, but I couldn't. I watched him, curled up on that chair, asleep. I bet he didn't sleep much last night either. There were and are so many horrid pictures sitting in my memory. I tried to send the tide to wash them away with happy ones.

I remember starting to draw. Mum and Dad are sitting watching us digging in the golden sand, trying to make a helter-skelter castle. We wanted our tennis ball to roll right from the top to the bottom. Dad kept offering to help, but we wanted to make it for ourselves. The sea was a long way from where we started and the sun kept drying out our sand so the walls we made to keep the ball from escaping, crumbled at the gentlest touch. Mum fetched two buckets of water which we used to cement our creation, but that just stuck to the fluffy ball and halted its progress. We're all laughing in my drawing. Failures on the beach – wonderful.

The WPC broke my smile. "Tom. Susie. Sorry to disturb you, but I need you to come with me now." She led us downstairs to a room where there was a desk with a pile of papers on it. "There are lots of fingerprints at your house. We have to sort out which belong to the family and which to any strangers that might have been there. I will ask you to put one finger at a time on to this pad of ink and then press it hard into the space on this form. I'll hold each finger to make sure it goes in the right place. Understand? Good. Who'd like to be first?"

In days gone by I would have been tempted to put my hands on Tom's cheeks, but that would have given me the black mark today, so I just went to the sink in the corner and washed the stains away. She gathered the two sets and took us back to our waiting room, to wait, again.

"Good, good. The prints are nice and clear. That's all we need from you today. I'll get a driver to take you back to the home," the Inspector said as he strode in.

Tom asked what I was hoping, "Our home?"

"No. Sorry. That's still a crime scene."

"A crime? We thought Dad had fallen asleep in the bath." The colour drained from Tom's face.

"I've got to be honest with you, although you are both very young." He searched for help, but the WPC knew it was his job. "The evidence strongly suggests that he was forced under the water."

Tom fainted on the floor whilst I threw up over the policeman's trousers.

When we got back here to the children's home, we were given special permission to sit together after we'd been up to change out of our outdoor shoes. I'd propped my drawing by the photograph I'd brought from the mantlepiece. It was of us all at the Bentalls' Staff Christmas Party. Mum had got it out especially because we looked so happy.

Our peace is shattered as a large group of girls burst in. They are screaming and pushing. "Quiet!" The large woman demands obedience and her authority is not challenged. "Room. Homework. You know the rules. Move!" They do. Tom and I smile at each other, thankful that we aren't residents here. "Why are you in here? Get to your room. Move."

I climb the stairs very slowly. The room is far from quiet. I recognise one girl's voice. These evil monstrosities are laughing, surrounding her, chanting. I stand at the doorway until they see me. Crystal is standing on my bed, waving my drawing and singing, "Oh I do like to be beside the seaside. Oh I do—"

I let out a primeval scream. "I'll kill you!"

She jumps off the bed, banging her foot into the bedside cupboard and sending my photo frame crashing onto the floor. She freezes. A corridor opens as I lunge towards her. I gasp at the smashed picture. I grab the largest shard of glass and point it towards her neck. "You're dead!"

"Stand by your beds!" Neither Crystal nor I flinch. The others melt away. I hear the heavy footsteps approaching. My eyes are burning with fury. "Give that to me!" I hesitate. I lower my blade and thrust it at her, turn on my heel and flee downstairs, out through the door and into the busy street.

65   SUPPOSITORY

'Pull yourself together, Lily.' I need a plan. My ultimate aim is escape. How do I achieve it? Alf would – stop – don't go there again. I must decide how I can escape and what I must do myself, just me.

I will need to be able to run if I get the chance. I must be fit, But how can I? I get out of the chair and climb the stairs, glance out and return. Three times up, three down and I have to sit down. I am unfit, a bit giddy. I need daylight. Up again.

There are weak shadows hitting the far-right corner of the fence and the far roofs. I think it's morning. There'll never be direct sun on this door. It won't budge, but pushing will strengthen my arms and hopefully keep my chest clear. Ooh. It's not helping my back much though. Down again.

I stretch up and bend down. Touch the floor, twist left, right, stretch wide, curl small. Do it all again. I've got to free this back up somehow. This mattress isn't helping, nor the cold, nor the diet. Think nurse. What would you give your patient? A suppository for starters to get things moving. Then a better diet. More liquid. I turn the tap on and view it suspiciously. I expect it is drinkable. I cup my hand under and take a sip. It's quite refreshing actually. The towel stops the dribbles down my chest. I really ought to change these clothes.

I hear a vague sound and move to the door. A box appears. "Excuse me. May I ask for some soap for washing?" I detect a grunt before the second box arrives. I pull open the lids. "Thank you. These look–" The hand places the mug on the floor and withdraws. "May I keep the mug for water from the tap?" The footsteps do not reply.

The drink might be tea, but it is gone rapidly. The sandwiches are curled at the edges and the biscuits do not look crunchy, but I am heartened to see a small apple. I decide that before I am allowed to eat anything, I must walk the length of the room twenty times. I count out loud. Seven paces there, turn, seven back. I calculate as I walk, recalling Mrs Bruce drilling the tables into us. "Nineteen times seven is one hundred and thirty-three. Twenty times seven is one hundred and forty." It feels good to have earnt my food. I eat the bread and fish paste more slowly to aid digestion. I stop. "Twenty more laps before biscuits. Oops. Laps means there and back. Get on with it, Lily."

I've slept since my exercise. The light now is much stronger. "Stairs three times." I allow myself to stare through the pane. There's a man, perched on the ridge of the terrace. I wave. My mind takes a while to register the impossibility of his seeing my fingers from there, even with binoculars. Enjoy seeing a human, Lily; they do still exist. I wonder what he's doing up there. His actions suggest he has tools, probably fixing some tiles that have slipped. These old houses do need maintenance. Oh, He's disappearing out of sight. Shame. I've nearly earnt my apple. I'll walk the room in a circle this time. Guess. I think twenty steps so I'll do ten clockwise and ten anti. I wish I hadn't changed out of my uniform so I had my watch to time myself. I'll count up in eights this time.

I've had my apple. It wasn't very sweet, but it will do me good. More water. I'd better put the mug back through with the boxes.

The time has passed a little more quickly today. Being active has helped. I'm tuned to hear footsteps approaching. "Thank you. I really enjoyed the apple." The hand comes through four times, the last being a brittle lump. "Thank you so much." I hear my primary school teacher's voice, "Politeness doesn't cost anything."

66 NECESSITATES

Why is he taking me without Susie? Why wasn't she in breakfast, or last night when we had that ghastly stew? Why can't I get answers?

I'm shown into the same interview room and the constable waits silently until the detective appears with his pack of papers. "Good morning, Tom. I hope you've slept well. Good. Now, I've more questions for you."

I stretch my hand out in front of his file. He looks at me for the first time. "Where's Susie?"

"That was going to be my first question to you. Where might she have gone?"

"I don't understand. We were sent up to the dorm when the others came in from school. That's all I know. I haven't seen her since."

"I'm surprised you hadn't heard what happened. The Assistant in Charge yesterday says here in her statement, 'Susie was screaming, I'll kill you, holding a dagger of glass to another girl's throat. She turned and lunged at me. I grabbed the weapon and she fled the building. I have had ten stiches inserted in my hand at Kingston Hospital.' You'd heard nothing?"

I sit in shock. "That's not Susie. "What on earth must that girl have done to her?" She's got her voice back is good, but has she been out on the streets ever since? "Is anyone looking for her?"

"All officers are aware of both her and your mother. It is a high priority. Where do you think she would go?"

"Home."

"No. There's been an officer there ever since–" He realises just before the words come out. "She couldn't get in. Where else might she go?"

"To Mr Penrose and Rachel's house, but they would ask about me."

"Yes. Maybe." The door opens and a flustered WPC Myers replaces the constable. "Where have you been this morning?"

"I have been on duty since six, Sir. As I am one of the few who Susie knows and trusts, I have been responding to all possible sightings."

"And?"

"Nothing. The last was a possible as a Miss Swanscombe saw a young girl she thought was Susie, dashing out of the main entrance of Bentalls just after they opened. She supposes she hid inside the store all night." I returned her smile as we both thought 'how sensible'. "They're checking each department carefully in case she has left anything, but all that had been reported were some missing chocolates; rather expensive ones, by all accounts."

"And mother?"

"Sorry Tom. Nothing, but we are all looking. Her photograph has been circulated throughout the Met. She'll turn up soon, don't worry." Why do adults say such stupid things? "Where else might Susie go near the town centre?"

"We would go through the market for food, maybe into Woolworths or one of those shops there and then walk home past the swimming baths. If we had a picnic, we would walk along the footpath beside the river until we found an empty bench and feed the ducks."

Both adults made notes. "Tell me Tom; are there any other men who ever come to the house; sorry, not tradesmen, but visitors who come inside?"

"No." I wonder why he asks that. "Oh, well there's George. He was with Dad in the army and was Best Man at their wedding. He always jokes that Mum should have chosen the best man."

They both scribble again. "Tom. You told me yesterday that Susie had run away before."

"Not run away. She went to the concert without permission, but she came home straight afterwards."

"Have you ever run away, Tom?"

"No."

"Really? That's not what a policeman put in this file a few years ago. 'Tom and Susie ran away and were found in the Hogsmill River by the Park Groundsman. Their mother came along some time afterwards and they returned to the family home. Mother said a bolt would be put on the allotment gate and Tom promised never to run away again.' Was the policeman lying Tom?"

This necessitates care. "I was very young and my head was full of stories. In books, all children go on adventures. I found the main allotment gate open and went down to explore the Space Station." He doesn't believe me. "It's what I used to think the Sewerage Works were, with their coloured lights that blinked messages each evening when I went to bed. When I got there, Susie frightened me. She'd watched me go and followed. I tried to take her home, but she ran off in the opposite direction. I thought about going for Mum, but realised that I had to look after Susie as best I could. She went to the train tunnel and then carried on. It was the route Mum always took us for a walk and we would come back over the railway bridge by the smelly public house." I pause as the Inspector pours me some water. "It's water that Susie wanted so I tried to jump across the stepping stones to get some. I don't remember what happened then, but I did have a very bad headache and couldn't go to school for a week." I'm not used to talking this much. My head is beginning to throb now.

"Okay Tom. Thank you. I got into some scrapes when I was a boy too." A knock and the door opens. A note is passed in. They don't look pleased. "Oh. What do you think, Myers?"

"We need somewhere else for Tom to stay tonight. Do you have any ideas yourself, Tom?"

"Aunt Alice?"

She shakes her head. "We had already asked before we sent you to the Children's Home. Aunt Alice is so sorry she can't because of working whatever hours are needed, now she's had promotion in the house. She said she'd love to, but couldn't give you any time when you came home from school, at weekends when she is busiest, or holidays, especially if you had one of your eye problems. She did say she would love to take you away somewhere really nice when she is allowed to have a holiday; you and Susie."

"What about your school friends? Could you stay with one of them until your Mum comes home?"

"Rachel's really my only friend; her and her father. I stay on my own at school. I don't really fit in there."

The Inspector gathers his papers together. "Canteen and rest room again. I think that's enough for now. Well done Tom."

"Er. What about that man, Jenkins. Did he know any more about Mum?"

The officers exchange glances. "Sorry, Tom. I can't say much. He seems to have vanished so we are looking for him too."

67 ELECTROPOSITIVE

My sleep is haunted by those images. Matron is approaching as I'm strapped on the torture table. The silver dome and wires lower menacingly. I feel the searing pain. The shocks pulsate through to my toenails. I feel the shakes, leaving every muscle twitching. As the power is turned off, tremors pulse on and on.

I wake in pools of sweat. My legs are weak as I try to reach the bathroom. I crawl in and turn on the taps. I'm electropositive; covered in salts. I must wash the memories. How can I?

I apologise for the state of my bedding, which Mary and Flo have stripped by the time I return from breakfast. Sylvie and I prepare to go through her exercises. They are rather boring for her, and for me. It's ten of this and ten of that. "I'm going to try something a little different. Let me know what you think." She's getting braver. "The first five in my chair, but then stand up for the second five. Turn round once. Next set. Five standing, five sitting. What do you think?" I smile and nod with my 'try it' face. Sylvie is concentrating so seriously, but the wobbles come from me which sets us both off into the giggles. Job satisfaction.

The knock on the door startles us. It's Ted. "Sorry to interrupt, ladies." He looks serious. "Sylvie. May I borrow your torturer for a few minutes please? I'll bring her back to the lounge for – what is it this morning?"

"Quiz time. We'll beat you to the chocolate again. Jo knows everything." Sylvie waves away my questioning gestures. "Go on, but be good. That means you, Ted."

Ted leads me up the stairs and into the craft room which is empty. He shuts the door and motions me to sit. "I've not slept very well, Jo. I don't know about you?" I close my eyes. "I'm sure we've uncovered criminal activity here, but I don't think anyone in authority would believe the two of us. I think we have got to confide in someone who we trust to do the right thing; someone who has some standing." I nod. "I can think of one person who I would approach. Can you?" I agree. "But is it the same person?" I look puzzled.

Ted pushes a paper and pencil towards me. "We should both write the name of the person we think, and then compare them." He turns away and writes. He waits for about a minute. "Okay?" He turns. I push my paper to him. He turns his over and smiles. "Isabel."

I write, 'When? She's not here this morning.'

"I expect she will be here at lunchtime. I'll ask her when she would be free to speak with us in private. That's the best we can hope for." I shrug a nod. "Right. It's quiz time. Are you ready to lose your crown? I fancy some chocolate."

68 REPOSITION

I'm dozing on my bed when a sudden light explodes through my eyelids. My brain is trying to comprehend. I cover my eyes before opening my lids. It's real. There is light. I take my time to allow for adjustment. It's coming from directly above the bed. It hurts.

"Sit by the table, facing the corner!" orders a voice. "Do not turn round when I come in." I follow the orders and hear the door creak open. "Stay there."

Nothing happens. I'm waiting. My mind is dreading the smell that knocked me out in the street, but it doesn't come. I'm being tested. Stay in control Lily. What have I learnt? Female voice, but no footsteps. She hasn't come in. She'll be watching me from the door. Relax and breathe, slow and calm.

"Good. You follow instructions. You have passed this test." Three steps. Not near enough to reach me. Breathe and listen. "You may answer my questions, but not turn. Do you understand?"

"Yes." My voice is wavering.

"Good. Would you like to earn more food?"

"Yes." I add, "Please."

"Okay. I am going to lead the way. You will follow, five seconds later, with your head down, up the stairs and into another room. Understood?"

"Yes. Thank you." I listen for her footsteps starting to climb and slowly get to my feet to follow. The light penetrates into another cellar, but I haven't time to look. The stairs are dimly lit and the door at the top on the right is open. I stand, looking at the brown linoleum.

"Walk to your left and turn left to face the window." The light source is natural and my eyes adjust slowly. There's rain falling on to a paving-slabbed courtyard. I'm disorientated.

"You said you were willing to work. You can start by washing all of this crockery, pots and pans. I want them spotless. I will sit here, watching."

"Is there any warm water?"

"I boiled a kettle on the stove to your right. You may move about in this area, but do not look my way. Get on with it."

The sink is full, as is the draining board to its right. I have to reposition all the plates together and stack the pans; my mugs are scattered amongst with cutlery too, before I find the bottom of the sink. It's disgusting. The plug has emerged so I push it home and turn for the kettle. It's hardly off the boil so I take the filthy dishcloth for protection and pour some into the sink. Steam drifts up to the cold window. A small turn on the tap brings a cooling squirt. I attack the grime with energy. I drain that, but the flow away is not rapid. Dare I ask? "Is there a sink plunger?"

"Cupboard underneath." I rummage and find it. It works. The stench fills my lungs and I cough it up, but the flow has improved. I'll never complain of emptying bedpans ever again.

237

I rinse the off-white china sink and cloth again before starting the real task I've been set. She's promised I will eat more so hygiene must be maintained. That's why I start with the mugs.

I'm beginning to enjoy meaningful activity. My hands are softening with the warmth and I feel my blood flowing. I sneak glances out of the window. I hear a clonk and realise my wedding ring has fallen in the water. Panic over. I put it on the windowsill. My fingers have lost weight too.

I've used up the hot water so I fill the kettle and relight the gas. The plates show signs of eggs, mingling with the daffodil patterns that are emerging. I'd noticed a metal scourer in the cupboards and some Ajax so these come into use on the pans. A thorough rinse causes another blockage, but I'm in full flow now with my plunger.

"Make a pot of tea when the kettle boils. I'm exhausted. The things are in the cupboard next to the cooker. In the larder there are vegetables. You can make soup for later."

She's exhausted? How am I feeling? I realise how much adrenalin I've used and fatigue kicks in. Don't buckle, Lily. Follow orders. I make the tea. "How would you like it?"

"Milky with three sugars. You may have one yourself."

"Thank you." I pour and place hers at the far end of the cupboard before returning to my station, staring out of the window at the clearing sky. The fence in front of me is the one I see on the side from my cell. The terrace is now to my right. This house is larger and sticks out into its bigger back garden. I can see windows above the fence at two levels before a dripping gutter sends damp and moulds down the red brickwork. Such details excite me. I savour my first hot tea in–
'How long have I been incarcerated?'

"Soup!"

I put the mug on to the windowsill and find the larder. The wicker basket has vegetables that could have come from our allotment. I select a good variety and a knife from the newly-filled drawer. The knife in my hand gives me an idea. I tackle the root vegetables first; carrots, a parsnip, potatoes are chopped into a sparkling saucepan and the rest of the kettle poured over them before lighting the gas once more. Matches; another idea. Onions, some celery, and tomatoes are added when it all comes to the boil. A pan of boiling soup would be a fearsome weapon.

"Enough! Downstairs. Now!"

69 REVISIT

It's been exciting, hiding from everyone. There are lots of back alleys and dustbins to slip behind. I don't like stealing, but I have to survive in this world without even a penny in my pocket. I nearly got caught in Boots. I needed the ointment for these cuts. I've washed them in the Ladies every time, but the edges have got very red and seem to be spreading.

I wonder if Mum has come home yet? I went home yesterday, through the hole in the fence into the allotments. Dad wouldn't mind me taking some carrots and raspberries. The juice really made my hand hurt, but not as much as thinking about Dad. Have they caught that man I drew? I hope so. I picked some fruit to give to the hens, but they weren't there. The run was empty. At least I could creep up the garden path unannounced. The back-door key was in its hiding place and I let myself in to the silent house. The cake tin had a bit left. I took my duffle bag from the hall and went upstairs. I listened before entering my room. Empty piggy-bank was no use. I needed clothes, warm ones for the nights, as well as bandages, scissors and Mum's special lotion for cuts from the bathroom cabinet. I peeped into Tom's room. Why should he have the big one, just because he's older? I spied his copy of the picture on the dressing table. Rage boiled inside me and I clenched my fist. "That Crystal." I wanted to take it.

Something fluttered to the floor. It was a photograph of Rachel. "I always knew you two were sweethearts."

I daren't stay sitting on a bench by the river in the sunshine although I want to. I feel a bit better today. I've washed and changed my clothes, eaten quite well. I mustn't stay here too long in case I fall asleep. It will be closing time soon and I want to get in before then. I need to revisit that comfy bed tonight.

70 POSITIVELY

I've been in the Police Station all day. I wish I had some homework to do – and I don't say that very often. They certainly pile it on at school. The Head is always rambling on about maintaining standards. He thinks anything less than trying for an Oxbridge place is a sign of weakness, unless you are going to join the Army or the RAF. We are crammed in how to pass exams, rather than to enjoy learning. I've found a pack of cards on the shelf. I'm trying to play all the different patience games I know. I wish Susie was here. At least we could play German Whist or something else.

The door opens and I see a dog come in. It's Jasper. He's pleased to see me, but hasn't been released as he leads his charge in. "Chair." The dog is inch perfect and Cyril feels for the seat. "Are you there, Tom?"

"Yes. It's lovely to see you." He releases the harness. "Hello Jasper." The nose and tail are in harmony as I fuss him. "Oh, such a friendly face."

"Isn't mine friendly enough for you, Tom?" I hadn't noticed her come in behind her father. I blush to my toes. "Come here."

"I'm not sure what you two are up to, but we are in a police station."

"Dad. On the way here I told you I was going to give Tom a hug."

"Well, let the lad breathe now, Rachel, and sit here beside me." His ears know she is obedient. I sit opposite, positively beaming, overcome with emotion. "Now then young man. I hear that your sister has gone missing and you both have been banned from returning to the Children's Home. Is that right?"

"Yes. No-one knows where Susie is. There have been some sightings, but she's proving elusive. I just hope she's coping."

Rachel offers her hand across the table, which I take, feeling her delicate fingers. I can finally understand how Mum and Dad felt about each other.

"So Tom. Are you okay with what has been planned?"

"Sorry? What has been planned?"

"Rachel and I have been asked if you can stay with us until your mother returns. We have a spare room and you can go to school just as easily as from your home. What do you say?"

"I – I – I'd love to. Are you sure? Are the police okay with it too?"

"Yes. They asked me."

"It's so kind of you, Mr Penrose. I won't be any trouble. I'm used to helping around the house; I always have."

"That's good to hear because my dear Rachel here has enough to do, looking after me. Now, Tom, one important rule." He looks serious behind his dark glasses. "Inside our house – my name's Cyril to my friends – and I think of you as an important friend to me."

Rachel lets go of my hand to cuddle her father. "That's a lovely thing to say, Dad."

"Thank you. I'd be honoured."

"That's enough of that then. Let's see if that car is ready to take us to your home first. You'll have to find some clothes and your uniform for school tomorrow."

71 HESITANTLY

The stairs seem dark as I stumble down after the brightness. I cannot hear footsteps following so I focus on this cellar. It's similar in shape to the kitchen above so some of it isn't in view. Dare I investigate?

Footsteps above focus my attention. There's more than one set. Chairs scrape. Voices are raised. Hesitantly, I go back up a few steps and sit, craning to hear. "Why not? What other use is she?" I'm tuned in to the woman's voice. The other sounds lower, more a growl. It's indistinct, but angry.

As the noise above dies down, I realise I mustn't be caught listening. I tiptoe down and into my prison. I've never seen its starkness before. The faded purple mattress without a sheet, the dark grey blankets, vermillion bricks covered in cobwebs that must house millions of dead flies and countless spiders. I shudder; never a fan. I open the drawers and cupboards. Lurking in the corners I find soap, a clean flannel and a small box of washing powder. Wonderful. Such simple luxuries. My hands are already so clean and soft from my washing up. I stare at them and sob.

72 WHATSIT

Ted and I are parked in a side road at the end of the street, watching the traffic coming from the Home. Isabel hadn't appeared for lunch, but Jasmine told Ted, "Her sister had a nasty fall so Isabel has gone to look after her. No. We don't know how long that will be for. Sorry Ted. We've all got extra work to do. Can't stop chatting."

Right on time, Matron's car pulls out. "Head down," he whispers. We hear the car pass and are off in pursuit. She stops outside a grocer's shop, then a chemist and then visits the library. Each time we park out of sight, but with a view of some part of the vehicle. "Where next I wonder?" Ted tries to keep a car in between us until it turns off into a drive or leafy avenue. As we reach the quieter streets with lots of terraced houses, she appears to be looking for somewhere to park. We have to pass by so I slide down beneath the window and Ted keeps looking away from her. He turns the car round at the next junction and heads back. "There." He nods towards her, carrying her bags up a garden path. "That's rather more than she bought. I wonder what else she's acquired?"

I hold up seven fingers to Ted. He agrees. "Waterloo Rise. But it's flat. What sort of name is that?" He passes the end semis and turns the car again. She's gone inside. Its looks like her, drawing the front curtains of the house next door. I hold up five fingers. "That's odd. Five. There's nothing more we can do here. It's not the address on her application. Ah well. Home James and don't spare the horses." We roar along the road until we see the hill coming into view. "Water in the loo does rise after all." I'm not sure about his sense of humour, or that of his sense of speed.

Everyone stares at us as we take our usual seats. The evening meal is half-way through. Sylvie's tutting into her mash. Jasmine plonks a plate in front of me without a word. I hear Ted's voice, "Sorry, we had a temporary breakdown. The whatsit had slipped off the umgrummit, but genius here has fixed everything!" Murmurs of disbelief spread and whispered comments abound. They change to delight when lemon meringue pie appears.

73 NECESSITATING

It feels really strange, pulling up outside our house, in a police car. My legs wobble as I try to get out, but Rachel holds on to me as the policeman opens the front door. "Please stay in the car with your father. Now young man. I must remind you that you must touch only the things you need to take. This is still a crime scene. I'll come with you."

The hall seems quiet, lifeless, and tears well in my eyes. I take my school bags from under the stairs before heading up to the bathroom. Get the worst over with first. The cabinet is open and there's a bandage unrolled on the floor. "This shouldn't be like this," I tell him.

"Please leave it there."

He makes notes. I take my toothbrush and paste, but leave Mum and Dad's alone. I can't look at the bath and exit rapidly to my own room.

I pull all of my clothes out of the cupboards and drawers. I look around. My childhood toys can stay. The suitcases are stored under my bed. As I pull out the largest, I see my photograph of Rachel we took in that booth in Woolies. It should be hidden behind– "Someone's been in here. My photograph of all of us has been moved."

He helps me load the case and carries it to the landing. "Susie's room has things missing. She must have been here."

"No. We had the lock changed which is why I could get in. She couldn't."

"What about through the back door?"

He carries the case down to the hall and I lead the way through to the kitchen door. It's locked. "She couldn't get in."

I rummage in the tools drawer and produce the key to swing it open. "Look. Those black marks. Susie knows where we hide the key in the coal hole. There it is. She's put it back, ready to come again."

"Quite the detective, aren't you? Well, she mustn't. We'll barricade it."

I go back in and find a sheet of paper and pen from my bag. 'SUSIE. Please come round to Mr Penrose's house where I am. We all love you! TOM' We fix it on the handle with two of Mum's pegs before shutting the door and locking it. He slides the two bolts.

We check into the dining and sitting rooms, but I need nothing from there except the homework I should have given in last week and the library books that were due back then too. We gather everything from the hall, my raincoat from the hallstand and I turn to look at the emptiness. "Miss you."

Rachel is on the path and takes one of my bags as the policeman loads the boot. We get back into the back seat and she says nothing, just rests her head on my shoulder and squeezes my hand. "Follow the road round and up the other side to join Burney Avenue, Officer, please. We're number 28, on your left."

As we open the door to let Cyril out, I realise that Jasper has been silently at his feet the whole journey. "Dog first please Tom. You hold him whilst Rachel helps me up. Thank you both. Yes, I know. You're home and deserve a treat." He follows his lead to the front door. "Manners Penrose. Thank you, Officer, for your help today. You have been most kind and I did ask my daughter to note your number so that we can commend you to your superiors."

We load everything into the hall. "First things first, Tom. Jasper. He's earnt his treat." I watch the pleasure shared in the room. "Now us. Tom, kettle on please. We're not here to wait on you. We'll be putting our feet up."

I love his wisdom. What better way could there be to make me feel at home? "I'll show you where we keep the biscuits." She takes me into the kitchen and gives me a kiss. "You're being so brave, Tom." She's blushing almost as much as I am. "The tin is high so as not to tempt the dog. Grab a plate."

"Rachel can pour when it's brewed. Come and sit here please Tom. I need to talk to you." I take the seat in front of him. I know he can sense my apprehension. "Don't worry, Tom, it's nothing difficult. You coming at short notice is necessitating a few changes in our routine which we have stuck to since Rachel was old enough to understand. You already tuck your chair in when you leave the table. I know you will continue to do so. The same must apply to things like your school bags so we'll find their own place. Rachel does her homework as soon as she gets in, unless I ask her not to for any reason. I will expect you to do the same. She will get up first each morning and when she has finished in the bathroom, she will knock on your bedroom door to let you know it's your turn. I can then take my time after you. We have our breakfasts separately on school days, but not at weekends. Is that okay with you, so far?"

"Thank you, Mr Penrose, sorry, Cyril. You are so kind to take me in like this. I'll do anything I can to help."

"We know you will, Tom. Now then, you two. You have a lot of things to take out of the hall and find places for in that small room. I suggest you don't try to carry anything too heavy up the stairs. I'll get on with sorting out some food for us."

We take a bag each and Rachel shows me the room at the top of the stairs, just like Susie's at home. "I hope you'll be very happy here, Tom."

I know I will. "Can I ask you a question, please Rachel?"

"Of course."

"Why do you like me?"

"Wow." She pulls her long dark hair away from her face and sits on the end of the bed. "Because you are always gentle and kind and slow to judge other people. When I went to school, I was bullied because of how I look. I was excluded by the girls and the boys were rude. Then, when we met you and your family, I was made to feel so welcome, important to all of you. When you came to school, you were bullied too. I stood up for you and faced the bullies. That gave me enormous courage to tackle anything. But most of all, you have never ever looked at me with pity, only kindness, despite this ugly mess of a face."

"But you are beautiful. It's who you are. I've grown up with a one-armed father who has shown us that anything is possible. Look how you help your father. You're perfect."

"Ouch! Hurry up and move this case!"

74 SIT ON THE TILES

I know which are the quietest entrances to Bentalls. I slip in as the nearest assistant is distracted and keep to the outside aisles. I was sad to cut off my long hair, but now my disguise is better. I've worn my duffle bag casually over my shoulder. I'm a teenager browsing, just like the others. I avoid the escalator in the middle and slip through the door to the customer stairs. Not many people use these so I can sit when I get half-way between floors, ready to move up or down if anyone comes.

The store's closing loudspeaker message is muffled, but I don't have to hear it. I make my way to the top and listen before sliding through the door. Toilet first. I lock myself in for a while in case there's a check.

That should be long enough. I unpin the bandage and roll it as I unwind. The smell is pungent. I run my hand under the warm tap to free the last layers. I daren't look. My legs buckle and I sit on the tiles before I fall. My free hand pulls at my duffle bag's front zip pocket. Why didn't I unzip it first? Mum's ointment; one clean bandage left. I pull myself up to the roller towel and pat at the wounds. The pain will ease. I've nearly used the whole tube. Save some. Mum had me practise bandaging myself with one hand and I'm so grateful she did. I hear her voice, "If Dad can, so can you." But I need her now.

This is not the right room for me. I need rest. I take my bag and listen before making my way to the bedding department. This is the one I chose last time. I'll curl up here again. The sun's final rays have warmed the ceiling and cast patterns through the blinds. I'll–

"Susie." I feel a hand on my shoulder. "Susie. It's time to wake up."

"Five more minutes, Mum."

"Susie. Open your eyes, dear." I do and I shake. "You know me. It's Iris. You'll be alright." I try to sit up, but can't. "They'll be here soon. I sent for an ambulance as soon as we found you. Just lie still." I'm ringing wet. I touch my forehead. It's a furnace. I start to shiver.

"She needs a blanket." I focus on another face I think I know. "It's WPC Myers, Susie. We've all been very worried about you. Ah, here are the ambulance men. Don't worry. I'll come with you. You're in safe hands now."

75 TRANSITORY

I hear footsteps echoing on the stairs through the open door. A book is tossed inside. "Chair facing the corner." I obey. "Good. Your work has been satisfactory today." I hear things being placed inside the threshold before the door slams shut. I wait a few moments, but hear retreating steps so can explore what has been left for me.

A spoon sits beside a bowl of hot soup. I inhale my creation with some pride, take it to the table and savour it. It feels good to have nourishing food, but my stomach won't cope if I gulp it. I fetch the rest. Some plain bread. That will help. Two raw carrots, two apples and two biscuits. Good. I can save some. I'll use one of the drawers as a larder. Hopefully the spiders won't get in there.

It feels a different world, here in the light, with warm food and even a book to read. I think I should finish that soup before it goes completely cold.

The cover tells me it's a romantic novel, set in a remote village in the north of England. Not the sort of book I'd choose, but who am I to complain? It's an escape from reality and I settle into the armchair with great expectations.

My eyes open to darkness. I've lost my bearings. I feel something on my lap. A book. I remember starting to read, but nothing sank in. I leave the chair and crawl under the blanket, hoping for the relief of sleep once more.

I awaken to a banging. "Ten minutes." Ten minutes for what? I visit the toilet, wash and hear the door as I dry my face. "Upstairs." I stagger after her in the gloom.

The floor and table are covered in clothing. "Kettle first. Your food's there. Make the tea. Then we'll start." I eat standing up, watching the sparrows dive-bomb each other in the hedge that separates the back yards. The whistling brings me back to duty. I make the tea. "Mine's—"

"Milky with three sugars." I'd been rehearsing that. Her silence earns me the satisfaction of a smile.

"Wash day." She broke the spell. "The washboard's under the sink with the buckets, powder and brush. Wash thoroughly in hot water. Rinse in cold three times. The mangle's just outside the back door beside the stairway. I'll unlock it when you're ready. Any questions?"

"Did you enjoy the soup?"

"Yes – we – I did. Now get on. I've a busy day today." Another victory.

I'm not used to smiling, but transitory triumphs are going to get me through this ordeal. So, he stayed to eat. Who is he? Is he someone I've upset, rather than her?

76 NOT VERY SENSITIVE

It's all hustle and bustle in the hospital as the trolley is pushed through the entrance and swung into a cubicle. "Susie Robertson. High fever. Hand injury. Been missing for several days so probably mal-nourished. Daughter of Nurse Robertson who is also missing."

I hear snatches of conversations from dismembered heads, looming above mine. None of the words are connected; it's a wilderness of sounds. I escape into oblivion.

My eyes have tried to open. I see machines and tubes, wires and blinking lights. I hear gentle breathing. "Hello Susie. It's nice to see you." I turn my head. Oh, that hurts. I move my feet and they hurt too. "You've not been very well, but you're getting better." My eyes close again and drift away.

I feel my legs being moved. I try to resist. "Welcome back, Susie. You've had a long, long sleep. We're just going to give you a wash to make you feel better." I feel hands in places only my mother has touched, followed by soapy water and a warm towel. Voices are chattering, but I cannot understand their words. It's exhausting being awake, so I drift away to fresh fields of fantasy.

My eyes open and focus on an array of faces, surrounding the bed. "Here she is. This is Robertson. She was brought in suffering from malnutrition, but more importantly, had lost a lot of blood from a palm wound which has festered. Remove the dressing, Nurse." A moustache almost touches my hand and I'm tempted. "Okay. Each of you look; then I'll ask for your opinions."

Five young men in white coats peer at my hand. The last is smirking, holding my wrist in a tight grip as if I'm a joke, so earns the swipe from my free hand. The other four suppress their amusement. The moustache is far from pleased. "Sister's Office, now! Re-dress this Nurse!"

A timid girl who doesn't look much older than me, gives me a lovely smile. "Great shot. I've been wanting to do that to the lout for weeks. Now, having used up all that energy, shall I get you a nice warm drink?" She's bandaging tightly. My head nods as pain sears through me. "Good. I'll just be a minute then."

I sense movement beside me and open an eye. "Hello Susie. It's WPC Myers. Do you remember me?" I focus both eyes on her. I try to move, but am still tied up. "Stay still. I'm just checking how you are. We've all been worried about you. Can you talk to me today?" I can, but just a croak comes out. "Don't worry, Susie. The doctors and nurses say you're doing very well, considering you have been here a week now."

Here a week? I look around at the small room with a window that looks out into a hospital ward, and another on the opposite side into an office where there are shelves of files on the wall. It's like the ward Mum used to work in. "Mum?"

"Sorry, Susie. We're still looking for her. Tom is staying with Mr Penrose."

"And Rachel. He loves her."

"Really? They do look to be very good friends. Now Susie, I've got to ask you a few difficult questions. Do you think you are ready?" I frown. How will I know before she asks? "How did you cut your hand, Susie?" I look down and see a white bandage over my palm. I bring it nearer to my eyes, but shake my head. "What had Crystal done to you?" I've never met a Crystal. "Where did you run away to?" Run away? I can't run anywhere.

The policewoman stands up and gently smooths my hair. "Don't worry, Susie. I'll come and see you another day. Your brother will be pleased to know you are awake." What were those questions about? They've got the wrong person. My eyes close as I yawn and–.

"Susie." I push away a hand that is moving my shoulder. "That's it. Wake up. It's doctors' rounds time and you need to be awake." I turn my head towards noise and see above people in beds to a gaggle of men around the far one. There're coming this way.

"Awake at last Sister." A nurse pulls a curtain to block my view. "Robertson. High time those tubes were out, Sister. Now she's awake she can feed herself. Cut that dressing to let us see, Nurse. Quickly girl." I feel shaky hands take mine and scissors cut through bandages. I'm not looking. "Good enough, I think, unless you want a closer examination, Goodman? No? I thought not. Don't want your pretty looks slapped. Get her up for exercise. Who's next?"

They exit in a swirl of coats, ready to pounce on their next victim. The nurse stays. "Mr Watkins. Sorry. He good save lifes, yes, but rude to..." She starts taking tubes away from me. "I bring breakfast soon. We get you see the toilet and then you can go. Good? Yes?"

I believe her when she re-appears with a milky porridge, a piece of toast and a dab each of margarine and marmalade. There's a child's beaker with a spout. "I butter, yes? And marmaduke?" I nod to both. "I back soon." It feels very strange as I pour a slop from the spoon. It's barely warm, but coats my throat before I try to swallow. I pause. Another dollop follows. I take three more mouthfuls before an eruption covers the tray, the bedclothes and starts to drip to the floor. I collapse onto my pillow and pass out.

I'm clean when I next wake. Fresh staff are buzzing around. I don't recognise any of them. What was I told to do? Toilet and go. I slide out of the bed, stagger across the ward, through the double doors and out along the corridor. I've seen the toilet sign. Now go. I can follow the signs for 'exit'. Is this an emergency? Probably. I push it open and see the metal staircase. I stumble down to the ground and stagger along the path. There are people walking so I'll follow. There's a car with an open door.

77 INQUISITIVENESS

Ted and I have a third rendezvous location now. We can sit and draw, paint or write, just like any other inmates, so we do. It's become a regular part of my day like physiotherapy with Sylvie, and although she doesn't approve of Ted, the rest of the tongues have tired of gossiping. He's been speculating about Waterloo Rise. Is Matron running another Care Home there, funded by this one. Perhaps it's a B&B for commercial travellers. She doesn't seem to arrive here very early and she leaves before the evening starts. Perhaps she has other properties to manage too? "Whatever it is she's doing there, Jo, I bet you it's illegal."

News of Isabel's return is non-existent. Francie seems to be acting as her replacement, but she's muttering about not being paid any more. "Doing two jobs at the same time. I think I'll go off sick." Our quiz sessions are shorter and we don't get a sniff of chocolate. Even Jasmine seems less good-natured than usual. At least we all cheer up when lovely Sally comes to sing to us. I'm beginning to remember some of the words in my head, even after she has gone away. I can practise silent singing in my bathroom.

Yesterday, Ted started croaking a wartime classic, "It's a long way to Tipperary, it's a long–" He smiled. "A man could take offence at the way the room clears whenever he bursts into song. It never fails to succeed." He checked that they had all departed and closed the door. "Right. I've been doing a dangerous thing – thinking. We need to gather more evidence for our case."

The office was rather a mess as we hadn't visited for a week or more. I tackled the shelves again as he found his figures. I suddenly realised what I needed to do and grabbed a pencil and paper. Ted just sat back and watched until I'd finished. "Two asses on the beach. Very good drawing Jo. You've copied it brilliantly. But why?" I couldn't tell him.

Today I've had to skip breakfast and physio as we're staking out Waterloo Rise. I'm armed with pencils and lots of paper, whilst Ted has 'liberated' the Home's camera, spare films and what looks like the week's supply of packets of biscuits from the Tearoom. A car pulls out as we approach and Ted slips his diagonally opposite our target with a clear sight of both front doors. "Perfect." He winds his window down and plays with the camera. "Just adjusting the speed and aperture." I haven't got a clue what he means. "I could do with a light meter." I settle to draw the street scene from number nine towards the end of the road. I like the way the tree canopies form an umbrella over the roofs.

"Someone coming." We tense. "Postman." Ted gets out of the car and follows him along the pavement. I watch the doorways. "That was useful. I told him I was looking for Mildred Carter's family, but wasn't sure if she lived at number three. He said she lived at seven and her brother at five." Ted looks very proud of himself. I suppose I'm impressed too. That explains why they would have a connecting door inside.

I'm glad I brought lots of paper. I've drawn the two doorways with their pretentious pedimented porches, the twisted branches and overhanging leaves, the cracked flagstones with distorted leaf shadows. I've recorded every pedestrian and noted the times from Ted's watch. None have gone to our properties.

"Stand by." Ted aims the camera as a man exits seven. I hear the shutter click three times. "Oops. Mustn't waste film." He walks down the road and we twist round to watch. Ted slips out to follow, but is back within seconds. "This is him in the green van." He clicks the camera as it passes. "Got it."

We settle down again. I wonder what the level of inquisitiveness is in this neighbourhood? I'm surprised if no-one has noticed us here for these hours. "Action." A large grey van pulls up in the middle of the road, blocking both directions. A man jumps out of the cab, swings open the back doors and pulls out a wicker basket. With the handle over his arm, he glances around before approaching seven. We watch, hardly daring to breathe. She looks out before exchanging the basket for a similar one and a handful of money. He counts it, tips his cap and glides back to the driver's seat and away. "Now that's not suspicious, is it?"

I've hardly written the details of time and registration plate down before a black van stops. It's a large cardboard box that goes to the door, along with a brown envelope. Nothing comes out. Ted keeps clicking. "Blast. Change films."

Before he has done so, Matron hurries out to her car. We follow her at a distance. We pull up short of our final destination. "It might be suspicious if we're too close behind her. We'll give it five minutes. Have you left me any biscuits?" Not many.

78 SENSITIVITY

I am so lucky. It's my wedding anniversary. The girl of my dreams wanted to marry me. Her father has been like a second father to me. He knows how much love we share. He was so proud when he walked her on his arm down the aisle at St Marks.

He said he'd expected it from when we were young children. It was how our voices changed just fractionally whenever we spoke to each other. He's never seen me, but he says he has always trusted me, like his faithful dogs, with his life, and that of the most precious person to him. I've never found such sensitivity in anyone else; it must be his years of blindness that has made him so intuitive.

I hope that I develop his skills now my failing eyesight is dropping its curtain. I've studied hard for the last three years since my office job became impossible. I wasn't really sad to go, although we have had to tighten our belts. Perhaps I was destined to be a piano tuner. I was never a gifted player, but had a good-enough ear. Now I have learnt where every wire leads and every connection has to be. My reputation is spreading and earnings increasing. Justin has become my eyes and the customers love to fuss him as soon as I am perched in front of their instrument. I suspect he has more treats there than at home.

Touch is so vital to me now. How our senses are under used when we are young. I still marvel at the silkiness of Rachel's hair; surpassed only by that of our wonderful daughter. I am so lucky to have seen her childhood and how she is blossoming with confidence. I never had any. We named her after her grandmothers; Rachel's and mine. Rachel never knew hers. I often think of my mother. It was a long time ago, but I did look for you every day until I couldn't.

79 SUPERSENSITIVE

Isabel's back. She just walked into lunch as if she'd never been away, but my, did she look tired. Everyone was pleased to see her and she stopped to speak at every table. I watched Ted whisper to her and she nodded. She was pleased to see how well Sylvie was doing. As she spoke to her, Isabel rested her hand on my shoulder with a gentle, caring touch. "I'll be seeing you later, Jo. My spies tell me you've been out gallivanting."

I am happy to miss Justine's bingo session, especially now that Sylvie can manage without me. I slip into the craft room where Ted is staring out of the window at his beloved car down below. It's a few minutes before he turns and sees me. He looks worried. "We've only got one chance at getting this right. Isabel has got to believe us. I just so wish you could speak. I'm afraid she'll just think I'm causing trouble for the fun of it."

I reach out to him, but withdraw my hand as I sense someone approaching. She comes in and we all sit around the table furthest from the door. "You sounded serious, Ted. What do you want to ask or tell me? But – before you do – I will not be able to give you any answers today. I've been worn out by my sister's three young children. Her husband has only just arrived back on shore to take over her care. She got knocked off her bike, broke her ankle and dislocated her shoulder, as well as cuts and bruises everywhere. Sorry. I'm rambling. Lack of sleep. I'm supposed to be listening."

I reach out to her and put my hand on her arm. Ted matches mine. "Take your time. We're here for you, like you have always been for us. That's why we trust you." I am touched by Ted's words. His bluff exterior hides a supersensitive side.

"Right. Ted, you said it was urgent and that you two have some important information to share with me in confidence."

Ted pulls a file out of his bag. "This all concerns Matron which is why we have said nothing to anyone else. She is a fraud and a thief and here are the figures to prove it." He has listed each month and then summarised the totals.

"How did you obtain these figures?"

I put my hand up and indicate the key turning. "Jo was told Matron's door was always open to her, but when it wasn't, she 'borrowed' a key. I followed her in one evening and wanted to see what was on my file about my medical conditions. I have some computer skills and came across irregularities. The more we looked, the more we discovered. Her job application is bogus; the dates don't work. She doesn't live where she says she does."

"How do you know that?" I point out of the window at the shiny car and pretend to steer the wheel. "So that's where you have been sneaking off to; on surveillance."

Ted pulls out another file. "These are our notes from that day. Jo did the sketches, which I think are brilliant, and I took these photographs. Matron and her brother own at least two houses together and there are deliveries made from plain vans and other things exchanged, along with money. We, well I, suspect they are fences for stolen goods as well."

"Thank you, Ted. May I take these to study further? I can see this does need dealing with today. Give me an hour and I'll catch up with you here. Okay?" Isabel stands to leave. "I'd better have that key please Jo. It's been missing a very long time." She doesn't sound cross.

We watch her go. "Let's go and see if they're ready for the quiz. They'll be suspicious if we miss that."

I can't concentrate. Sylvie gets lots right, but I don't offer many suggestions for her wrong ones. Ted and Joe don't do much better so it causes quite a stir when the two latest arrivals win. Ted gives me a wink which I take to mean that he's lost on purpose. That's hard to swallow.

I head up to the room and stare out of the window at the squirrel leaping from bough to bough and frightening off the collared doves. Isabel and Ted aren't far behind me. "Let's sit down. Good. I want to start by saying – I believe you. I was very surprised to see the log of her arrival and departure times here. I have telephoned the owner of this Home and he is quite clear that we need to go to the police."

Ted and I feel relieved. "What do we do next then?"

"Nothing. Nothing today. We must carry on as normal. When Matron has gone home, I will make copies of all the files on the office computer. Then I will take them and your evidence to the police station. They will take over and so it is important that we carry on as if nothing has happened. We wouldn't want anyone to tell Matron there was something odd. Any questions?"

I look at Ted. He's not usually speechless. "No. Well. There are a few things that I've been wondering about, Jo. Some months ago I asked you both to write or draw some answers. I've kept them all. I was struck by the similarity of those drawings to Ted's photographs. Anyway, we'll see what the police do next. Our job is to carry on as normal, so, I expect it's time for tea."

80   WITHOUT HESITATION

I've been a prisoner here for years. I'm just slave labour. Washing, ironing, cooking, cleaning, even wallpapering and painting rooms. I had hoped to find an escape route from the back yard, but even when I'm mangling or hanging the washing on the line, there is only one locked gate, high fences and thick prickly hedges. Even the gate and fences have barbed wire near the top. I've thought about jumping from an upstairs window, but none of them open. And anyway, I'm watched by her, every step of the way.

I watch her when she doesn't realise. Her reflection is quite clear in some windows. She does get very bored. She reads the newspaper each day and has at least provided me with library books. I did take an old paper once and hide it in my clothes, but it was missed and I lost my food for two days.

When I got sick, she threatened me; thrown into a deep lake or act as a mute to a doctor. She did all the talking, as if she was a benevolent aunt, giving false names and address; I'm sure this isn't Banstead. She did allow me less work and more nourishing food which has continued as even she must have realised that I work better when well.

I do get cold down here. I've got extra blankets and a pillow now. Some thicker clothes too have helped. I was allowed a bath before the doctor saw me; it was bliss.

She's got into the habit of putting the food at the top of the stairs now which is good. I get the freedom of controlling the light; such simple power. There it is now. No words; just the sounds of opening, tray down, closing and bolts sliding. Tea, porridge, toast and an apple is normal so why would I crave scrambled eggs with lashings of butter? I just perch on the top steps and watch the shadows' stillness as I eat and sip my tea.

A mighty knocking echoes through the house, followed by raised voices. The door behind me swings open and a body trips, scattering the precious food into the darkness. The door slams shut and bolts slide across. I hear groans from below. "Help me hide."

I edge my way down and without hesitation my nursing training kicks in. "Stay still. Don't move. Where are you hurt?"

"Everywhere." It's a man's voice, but the gloom at the bend of the stairs is no place for an examination. His shoulders are lowest so I ease past and pull him down and into the light. There's no major blood flows and he's conscious, but his attempts to muffle his cries tell me to investigate for breaks. There could be internal injuries to watch out for.

"Slowly, move your head. Good. Now your hands." I watch him grimace, but the fingers are twitching. "What about your feet?" A cry accompanies his effort. One or both legs – could be spinal breaks. "Lay flat on the floor and don't move. I'll go and bang for help."

"No." His hand has gripped my ankle like a vice. "You will do nothing. Stay here. Sit." His snarls exude menace as he pulls me to the floor. "Be still and silent."

I can hear both of us breathing heavily. His grip tightens further as I sense a surge of pain pulse through him. I look towards the loud footsteps above which are accompanied by many voices and a cacophony of sound.

"Why are you hiding?" He doesn't answer. His face has gone grey. There's a gold chain around his neck. I pull to check he's not being choked by it. Two rings jangle together. That one looks like mine. "And that's like the one I gave Alf."

I prise the fingers from my leg without him resisting. I race up the stairs and bang my fists against the wooden panels, screaming as hard as I can.

I pause to listen. "Where are you?"

"Cellar! It's a hidden doorway beside the back door!"

"Stand back. We'll break it down."

I return to the patient and check his pulse. There is a feint one. I hear splintering wood and then the bolts being drawn. "Down here! Get an ambulance!"

Four policemen fill the room. One helps me into the armchair. They look at the squalor. "Do you live here?"

"Not by choice." I'm given a mug of water which I spill over myself. The shakes have kicked in. I'm wrapped in a blanket, but it doesn't stop me passing out.

The lights are bright as I awake. Where am I? I can't focus my mind. This is familiar, but different. I'm coming through a murky dream. I try to move, but my arm cannot. I look. I'm tethered to a rail. "What?"

A policewoman appears in front of me. "Hello. Can you see me okay?"

"Yes. Why am I chained up?"

"I can't say. I'll go and let the detective know you're awake."

I watch her leave and try to see past the door into the corridor. This is Kingston Hospital. This is Women's Ward C, the isolation room next to Sister's Office. I pull myself up as far as I can. I can see Sister's uniform and as she turns, I think I recognise her face. It brings tears to my eyes. "Glynis?"

It's as if she's heard me. She comes into the room and gives me an enormous hug. Our tears are intermingled. My one free hand is gripping her blouse as I shake uncontrollably. "Now then. What's all this about?" Glynis breaks away and searches for her handkerchief, still holding on to my hand. We both look at a tall man in a suit. "I asked what was happening?"

"You silly man. Take these cuffs off immediately. This is Lily, Lily Robertson. My best friend who has been missing for so many years. We all thought she was dead and here she is, in my ward when I come on duty. It's a miracle."

"That may be so, but she is suspected of being a member of a criminal gang."

"Who's the senior officer at the station today? We're going next door to my office and you are going to tell him you have found Lily. Understood?" Definitely Sister material. I love my best friend. "Move man!" I watch the backs and try to hear the conversation. It's brief. My released wrist displays the evidence.

"I am delighted to see you Mrs Robertson. I apologise we had to restrain you. You were found in the company of the ring-leader and we jumped to a wrong conclusion." I look into Glynis's face and mouth my thanks. "I've got to ask you some basic questions. We'll let you recover before we go into the details. Sister, will that be alright with you?"

Glynis looks to me. "Are you strong enough?" I nod.

"Good. Thank you. The WPC here will take notes. How long had you been in Waterloo Rise?"

"Where's that? I have had no idea where I was since I was kidnapped."

He pauses while she writes. "I see. Can you remember what happened just before you were taken?"

"Like it was yesterday. I was talking to Glynis about a nasty little man called Jenkins. We lost him in a crowd of people and then I ran for the bus, but it wouldn't wait for me. I walked on and a car pulled up. The woman with the black ring, asked me for directions. As I bent to answer I had my face covered with a rag of chemicals and I woke up in the cellar where I was found."

"Do you think it was Jenkins?"

"No. I've relived it every day since. The man was taller. His arm as he caught me convinced me of that. It could have been that man who fell on me on the stairs."

"Do you know him?"

"I don't think so. Should I?"

"We're not sure. We've been told his name is Roderick Cartwright."

"Rod?"

"I think that's enough, officer. Lily needs to rest. Tomorrow will be another day."

81 SITTING ROOM

I'm feeling a little bit guilty. I'd heard some of the staff moaning that they didn't know what to do if there was an emergency. "What if there was a fire in the night?" Jasmine had asked.

There hasn't been a fire drill since I've been here. I did wait till everyone had finished their lunch. The staff need that peaceful time to eat before the activities of the afternoon kick in. It's a nice day. Warm enough to be out amongst the flower beds. I knew that box of matches the workman had dropped would come in handy. It only took one strike, held beneath the ceiling sensor in the small rest room.

I see Sally in the sitting room, waiting for us as we troop in from the garden. I get to the corner seat from where I can see them all and save a chair for Sylvie. It takes an age for everyone to settle. There's always a full house when young Sally sings. I wonder which song she'll start with today. She gives a gentle cough and a hush descends. "I've got to begin with an apology. My throat has been rather tender this week and so I need you all to sing loudly. Ready? Daddy wouldn't buy me a bow-wow."

Most of the audience join in, if only with the bow-wows. There's a lot of laughter as the song finishes with the bow-wow-wow. The door to the Reception Area opens and Isabel ushers in a real dog, followed by a man. Sally takes his arm and guides him to a spare seat beside her. The dog sits at his feet until the man unhitches his harness. He immediately wags his tail, demanding Sally's strokes. "Well, Ladies and Gentlemen. I chose that song because this is why my Daddy wouldn't buy me a bow-wow. We have the pleasure of a beautiful dog, living with us, that is, with my father, mother and myself." There are lots of mutterings.

"To save my voice, I've asked Dad to recite some of the poetry that he writes. I'm sure you won't mind if he stays sitting. His first poem is called, Make sense?"

The man gives us all a cheerful wave. "Hello out there!" I like his voice. It's full of confidence. "As Sally says, my poem is called, Make sense?

It's obvious to the world that I am blind.
Dark glasses and white stick are quite a clue –
yet strangers seem to think I have no mind –
they need to shout and tell me what to do.

Without my sight I rely on my ears
to pinpoint the directions of soft sounds.
These skills have been developed through the years,
but what I hear brings pleasures beyond bounds.

Touch too can offer happiness – or pain.
A kindly, helping hand is full of joy,
yet danger lurks when cooking, or my brain
mistakes the hair of maiden for a boy.

Locations give their clues away by smell
as evergreens compete with forest pines.
The nose detects what any shop will sell
from boots to fruits or suits to fragrance lines.

My sense of taste though has developed less.
I seem to favour simple foods the best
like salad crops grown in my garden mess –
just like my fashion sense – not the best-dressed.

But what I value most in other folk
is – when they have their fun and laugh out loud,
they include me – so I can share the joke
and feel an in – not out-cast, from the crowd.

And so my wish for all is – common sense.
If you observe a blind man, think of me.
Remember – if you treat him as if dense –
there's none so blind as them that cannot see!"

There's a long moment of thought before loud clapping breaks out. "Why thank you – thank you very much. I started writing poetry when I was in primary school and often find simple things move me to scribble down thoughts. Luckily, I have a patient wife and daughter who can read most of my ramblings and translate them into print for all. The very first poem I remember making up was about another lovely girl.

Sister Susie sits and stares upon the stair
with rainbow ribbons in her hair.
What she is thinking, no-one ever knows.
She is a mystery from head to toes."

"Mumble, tumble, hear him rumble, monster now will squeal and grumble!"

The whole room is turning to look. My voice was loud and clear. The man feels for the arms of the chair as he stands. "Susie?"

"Tom!"

MALCOLM BULLER

Malcolm was born just after the Second World War in a house in Surbiton as the youngest of four boys. Their garden led to a chicken house at the end of their allotment and overlooked the Hogsmill Valley and beyond to Richmond Park. He had a short spell as a Saturday shop assistant in Bentalls which was then the largest department store outside of central London. His eldest brother was a police constable stationed in Kingston.

Sitting in Malcolm's memory is the time he was led to the Hogsmill by an older boy to play in the stream. Having got wet, he waited to dry in the sun before returning home, many hours later, oblivious to the trauma this had caused.

Malcolm and his wife Joan live in a village in Kent where they are very active members of the community. He has taken many supporting roles as Joan has served as a Parish Councillor for forty years. They founded a morning 'Interest Group' in 2002 which they continue to run weekly, providing social interaction opportunities through activities and talks, all with laughter and friendship at their core. In 2022 Malcolm instigated a Poetry Group to further encourage the 'have-a-go' spirit.

Andrew, his elder son, has developed his writing, design and publishing career which has prompted Malcolm to turn to writing both poetry and this, his second novel.

Parallel Lies – a novel set in a few weeks of 1964 London sees how a chance event impacts young lives and how they run in parallel yet become irreversibly intertwined. Are untold truths really lies in disguise?

What's in the Box? – a poetical miscellany – captures some of the poetry Malcolm wrote in his early years, through his primary school teaching career and during the months of lockdown in 2020. One poem 'Who's the Traitor?' was selected for publication in the 'Lucent Dreaming' Arts Book in that year. Others appeared in local publications.

Leeds Castle – a poetic tour – was inspired by the grounds, buildings, seasonal variations and characters to be met in 'the loveliest castle in the world'. Malcolm indicates places that have inspired poetry and encourages others to become 'Have-a-go poets'.

Printed in Great Britain
by Amazon

19092808R00164